A PRIVATE PERFORMANCE

by

CAROL ANDERSON

Published by **CHIMERA**

ISBN 9781780806976

This novel is fiction - in real life practice safe sex.

Chapter 1

Saturday, 2 December 1922

Jessica Harper accepted the cup and saucer Charlie Foster offered her, trying hard not to notice he was naked beneath the maroon silk dressing gown.

'I'm really so glad you dropped in,' said Charlie, sliding a cigarette into a long ebony holder. 'Do have a cream cake. It's been awfully quiet this week. Alice has been putting the finishing touches to the new costumes for the pantomime at the Grand. He rolled his eyes heavenwards. 'Puss in Boots, for God's sake.' He glanced at the clock on the mantelpiece. 'No matinee performance for me today, so we're all right until about six, then I really must dash. But do feel free to stay as long as you like. Alice shouldn't be very long. Let me tell you all the gossip. Did she tell you I'm playing Buttons this year? At the Empire, no less. Well...'

Jessica herself settled back into the armchair. The cramped sitting room was warm and dark. Outside the arc of lamplight there might well be complete chaos, but Charlie, ever mindful of the effects of good lighting and with a natural desire to be centre stage, had artfully arranged the shades to light him to the best advantage. While Jessica sat in shadow, he was bathed in a soft golden glow which picked out his perfectly chiselled cheekbones and tumble of white-gold curls.

Arranged around Jessica's feet were bags and boxes of Christmas shopping. She hadn't really called in to Alice's flat to talk, just catch her breath and ease off her tight, damp shoes for a while before catching the train back home.

Across the low table, Charlie Foster was already in full flood, spinning an outrageous story about someone she had never heard of - acting out each character, mimicking their voices and mannerisms - while drawing pictures in the air with his long expressive fingers. It was impossible not to be mesmerised by the performance.

Jessica didn't hear the door to the flat open.

'Take no notice of him, Jess, it's all lies,' said a familiar voice.

Jessica turned round smiling, as her friend, Alice Fallon, struggled across the room carrying an unwieldy bolt of fabric. She looked frozen despite her exertions, manfully heaving the cloth onto a table just outside the lamp's arc of light.

Jessica was already on her feet, hurrying to help.

Alice waved her away, pulling off her hat and coat.

'Sorry I wasn't here when you arrived,' she said breathlessly. 'How did the shopping expedition go?' She peered at the evidence around Jessica's feet and grinned. 'No problems finding what you wanted, then?'

Jessica giggled and shook her head. 'No, I've had a lovely day out. Charlie was just—'

Alice sniffed, eyes travelling up over Charlie Foster's long muscular legs.

'Posing for you.' She pulled a face, and stared with resignation at the beautiful young man arranged on the *chaise longue.*

'I told you Jessie was going to drop in,' she said flatly. 'You might have made the effort to get dressed.'

Charlie shrugged. 'I must have forgotten,' he said and sprung to his feet. 'I'm sure Jessica wasn't offended in the least by my deshabille. Were you, my dear?' Before Jessica could reply, he sauntered slowly towards the bedroom, the light glowing through his robe so that his muscular frame was picked out in stunning silhouette.

Alice frowned and turned up the lamps.

'You really shouldn't encourage him,' she said crossly to Jessica.

'I didn't, he was dressed like that when I arrived. He seems quite sweet.'

Alice refilled the teapot with hot water. 'He's got a good heart, but he really is the most awful tart.' She stretched, easing her shoulders back to relieve the muscles. 'I'm so glad you called in. What did you think of the suggestion in my letter?'

Jessica frowned. 'I'm not sure. I mean, I'm a school teacher, not a stage manager. Surely Charlie could help find you someone more suitable.'

Alice shook her head. 'That's just the point. He can't. Almost everyone we know is already in a show somewhere or a pantomime. Christmas is such a hectic time of the year, and the only time when there is more work than people looking for it. This is just a small revue thing, a dozen or so sketches and skits, a few songs. I thought you'd be perfect. You used to sing like an angel at school and were awfully good in all those dreadful school plays. And really, all I want is a glorified skivvy.'

Jessica smiled. 'Who else has said yes?'

Alice looked up, trying to think. 'Rupert and Bobby, the Haywood twins? You must remember them from the Christmas party at the Bellwoods? Bunty Redknap, Miranda - she's the latest little starlet on the block.' She pulled a little notebook out of her handbag. 'Lots of my old crowd, Tilly, Helen, Henry Foss. It should be great fun. My plan is to ship us all down there on the train, do the show, have a really super time and come home. Simple.'

Jessica stared at her. 'What about rehearsals?'

'Oh, come on, Jessica.' Alice groaned. 'A few well known songs and skits a monkey could memorise in an afternoon? We'll only be there for a few days. Rehearse Friday, big performance Saturday night. Sing for our supper again around the tree on Christmas Eve which is the Sunday, have a buckshee Christmas dinner on Monday as Jack's guests and then leave on Boxing Day after lunch. What could be simpler? It'll be great fun and you'll get paid as well. What more could a girl want?'

Charlie reappeared through the bedroom door, dressed in soft, cream-coloured jodhpurs and an open neck shirt. The outfit was complimented by a flamboyant brocade waistcoat and high patent leather boots.

3

Alice looked up in disapproval. 'He is never off stage,' she said in a low hiss. 'Give him a new face and he is determined we should all have to suffer his performances. He'd tap dance under the street lamp if you'd let him.'

Charlie feigned insult. 'Bitch,' he hissed.

Alice got up. 'I'll just see if I can find the letter from Jack.' Anxious not to be left sitting eye to eye with Charlie, Jessica got to her feet and began to look distractedly at the piles of papers and books. Every surface seemed to be covered - there were books, handbills, paper patterns, magazines, newspapers, sketches and scripts mingled with empty bottles, folds of fabric and twists of lace. Here and there, piles had fallen over and settled in precariously balanced landslides.

While Alice rifled through the debris on a bureau, Jessica tried to avoid eye contact with Charlie, who had uncurled himself onto the sofa. His jodhpurs were very tight, revealing every unnerving plain and curve of his body. Looking up, she blushed furiously - he was watching her every move. His hand lingered casually in his groin, a long finger delicately stroking his muscular thighs.

Jessica's colour intensified. She swung back to look at the pile immediately in front of her and instinctively picked up the first thing that came to hand - a handful of postcards. What she saw on them made her breath catch in her throat. She dropped them as if they were red hot. Alice, still sifting through the pile of letters, was oblivious.

Jessica stared at the cards in disbelief. She had never seen anything like it. A blonde masked woman was crouched on all fours on a dais. She was wearing a tail and whiskers so that she looked cat-like. In front of her a tall muscular man was... Jessica shivered.

Naked, the man was guiding his huge arching cock between the woman's pouting lips. Behind them, an equally impressive, shorter, more muscular man had his shaft buried to the hilt in the woman's compliant sex.

Jessica felt the heat rising in her belly. She found it almost impossible to tear her eyes away from the erotic tableau. Without looking, she guessed the other postcards showed more astonishing couplings. Casually, she picked up a magazine, intending to cover her discovery, when she realised with a breath-stopping certainty that the woman in the picture was her friend Alice Fallon and the man... Jessica glanced over her shoulder towards Charlie Foster.

He grinned, as if he knew exactly what it was she had found. He turned slightly in the lamplight so his face was caught in three-quarter profile, leaving her in no doubt that the cat-woman's extraordinarily well endowed companion was Charlie Foster.

Jessica took a deep, steadying breath.

'Have you found the letter yet, Alice?' she said in an uneven voice.

Alice snorted. 'No, just about everything else, though. Damn, damn, damn! I know that letter's here somewhere. The gist of it is that Jack Heally is throwing a Christmas bash for some friends and would like us to provide the entertainment.'

She snatched a sheet of paper off the pile and grinned triumphantly.

'Yes, here we are: "Dear Alice, long time no see," da-di-da-di "a Christmas house party at my place in Norfolk. I rather fancied a concert-party-style evening, a few rousing songs, silly sketches and maybe we could round the evening off with a few carols around the old piano? I realise it's terribly short notice but I was rather hoping that you could see your way clear to arranging it. Of course, it goes without saying, it's all expenses paid, all found, and the usual going rate for your poverty-stricken theatrical cronies. I look forward to hearing from you. With all best wishes, Jack.'"

Alice looked up, smiling. 'It will be terrific fun. Jack Heally is a really charming chap. He served with my brother in the war. Presumably your ma and pa are still in America?'

Before Jessica could do anything more than nod, Alice continued, 'Well, in that case you just have to say yes. Anything's got to be better than spending Christmas with your godmother in Crewe or wherever it is the ghastly woman lives. Term finishes soon, doesn't it?'

'I wave goodbye to the last of the young ladies of St Winifred's Academy on the fifteenth. They won't darken our doors again until mid-January. Actually, the headmaster and his wife have already invited me to spend Christmas with them this year. My little flat tucked up under the eaves is very cosy.'

Alice sighed and lit a cigarette. 'I really can't imagine you as a house mistress, Jess. You're not the school ma'am type at all. Why don't you come down to Norfolk with us? It'll be a hoot.' She glanced fleetingly at Charlie, who was flicking through a magazine. 'Our egocentric little friend here is in panto so it will be you and me together. Just like the good old days at St Faith's. I really could do with your help, darling. A friendly face and a safe pair of hands to help keep everyone else in order - and Jack Heally is a superb host.'

Jessica held up her hands in mock surrender. 'Stop it, stop it. I can feel myself being railroaded into this.'

Alice grinned. 'Is it that obvious? I really wouldn't ask if I didn't need you, Jessica. Do say you'll come.'

Jessica, surreptitiously sliding a newspaper over the pile of erotic postcards, laughed.

'All right, you win. You've persuaded me. When do we leave?'

'I'll send Jack a telegram tomorrow and get him to confirm all the details.' Alice smiled broadly. 'You'll love this, Jessie, it's going to be so much fun.'

Jack Heally reined the chestnut gelding back, slowing its pace so that it was set up for the last brush fence. He barely had to encourage it on - ears pricked, the animal knew exactly what was expected. Jack sensed the tension in the horse's body, feeling its anticipation. He made a soft noise of encouragement in the back of his throat and instantly the horse exploded forward, unleashed like a shimmering, flame-red arrow at the huge fence.

Gauging the distance perfectly, man and animal took off, stretching outward and upwards, smoothly, seamlessly, in a stunning arc, clearing the jump with at least eighteen inches to spare beneath the horse's tight muscular belly.

Jack smiled and turned the horse sharply to accept the flurry of appreciative applause from Lady Felicia Gudgeon, her husband, George, and a handful of their friends.

'Splendid. Bravo,' Felicia said loudly, hurrying across the paddock towards horse and rider. 'I'm surprised you can bear to part with him, Jack. He is a truly magnificent animal. All those stunning jumps and barely sweated up.'

As she approached, lifting her hands to rub the horse's neck, she looked up into Jack Heally's dark, handsome face. Her tone dropped to a conspiratorial purr.

'Are you satisfied now George is here to watch us together? Does it excite you to see me with him?' She paused, eyes sparkling with mischief. 'He made love to me this morning. He is so rough. I can still feel his body pressing me down onto the mattress. That great fat belly of his rubbing against mine, wet lips closed around my nipples, cock rammed home.'

Jack doffed his cap. 'I thought you'd appreciate a good sturdy mount, ma'am,' he said in a clearly audible voice, his handsome features impassive.

Lady Felicia Gudgeon lifted an eyebrow. 'George leaves for London this evening,' she whispered. 'I'll be free for dinner.'

Jack nodded and then waved towards the small group of onlookers.

'George,' he called cheerfully. 'How are you this morning? Have you thought any more about my invitation to join me up at Malestone for Christmas?'

Lord George Gudgeon, red faced, and leaning heavily on a cane, lifted a hand in salute.

'Morning, old chap. Impressive piece of horsemanship.' The brisk wind had lifted the colour in the old man's cheeks so that they seemed to be almost purple. 'Ask my good lady about Christmas,' he continued, indicating Felicia. 'She makes all our social arrangements.' He nodded towards the gelding. 'And buys all our best horse flesh, too. What do you think, m'dear?'

Lady Felicia turned, smiling artfully. 'What about, George darling? Jack's invitation or the gelding?'

George snorted good naturedly. 'Both, damn you, woman. Make up your mind. Too dashed cold to be standing around out here. A chap could get set.' He grimaced, obviously in some pain. He glanced over his shoulder at his companions. They were weekend guests, up from London, and were quite obviously bored stiff and frozen to the marrow.

Jack Heally waved his groom over and gracefully dismounted, passing the reins to his man.

'Forgive me. Didn't mean to keep you all standing around so long, George. Why don't we go back to the house and talk about this over a brandy? I've asked cook to lay on some lunch for us.'

George sniffed and then nodded. 'We've got the cars parked in the chase. Would you like a lift?'

Before Jack could reply, Felicia shook her head. 'Jack's going to walk back, aren't you? Let the horse cool off.' Behind them, the groom had already slipped off the beast's saddle and thrown a blanket over it.

Jack reclaimed the reins while Felicia continued, 'I shall walk with him, if you don't mind, darling. Try and beat him down on the price. Use all my womanly wiles to get his best offer.'

George snorted. 'Women, eh?' he said, to no one in particular, and limped slowly back towards his car, followed by his house guests.

They were barely out of sight when Felicia stretched up on tiptoe to kiss Jack on the cheek. Her breath was warm on his face - a scintillating caress that was both exciting and at the same time totally infuriating.

'For God's sake, Felicia,' he snapped. 'Do you want us to get caught?'

She pulled a face and slipped her arm through his. A stray tendril of blonde hair had crept out from under her cossack bonnet, adding a certain winsome vulnerability to her small, perfect features.

She crept closer still. 'Sometimes,' she said in a whisper. 'But then I very quickly remind myself of all George's lovely, lovely money, his title, Tideacre Hall, the London house, that sweet little estate he has in Scotland, the chalet near Geneva, and the way he loves me so very much. It would be a terrible shame to give up all those wonderful, wonderful things for a rogue like you.'

Jack grinned and shook his head. 'You really are a black-hearted whore,' he said, with more than a hint of admiration.

Felicia Gudgeon peeked coquettishly at him over her shoulder. 'Oh, how good of you to notice,' she said softly. 'It would be a dreadful shame to have worked so hard at it all this time, only to fall in the final furlong. Now, do you think we have time to make love on the way back? Or shall I call on you this evening after George and all those tiresome friends of his have left?'

Jack sighed. 'Are you coming to stay at Malestone House for Christmas?' he said softly.

Felicia ran the tip of her tongue provocatively around her lips. 'Perhaps. It rather depends on what you have in mind for me. For Christmas and tonight—'

Jack sprung forward and grabbed her, making her squeal with a mixture of surprise and delight. His hands tore furiously at the fastenings of her coat, seeking out the swell of her heavy breasts. As the buttons gave way, he felt the compelling warmth of her body, suffused with a heady mix of perfume and the musky scent of her sex. She shivered as he jerked her closer, pressing his lips to hers. Under his palms, her nipples contracted instantly, making him almost breathless with desire.

Behind them the horse whinnied nervously. Jack's eyes darkened.

'What makes you think I'm going to wait until tonight?' he said thickly. Dragging her skirt up over her stocking tops, one hand tugged at the waistband of her knickers. His fingers locked in the thin fabric, ripping the material down over her voluptuous hips, exposing her soft pink quim to the bitter winter wind.

She shivered, her excited kisses encouraging him on. Her sex was fringed by a corona of golden hair - a holy grail of pure delight. He ran an appreciative hand over her rounded belly, parting the lips of her sex, stunned as always by the intense heat that glowed within.

As his fingers worked deeper, he heard a noise behind him and half turned, catching a fleeting impression of his groom, hidden amongst the trees that ringed the bottom paddock.

He grinned. 'Don't skulk there, old man. Come and help me with this bloody filly. Can't you see I've got my hands full?'

The man hesitated.

'I said come here,' Jack said briskly, stepping to one side to reveal his blonde companion.

The groom lumbered eagerly across the frosted grass. His eyes worked their way across Felicia's exposed body with an expression akin to hunger. Though her refined features were ashen, Jack could feel Felicia's pulse quickening under his fingertips.

'What d'you want me t'do, sir?' said the man, licking his lips.

Jack handed him the reins of the gelding. 'First tie this fellow up, then I thought I'd hold this pretty little filly still whilst you mount up.'

Felicia flushed crimson. 'Jack!' she protested.

Jack Heally tightened his hold on her wrists.

'Don't worry,' he said with a smile, pressing his lips to hers, 'my man here is an expert at dealing with spirited rides. I had him brought over especially from Ireland, he's a natural jockey.'

He saw Felicia swallowing hard, her eyes reduced to dark pin pricks, alight with expectation.

'You bastard. Do you promise you'll come and see me this evening?' she said thickly, looking the groom up and down.

Jack nodded. Gently, he turned Felicia in his arms, lifting her skirt with one hand while the other cupped her ample breasts, teasing and nipping at the ripe, hard peaks.

She groaned, writhing and pressing her buttocks back into Jack's groin as if relishing in her exposure. The swarthy groom closed on her, moving towards them with slow determination. He unbuttoned his fly with one callused hand, opening her sex with the other.

Jack glanced down, admiring the stature of his servant, who cradled his great manly cock like a rifle primed and ready.

In his arms Felicia gasped, as without prelude, the man lunged into her. His huge hands grabbed frantically at her rounded backside, dragging her closer and closer. Jack eased his grip so that the man could take more of the shapely blonde's weight, then slowly worked his fingers lower, down towards the warm inviting folds of Felicia's quim. He was almost pinned by the body of his groom. He waited until he could read the rhythm, sliding lower and lower with each earth-shattering thrust, until he could finally stroke the junction where their two bodies joined.

Lady Felicia's delicate little sex oozed excitement, fragrant juices trickling out, as it opened and closed like a hungry mouth around the meaty shaft of her swarthy rider. Jack shivered with delight as her pleasure dripped out onto his fingers.

He closed his eyes, concentrating on the sounds and the smells and the raw sensual heat between the three of them. He had no great desire to see his groom's unshaven face, contorted in a grimace of sheer ecstasy no more than a foot away from his. Standing so close, Jack could smell the heavy scent of the stable yard mixed with tobacco and cheap Irish whisky.

He felt the man strain and surge forward again and again, each thrust like a hammer blow. Jack could sense Felicia fighting her way towards release. Her breath came in shuddering angry snorts, whilst her body contorted. She thrust her hips forward to seek out the bruising touch of her lover's body.

Jack slid his finger down over the hood of her clitoris. The lightest pressure was enough. Felicia let out a long wail of delight, thrusting wildly, while the groom, caught unawares, hurried to catch her up on the final chase. They bucked, they twisted, all three caught up in the last frantic thrashing of release.

Suddenly, it was over. Felicia clumped back onto Jack, breathless, sweat running over the swell of her little heaving belly. The groom slithered out of her quim, all spent, and dropped onto his hands and knees.

Only Jack Healy remained standing.

His excitement still brewed, glowing like a red coal low in his belly. The ache in his cock was almost more than he could bear, but even now he did not intend to spoil the pleasure by being in too much of a hurry.

He looked first at his groom. The man was struggling to catch his breath. He had thick slack lips. There was a trickle of saliva clinging to his unshaven chin. For an instant, Jack imagined slipping his raging shaft into that rancid mouth with its tobacco stained teeth and long serpentine tongue.

In his arms, Lady Felicia wriggled. Her lips were sugar pink. Her mouth, like her sex, was warm and fragrant and delicate as a summer rose. He smiled and gently turned her again in his arms, this time guiding her onto her knees.

She looked up at him.

'What about George? Won't we be awfully late for lunch?' she said, as he guided her fingers to his straining fly. 'We'll tell him one of the horses broke out.'

Felicia giggled and almost before he had finished the sentence, she had him in her mouth, sucking him deep. Her quicksilver tongue worked up and down, aided and abetted by cunning, knowing fingers that set a heady counter rhythm.

'Will you accept my invitation to spend Christmas at Malestone House?' he snorted between excited breaths.

She looked up at him, her eyes now returned to their normal mischievous blue. She trailed her tongue to the end of his shaft, running the very tip beneath his foreskin.

'It's terribly rude to talk with your mouth full,' she said, lapping at the scarlet glans.

Jack shuddered. When he looked down, he realised he could still see the pink wind-nipped cheeks of her backside peeping out provocatively from under her coat.

'Will you say yes?' he gasped.

Felicia giggled again, the laughter vibrating along the length of his cock. It was enough, tipping him into a stunning climax, a great wave of pleasure that drowned out all other thoughts. When he looked down again, Felicia was licking her lips, swallowing down every last drop of his salty offering.

She got to her feet with exaggerated dignity, rearranged her dress, patting her coat, tidying her hair. She appeared not to notice the torn remains of her silk panties lying amongst the trampled grass.

'George and I would be absolutely delighted to accept your invitation,' she said, in her most cultured voice.

Jack offered her his hand. 'Good show,' he said evenly. He signalled to the groom. 'Take the horse up to the house. Lady Felicia and I are going to take the short-cut through Hall Wood.'

The man touched his cap. 'Right you are, sir.'

Chapter 2

Monday, 18 December

Jessica Harper glanced up and down the railway platform as she struggled to drag her suitcase off the train. She slammed the carriage door shut. Surely there had to be a porter somewhere? Steam billowed out from under the bellies of the carriages. A flurry of snow blew along the darkened platform. Close by she heard the whistle blow. The stationmaster, she thought with relief. He was standing at the far end of the platform waving the train off. Perhaps he'd be able to help her.

Slowly, the train pulled out of the station, leaving a miasma of fire and brimstone in its wake. The hiss of the great pistons working sounded like a dragon taking a breath. Jessica tugged her hat straight and, abandoning her luggage, hurried towards the station master's office.

'Good evening.'

A rotund man, rolling up a green flag, peered at her from behind wire-framed glasses.

'Is there a porter?'

The man sniffed. 'No, I'm afraid there isn't, Miss. He won't be back till tomorrow morning.' He screwed up his face, as if struggling to focus. 'We usually only get mail on the late train.' He nodded towards a stout canvas sack resting against the door of his office. 'Sometimes we get two bags but we don't usually have no people. Not on a weekday night.'

Jessica wondered if perhaps she had ended up in the wrong place by mistake. She squared her shoulders and extended a hand.

'Jessica Harper,' she said briskly. 'I wonder if I might use your telephone? Miss Alice Fallon said she would arrange to pick me up. She's staying at Malestone

House. It looks as if she may have forgotten I was coming.'

The stationmaster hadn't moved. 'Alice Fallon?' he said, eyes narrowing.

'Alice Fallon,' she repeated.

The man grinned and began to pump her hand enthusiastically.

'Well, I'll be blowed. You must be one of them theatricals, then? The rest of them came down on the six-thirty. Miss Fallon used to live round here, you know. Up at the Old Rectory.' As he spoke, he guided Jessica into the warmth and comfort of his office. A fire burned in the stove, a black kettle was boiling on the hot plate. He indicated his desk.

'Feel free to use the telephone, Miss. Would you like a cup of tea while you're waiting?'

Jessica smiled. 'How far away is Malestone House?'

The man pulled a face. 'Not far by car, shouldn't take them too long to come out and fetch you. There's plenty of time for a cup of tea though, if you'd like one.'

Nearly an hour later, Jessica was heading out towards Malestone House with Alice Fallon at the wheel. Alice crashed the car down a gear and pulled her face into an exaggerated grimace. Something under the bonnet complained, as she swung the little roadster wildly around the next bend. The headlights, reflecting the frost in the trees along the lane, made the leaves glitter like opals.

'I thought you'd chickened out,' Alice called above the sound of the engine. 'Everyone else has already arrived.'

Jessica snorted. 'If I remember, you said we'd rehearse Friday, big performance Saturday night. Sing for our supper again on Christmas Eve. Have Christmas dinner on Monday as Jack Heally's guests. Leave Boxing Day after lunch.' She looked across at her friend. 'Today is Monday, if you hadn't noticed.'

Alice shrugged. 'Sorry, darling. Change of plan. I wasn't sure that you'd got my telegram. I knew school had broken up. I didn't think it would be a problem.'

The car complained bitterly as Alice braked hard. With more determination than skill, she whipped the steering wheel round and drove between a set of ornate gates.

'Everyone else is settling in with a late supper and a sherry or two. People have been turning up all day. Most arrived on the teatime train. The twins drove down. This is Bunty Redknap's new roadster.' She gave the horn a friendly toot-toot. 'Rather smart, don't you think? He said I could borrow it if I drove carefully.' She glanced over towards Jessica. 'So, if he asks, you must say we crept home at a snail's pace. Right?'

Jessica nodded and stared out of the windscreen. She had forgotten how isolated the north Norfolk coast was. In the distance she could just make out the glittering inky black sea between the trees.

The London train had travelled from Cambridge on a steep embankment far above the fenland, out past King's Lynn towards Hunstanton. The stop closest to Malestone, Beachhill, was between the two; a remote rural halt set amongst heavy pine woodland.

Jessica peered out of the windscreen. There didn't seem to be a light or a house anywhere. Above them, the moon broke through the clouds. A tiny sliver of silver, the newest of new moons, it looked like a winking eye against a velvet black sky.

Alice grinned and pointed. 'Turn your money over, Jess, makes it grow. Isn't that what they say?' She paused. 'Good to be back?'

'I'm not sure yet. It seems like an age since I was in Norfolk.'

Alice threw back her head and giggled. 'That's because it is, you pickle. Look, there's Malestone.' As the car took another dramatic turn through the pines, she pointed into the night.

In the far distance, Jessica could just pick out a cluster of lights.

'Malestone House. Have you been here before? I couldn't remember,' said Alice.

'No, and I haven't met Jack Heally either. Remember that when you start waxing lyrical about the good old days.'

Alice snorted. 'Really? I'm surprised. I thought we all used to come here when...' She stopped, silence falling. Thinking would take them both back to the people they had lost in the Great War. It was still too painful, too close.

Jessica reached out and touched Alice's hand, before saying cheerfully. 'I just wanted to remind you - don't forget to introduce me.'

Alice pulled a face. 'As if I would.'

The little roadster cut up a plume of gravel as Alice jerked the brake on, stopping the car right outside the main door of Malestone House. Jessica climbed out stiffly, stretching, relieved to finally be at her destination. She peered into the gloom, trying to pick out details of what was a very large country house. It was difficult to get any real impression of it in the darkness. Here and there lights glittered through the windows.

Alice clambered out, peeling off her driving gloves. 'Leave your suitcase, the servants will take care of it. Let's get inside and get warm. I bet you're dying for a drink, aren't you?'

Jessica nodded, hoping that Alice meant a pot of tea, but doubting it.

The main hall was huge, dotted with gas lamps but not quite enough to dispel the shadows. Jessica took a few seconds to get her bearings, while the footman helped them with their coats. The ceiling was high, the lights barely piercing the gloom above them. The vast expanse of floor was covered with black and white tiles, while the centre of the hall was dominated by a large staircase that led up to a galleried landing. Around an inglenook fireplace in the far wall sat a group of people, cradling glasses.

Their jovial conversation faded as Alice and Jessica came in. Everyone looked up at the new arrivals. Alice waved as the men got politely to their feet to welcome them. Jessica coloured under their undisguised interest. She had bought a new navy blue suit to travel in, which fitted like a glove over her slim frame. She had been afraid of looking dull by comparison to Alice's actor friends -

obviously the new outfit had worked.

Alice grinned at the man nearest to them. 'Stop staring, Bunty, and get us both a brandy. God, it's freezing out there.' She handed him her driving gloves. 'And don't worry, your precious little baby car is fine. It went like a dream.'

She guided Jessica closer to the fire. 'This is Jessica Harper, an old friend of mine. I'm sure most of you have met.' She peered into the shadows. 'Where's Jack gone to now?'

Bunty snorted. 'Gone off to do something businesslike in the study. He said he'd be down again in a little while.' He smiled at Jessica, extending a chubby, pale pink hand. 'I'm delighted to meet you, my dear.'

Beside him, Alice rolled her eyes heavenwards.

'Work, work, work,' she said. 'I'll just nip upstairs and find Jack. Bunty, will you do the honours?'

The plump man smiled at Jessica. 'Didn't we meet at the midsummer ball in Cambridge?'

Jessica was about to shake her head, when Bunty's limp, damp hand engulfed hers. She suppressed a shiver, forcing a smile.

Bunty poured a brandy and handed it to Jessica.

'Now,' he said, 'let's introduce you to everyone. You were at school with Alice, weren't you?'

Jessica nodded, keenly aware that everyone in the room was still watching her.

'That's right, seems an awfully long time ago now though,' she laughed.

'Oh, not so long, I'm sure,' said Bunty with exaggerated politeness. 'Now, this is Johnny Fellowes, and this...' Jessica made her way round the small group, nodding and shaking hands, exchanging social niceties. There were more than a dozen or so people in the hall. Some of the faces were familiar but other than Alice Fallon, Jessica realised that she didn't really know anyone well. There was something else; a little tension in the air between them all. It was something just below the surface, an unidentifiable flutter of expectation that tightened her stomach.

As Bunty introduced her to everyone, she struggled to try and work out what it was that was making her feel so uneasy. She'd been in the company of strangers before. As she sipped her brandy, one of the girls uncurled herself from the sofa.

'Is someone going to wind up the gramophone or play the piano or something? Bunty, come along, darling. Stop playing *meine host* and get something organised before we all *die* of boredom.'

Jessica stared at her in astonishment. The girl was tall and blonde, with long, long legs which were exposed to mid-thigh through the split sides of her silky sheath dress. She just had to be a dancer, Jessica thought.

Despite the weather outside, the girl's dress was so thin that it was practically transparent. Barely more than a chemise, it revealed every curve of her voluptuous body. She looked pointedly at Bunty, her plump nipples pressed against the bodice of her frock like bugle beads.

Bunty snorted. 'Miranda, darling, how very remiss of me. I'd forgotten you have the attention span of a maggot. I thought you'd enjoy all the gossiping. We've been catching up with everyone's news,' he whispered, as an aside to Jessica, who was still staring at the tall slim blonde.

Across the room, Miranda mimed a very theatrical yawn. One of the young men close to the fire, who was in the middle of a hand of cards with the man opposite him, grinned broadly.

'Oh, come on, Bunty, you know what Miranda's like. Unless we're talking about her she's not in the least bit interested.'

Everyone, except Jessica and the scantily clad blonde, whooped and giggled with delight. Jessica wondered fleetingly if Alice might have invited her to Malestone to keep order. The theatrical troupe reminded her of a classroom full of naughty children.

Miranda pouted. Beside her, one of the men leaned forward and slid his hand up over her slim muscular legs.

'Don't sulk, darling,' he said in an undertone. 'I'm sure Bunty will organise some music for us, won't you, Bunty?'

Bunty raised his soft pink hands to quieten them all. 'I'll see what I can do. Jack will be back in just a few minutes. I'll have a word with him.'

Jessica felt her colour rising, as Miranda's companion slid his hand higher still. The blonde, without any shred of self-consciousness, threw back her head and shivered with sheer delight.

Blushing furiously, Jessica turned to Bunty. 'I was wondering about my room? I'd really like to go and freshen up.'

Bunty nodded. 'Oh, I'm so sorry, of course. I'll ring for the footman; I'm not exactly sure where Alice has got to.'

Across the room, Miranda had plonked herself into the lap of the man stroking her legs. His hand was now out of sight under the silky sheath. No one else seemed to be in the least bit embarrassed by Miranda's outrageous behaviour. Her companion tipped his face close to hers, pressing a wet eager kiss to her pouting lips. The blonde giggled, moving her shoulders so her pert breasts brushed the man's shirt.

Stunned, Jessica looked away.

From the shadows a man in uniform appeared.

'Miss Harper would like to be shown to her room,' said Bunty.

The uniformed man nodded. 'If you'd like to follow me, Miss.'

Gratefully, Jessica fell into step behind him and climbed the impressive staircase up into the body of the house.

Her bedroom, tucked away in one of the passageways off the main corridor, was quite small, but comfortably furnished. Jessica's suitcase had already been unpacked, clothes neatly folded and hung, all tidied away in the wardrobe and dresser.

A fire glowed in the grate. A comfortable chair and a side table had been pulled up beside the hearth. Jessica slipped off her shoes and looked around. The bed with its heavy silk counterpane looked very tempting. It felt as if she had been travelling all day.

The footman hesitated in the doorway.

'The bathroom is across the hall, Miss. I wondered whether you might like a supper tray? I'm afraid it will only be sandwiches and a pot of tea.'

Jessica nodded gratefully. 'That would be wonderful, thank you.'

When the man had gone, Jessica stared into the mirror above the washstand and tidied her sleek dark bob. Coming to Malestone House really hadn't been a very good idea. She had barely seen Alice Fallon in years. They'd kept in touch by letter, exchanged cards at Christmas and she had visited Alice when she was in London, which wasn't very often. They could hardly be described as close friends after all this time. Jessica ran a finger over her lips, smoothing the touch of lipstick she was wearing.

She felt tired; maybe going to bed early wasn't such a bad idea.

The invitation to come to Malestone had come out of the blue. Jessica wasn't all together sure now why she had accepted it. She smiled wryly at her reflection - a little bit of envy perhaps?

Alice's life in London always sounded so glamorous in her letters. All those first nights and theatrical parties, mixing with a bevy of famous names. Life as house mistress of St Winifred's school for young ladies sounded very dull by comparison.

Jessica made up her mind. She would stay the night, make her apologies and leave first thing in the morning. What on earth had Alice been thinking of inviting her in the first place? She shuddered, thinking fleetingly about the postcards she had seen in Alice's flat, and the man downstairs caressing Miranda's sleek thigh.

Jessica slipped off her jacket and unbuttoned the neck of her blouse before stretching out in the armchair. A few minutes later the footman returned with a tray.

She felt better after she had eaten. There was still plenty of time to get back to her rooms at the school and accept the invitation to have Christmas dinner with the headmaster and his wife.

Jessica glanced at her watch. She'd get up early and ring for a cab to pick her up. No need to disturb anyone else, although she was certain Bunty Redknap would take her to the station if she asked. Perhaps she ought to let Alice know about her plans.

Slipping on her shoes, Jessica tiptoed back out onto the landing. Downstairs she could hear the sound of music playing and voices raised in laughter. They really wouldn't miss her if she slipped off to bed now. She glanced over the ornate banisters into the circle of light below, where people were dancing, Miranda and her beau amongst them. The expression on Miranda's uptilted face and the way her sinuous body snaked against her partner made Jessica's mind up for her. She wouldn't go back downstairs, she didn't really want to socialise with people who thought Miranda's scandalous behaviour acceptable.

She strained to try and pick out Alice's voice amongst the mêlée - perhaps she was still with their host, Jack Heally. Not that it really mattered.

As Jessica turned to go back to the bedroom she heard a soft desperate sound close by. It was an enticing murmur, so compelling it stopped her in her tracks. And again, louder now, a shuddering electric sound that made the hair on the back of her neck stand up. Across the hallway, one of the doors stood slightly ajar. Even though she knew she was eavesdropping, Jessica couldn't resist the temptation to peek inside. Instinctively, she already knew what she would find.

In the soft glow of a table lamp a man was making love to a slim redheaded girl. She was stretched out across his desk, naked, her legs wrapped tightly around her lover's waist as he plunged deep inside her. She mewled again, arching up to engulf him.

His shirt was open, revealing a dark hairy chest, breathtakingly muscular, gilded here and there with glittering diamonds of sweat.

His fingers moved constantly between the girl's legs, seeking out the soft moist folds and that tiny sensitive peak that would bring his lover to a stunning climax. The girl moaned, revelling in her exposure, lifting herself again and again for her lover's caresses.

Jessica felt the heat rising in her belly. She was torn between stunned curiosity and shock. She knew she ought to turn away but her legs refused to obey her. She swallowed hard, feeling dizzy, stretching out a hand to steady herself against the door frame.

The tiny movement was enough to announce her presence. The man looked up, his face alight with pure animal pleasure. There was no doubting that he had seen her. He smiled, capturing Jessica with his eyes. His hands circled the redhead's heavy creamy breasts, fingers working at the scarlet-tipped peaks. He smeared the juices from her sex across her nipples, making her writhe with delight.

Jessica blushed crimson as his eyes held hers, then gasped as he bent down, lapping and sucking at the pert orbs. When he looked up again, he licked his lips, his expression holding a tantalising invitation.

The girl beneath him shuddered and for an instant Jessica felt her own breasts ache in response to his expert touch. Still holding her gaze, he changed pace, hips grinding more slowly against the prone girl's eager body.

Jessica felt as if she was struggling to breathe. The redhead arched upward against her lover and instantly Jessica felt her whole body respond. She closed her eyes, imagining that she was on the desk, her sex hungrily accepting the man's throbbing cock. The girl let out another excited tortured sob.

Head spinning, Jessica tore herself away and ran along the corridor to her bedroom, slamming the door shut behind her, trying to close out the sounds of the final desperate gasps of the redhead as her body convulsed with waves of pleasure.

Jessica stood with her back to the door, arms spread wide as if to hold it shut. She had to leave. Her head throbbed. She could feel the expectation glowing in the soft wet depths of her sex. Her body ached for a lover's touch, for the delight of feeling a man buried to the hilt inside her. At the same time she was angry with herself for looking into the room.

What would the man think of her? She blushed - what a ridiculous thought, if anyone should be embarrassed it ought to be him, not her. What did it matter what he thought? But she knew by his expression that far from being unhappy about her watching, he had revelled in her voyeurism. Perhaps, she realised, he had left the door open so that he would be discovered.

Never mind, she would be gone tomorrow. Just as she felt the tension ease, someone knocked on the door behind her. It was all she could do to suppress a shriek of panic.

'Hello?' said a familiar voice. 'Are you in there, Jessica?'

Alice Fallon - Jessica sighed with relief. She hurried across to the mirror, wondering if her face would give her away. Cool blue eyes looked back, only the dark, jet-bright pupils betraying her excitement.

'I won't be a minute,' she said with forced cheerfulness and splashed cold water onto her face from the jug on the washstand. 'Come in.'

Alice smiled sheepishly. 'Sorry I've been so long. I couldn't find Jack, but just thought I'd better see if the trunks of costumes had arrived. I wondered where you'd got to. Are you coming downstairs? Bunty has managed to get a piano moved into the hall and some dance records for the gramophone.'

Jessica hesitated. 'I'm really very tired,' she protested, glancing towards the bed. 'I was just about to get undressed.'

Alice groaned. 'Rubbish. Come downstairs and mingle. There was hardly any point your coming at all if you don't get a chance to mix with all my favourite drunks and reprobates. Besides, we need a decent contralto for a sing song.' She picked up Jessica's jacket.

Jessica forced a smile. Her mind was still full of the images of the dark muscular man and the red-headed girl. She swallowed; perhaps it would be better to be in company than alone with her feverish thoughts. She would be able to talk to Alice downstairs and explain to her she was leaving.

'All right,' she said finally and let Alice lead the way. She was relieved, when they stepped out into the hall, to see that the door she had been spying through was now firmly closed.

They were barely at the bottom of the staircase before Bunty Redknap had pressed an enormous brandy into Jessica's hands. Without hesitation Jessica drained the glass and stood it on a side table.

If Bunty noticed he said nothing, turning his attention instead to Alice.

'Dance with me, darling?' he said in a mocking falsetto, as they crossed the room.

Alice snorted. 'Oh Bunty, I've just promised Jessica a jolly time and you come and steal me away. May we dance in a minute?'

Bunty pulled a hurt face and Jessica was about to insist that Alice dance with him, when someone touched her arm. She turned and felt her stomach contract. The dark man she had seen upstairs with the redhead was standing beside her. He smiled warmly and inclined his head.

17

'Good evening,' he said, looking across at Alice. 'Maybe I can give your friend a jolly time instead.'

Alice grinned. 'Oh Jack, darling, there you are. I've been looking everywhere for you. Have you met my old school chum, Jessica Harper? Jessica, this is our host, Jack Heally.'

Jack lifted Jessica's hand to his mouth, pressing a soft kiss to her fingertips.

'No, I don't think we've ever met,' he said in a low, hypnotic voice, 'but I'm certain I've seen her somewhere before.'

Jessica blushed furiously, while Alice groaned.

'If you say in your dreams, Jack Heally, I swear I shall be sick.'

Jack grinned. 'No, not exactly my dreams, was it, Miss Harper?' Jessica was speechless. He held tight to her hand. 'Would you care for this dance?'

She felt rooted to the spot. Every part of her felt as if it was glowing red hot with sheer embarrassment. Beside her, Bunty Redknap folded Alice into his capacious arms. Jack Heally stepped closer to Jessica, his hand sliding around her waist as he drew her closer. Behind them the music began again, and he led her into the space that had been cleared for dancing.

She swallowed hard, fighting to regain her composure. 'So, Miss Harper,' said Jack Heally, eyes alight with mischief. 'Where was it we met before? Do you remember?'

Jessica stared up at him.

He grinned. 'Come, come now, was it Henley? Or perhaps at Ascot? Or Cowes?' His hand rested lightly in the small of her back, guiding her this way and that in time with the music. As the tempo slowed he pulled her closer to him. 'Perhaps it was in Cannes? I went for the first time last year. Rather charming. Were you there too?'

She could smell the scent of his body and on the very periphery of her senses, the perfume of the red-headed girl. She closed her eyes, groaning softly. Jack Heally held her closer still. She didn't resist him, instead her body moulded itself against his, every pore, every sinew crying out for his touch. She rested her head on his shoulder, relishing the heat and the strength she sensed beneath her cheek.

'Oh, I remember now,' he said, in a whisper, pressing his lips to her neck. His fingers delicately traced the contours of her spine, making her shiver with anticipation. He tipped her face up towards him and with infinite tenderness, he kissed her. The sensation lit a thousand tiny flares inside her mind.

As he pulled away, he said quietly, 'You're the young lady who likes to watch, aren't you?'

His words were like a body blow. Jessica jerked upright, her growing excitement snatched away, to be replaced by indignation.

Jack smiled at her. 'You should have come in and joined us. I'm sure my friend wouldn't have minded in the least. In fact, I've always thought she had a penchant for female flesh. Next time don't be so coy. My door is always open.'

Jessica was crimson. She struggled to swallow and then stepped back and slapped Jack Heally hard across the face. The blow sounded like a whip cracking and before it had finished echoing round the room, Jessica ran up the stairs, tears tumbling down her face. Everyone else, caught like musical statues, stared in astonishment at Jessica, then Jack and finally Alice, who hurried over to him.

Jack grinned ruefully and rubbed his cheek before waving the dancing to continue, then looked at Alice for some kind of explanation.

Alice slipped her arm through his. 'Oh God, I'm so sorry. I should have said something about Jessica. I invited her out of kindness really. She was always such a fun person and then she lost her fiancé in the war and really never got over it. You know what it was like.' She paused. 'I thought coming to help with our Christmas party would be wonderful for her.'

Jack, still rubbing his cheek, smiled wryly. 'And there was me thinking all you theatrical types were open minded amoral hedonists.'

'Jessica isn't a theatrical, darling, she's a school teacher.' Alice laughed.

Jack raised his eyebrows.

'No, honestly, it's true, Jack. She's a house mistress at some dreary girls' academy down in a little backwater in Somerset. We were at school together.'

Jack shook his head. 'Poor girl, she must think she's found herself in Sodom and Gomorrah.'

Alice pulled a face. 'I'm not with you.'

Jack smiled. 'Why don't you go and have a word with your friend? I think I may have upset her.'

'What exactly did you say?'

'It doesn't matter. Go and say something sweet and supportive.'

He watched Alice Fallon climb the stairs, but his mind was on Jessica Harper with her glittering eyes and her eager, hungry body. He had interpreted her interest as mutual lust, now he realised, with a flicker of excitement, it was genuine desire. A desire he would be only too happy to satisfy.

Chapter 3

19 December

The following morning, Jessica stood by her bedroom window and looked out at the grey, forbidding, Norfolk sky. A bitter wind tore at the bare trees, whipping up remnants of the autumn leaves into curling twists. Jessica shivered. On the bed was her suitcase, its contents all neatly packed and ready for her departure.

She had woken up quite determined to leave, but now wondered if perhaps she had overreacted to the events of the previous nights. Everyone had had a few drinks. The guests had let go of their inhibitions - she smiled - always assuming Alice's friends ever had any inhibitions. What had she expected? Hadn't Charlie Foster, Alice's lover, and the photographs she had found in their flat, given her an idea of what awaited her at Malestone? She glanced back at the suitcase. There was some part of her which was terribly tempted to stay.

All night long her dreams had been full of electrifying caresses. Jack Heally had pursued her through the darkness, his eyes alight with desire. When she'd woken up the sheets had been tangled into a plait and soaked with sweat. Even now, she felt a dull, unfulfilled ache in the pit of her stomach. She stared into the grounds of Malestone House, eyes unfocused, as she imagined Jack Heally's body pressed hard against hers, his hands cupping and caressing her breasts. Images of the redhead writhing under him mingled with her own memories of the way his hands had touched her. She could feel the excitement building in the moist depths of her sex, and she shivered.

'Jessica?' said Alice, through the closed door. The sound of her friend's voice broke Jessica's train of thought. 'Are you coming down to breakfast?'

Jessica pulled her cardigan on, aware of the flush of colour in her cheeks. Torn between wanting to stay and knowing she ought to leave, she opened the door. During breakfast there might be a chance to have a quiet word with Bunty Redknap.

Alice grinned at her.

'Morning, darling. Did you sleep well? I hope you're fighting fit and raring to go. We've got to sort through all the costumes and props this morning. I thought you could help me with that, while the twins put the scenery up in the music room.'

'I'm not sure I'm going to stay, Alice,' Jessica said in a small uneven voice.

Alice stared at her. 'Oh Jessica, for goodness' sake. You're not still upset about last night are you? I've already said that Jack is terribly sorry. He just assumed that you were fair game.' She paused. 'I'd forgotten that not everyone is like Miranda or the rest of them. I'm sorry. Just try and put it behind you. I'm counting on your help. Can you imagine me asking Miranda to sort things out? It would be a complete disaster. Please say you'll stay.'

Jessica sighed, feeling her resolve faltering.

'I'm just not used to people being so - so...' she reddened, struggling to find a word to describe Alice's debauched friends.

Alice giggled and slipped her arm through Jessica's.

'I know, they are terribly naughty, but they're very nice, once you get to know them. Come on, let's go and get some breakfast. I could cheerfully eat a pit pony.'

Jessica followed Alice without protest down to the dining room, where everyone was tucking into plates of bacon and eggs. The smell made Jessica's mouth water. Her stomach reminded her she had only had a sandwich the day before.

At the head of the table, Jack Heally was deep in conversation with Bunty Redknap about the merits of their respective cars. The others had formed into little groups, talking in low voices and eating heartily. Jessica noticed the statuesque redhead - Jack's eager companion in the office - had turned her attentions to another member of the troupe.

Jack looked up as Jessica came in. For a second their eyes met and Jessica instantly blushed crimson. Jack smiled, his gaze moving on to Alice.

'Good morning, ladies, I hope you both slept well.'

Alice groaned. 'Like a top. I think it must be all this appalling, healthy country air - and I'm absolutely ravenous.'

She poked Bunty Redknap playfully as she made her way to the sideboard. 'I do hope you've left some of that bacon for me. You might have been better off just ordering a whole pig by the amount on your plate.'

Bunty coloured. 'I was hungry too,' he said defensively. Alice lifted the cover on the first of the serving dishes and made a little noise of satisfaction.

'Come on, Jessica,' she said, over her shoulder. 'Best we get something before everyone comes back for second helpings.' She turned her attention to her plate and then, almost as an afterthought added, 'By the way, I'd like everyone in the drawing room at twelve for a costume fitting. No excuses.'

Bunty waved his knife to attract everyone's attention to him. 'And I want everyone in the music room for rehearsals straight after breakfast. Same applies. We've got an awful lot to get through.'

As they spoke, Jessica was aware of Jack Heally's eyes on her. They were as compelling as his fingertips. As she took the plate Alice offered her, she could detect the slightest tremor in her hands.

Jack got to his feet. Standing between her and Alice as he helped them to breakfast, he was so close that Jessica could feel the heat from his body. She swallowed hard, trying to dispel the nervous tension in her stomach.

'And what have you got planned this morning?' said Jack, turning towards her. She thought for one awe-inspiring moment that he was going to kiss her. He tipped his head, adding emphasis to his enquiry, his dark eyes softened by laughter lines.

Jessica forced a smile, feeling the little flurry of excitement she had felt earlier returning. 'I'm helping Alice with the costumes,' she said in an undertone.

Jack nodded.

Alice turned round, popping a tiny sliver of bacon into her mouth. 'Why, what had you got planned, Jack?'

He shrugged. 'Nothing really. I've arranged to go riding after breakfast and then I'm at a loose end for the rest of the morning. I thought perhaps you might like an extra pair of hands.'

Alice grinned. 'Why don't you come to the drawing room? I could fit you for a costume, if you like.'

Jack grinned and moved back towards the table.

Jessica let out a long sigh of relief.

'Sounds like a wonderful idea,' he said, 'but if you'll excuse me, I really have to go. I'll see you around twelve, or do I get a private fitting?'

Alice laughed. 'Turn up whenever you like, only be warned, I may press you into service.'

Later that morning, Alice sat back on her heels and looked at the row of costumes hung out along a makeshift rail in the drawing room. She was surrounded by a mountain of shoes, boots, hats and gloves.

Jessica hung another dress up on a hanger and tugged it straight. 'There are just so many things,' she said with a hint of wonder in her voice. 'Why did you bring so much?'

Alice laughed. 'I'd got no idea who would actually turn up. They all said they'd come, but, amongst other things, they're all terribly unreliable. I had to bring a few alternatives in case we had to alter the plan.'

Jessica tugged a cream wig onto a stand. 'Which is?'

Alice stretched. 'We've got enough people here to do Cinderella. Bunty makes a perfect ugly sister. We talked about doing a pantomime before you arrived last night and everyone seems very happy about the idea.'

Jessica stared at her. 'I thought you said we were going to do a revue?'

Alice's attention had turned back to her seemingly bottomless box of tricks.

'Yes, I know. We're going to do that too, but panto is such good fun. Oh, damn.' She pulled out a small metal cage containing six plaster mice. 'Would you mind nipping and finding Jack? I don't seem to have packed a whip for the coachmen.' She lifted out another small ornate box. 'I've remembered the flash powder, thank God. I'm sure we wouldn't be able to find any of that round here.'

Jessica stared down at her. Hunting for Jack Heally was the last thing she wanted to do.

'I thought he said he was going out riding?'

Alice sniffed distractedly. 'That was ages ago, but don't worry, if he's not around, just find a groom and ask him. I'm sure Jack wouldn't mind.'

Jessica went upstairs to the office and was both relieved and slightly disappointed to find it empty. Malestone was a large place, built in the shape of a squared off letter U, and it took Jessica a little while to discover he wasn't in the house. In the music room, Bunty and the others were gathered around the piano, busy rehearsing.

Just as Jessica was about to give up she came across a footman, who directed her to the stables.

After getting her coat, Jessica headed out towards the stable block that stood a little way from the house, half hidden amongst a stand of conifers. Outside it was bitterly cold; the sharp wind blowing up from the sea whipped her breath away. Dragging her coat up around her, Jessica hurried towards the stables. Everywhere seemed very quiet. A heavy horse whinnied over the top of an open stable door. Surely there had to be someone around? She pushed open the door of a shed and stepped inside, glad to be out of the cold wind.

Jack Heally stared down at Felicia Gudgeon and grinned. 'What about George, won't he be worried that you haven't arrived home yet?'

Felicia let her fingers glide down the buttons of her riding jacket, tugging each one undone with practised ease. Beneath the thin silk of her blouse, Jack could see the stark outline of her breasts jutting forward, her nipples hard and dark in the cold air.

'Oh, Jack, don't be such a tease. George is entertaining some boring chap from the ministry this morning. You know he won't even notice I'm gone. It was far too cold for any grand passion outdoors with this wind blowing. Don't be such a spoil sport.' She posed provocatively. 'Or is this your way of turning me down? Don't tell me you've gone off me already?' She tugged the blouse out of her skirt and let her fingers stroke the tight little peaks of her nipples before shimmying the thin fabric down over her slim shoulders.

Jack snorted, pretending to be reluctant, although he could already feel his cock hardening and his mouth watering in anticipation of drawing one of those ripe, swollen cherries into his mouth.

'I ought to be getting back. I've got a house full of itinerant actors,' he began.

Felicia giggled. 'Oh, yes, your Christmas entertainment. How's it going?'

As she spoke, she unfastened her skirt, rolling it down over her hips.

Jack grunted. 'Do you want me to talk or make love to you?'

Felicia pouted. 'You really have to ask? What I want is to feel your tongue lapping up inside me, kissing all those soft wet places you know so very well. I want you to make me faint with sheer bliss - and if you call that bloody groom of yours in here, I shall scream. I had a rash on my face for a week from his unshaven, stubbly chin.'

She threw her skirt down onto the hay behind them and then turned to demand his attention. Not that she needed to demand. She looked astonishing. Her thick blonde hair was caught up in a bun under a top hat and veil, her naked breasts jutted towards him, her sex was outlined by the sheerest of silk drawers, and finally, her slim legs were covered in silk stockings and tiny, high heeled, buttoned riding boots. Jack grinned. She was delectable.

'Are you going to take your hat off?' he said in a soft, teasing voice.

Felicia grinned and stepped into his arms, breasts thrusting up against his chest.

'No,' she said with a pout, 'it's new, and besides, you squashed the last one. I did think about sending you the bill.'

Her lips brushed his. She smelt of horses and expensive French perfume - a heady combination he couldn't resist. He ran his hand down over her belly, working lower until he found a way under the waistband of her knickers. She gave a little throaty moan as he found the mark and eased a single finger in and out of the slick, tight confines of her fragrant sex. Now, mingled with her perfume, he could detect the subtle, mesmerising scent of her excitement.

Gently, he guided her back towards the hay, imagining the taste of her juices on his tongue and the way she would move against him, getting sweeter and wetter. He could feel his mouth watering - when Felicia was excited it felt as if he would drown in her body.

She sank back into the soft hay, pulling him down with her. Her eyes were hooded, her skin flushed with anticipation. She opened her legs, lifting herself up towards him. 'What are you waiting for?' she purred. 'An engraved invitation?'

He grinned and pressed his lips to her throat, lapping at the salty pit between her collar bones. Next he caressed her breasts, spiralling his tongue around their firm buds, all the time aware of her breath quickening and the little animal noises of pleasure trickling from her perfect, bow-shaped mouth.

She lifted her hips higher, offering herself to him like an exotic dish. Her belly brushed up against him, making him shiver, until neither of them could resist any more. He pressed his mouth to her sex, breathing deeply, relishing the smell and the taste of her body through the thin silk.

'Please,' she whispered. 'Kiss me, make me cry out for more.'

As if he might consider denying her. Jerking down her panties, he plunged his tongue into the swollen depth of her quim, seeking out the hard ridge and the sensitive hood of her clitoris. She gasped at his brutality and then opened her legs wider. As always, his senses were overwhelmed by the sheer power of her desire.

Fingers and tongue worked together, dipping into the soft folds, sliding back to stroke the tiny rosebud of her backside. The sensation made her snort with pleasure. Her body opened up for him like a flower coming into bloom, so that he could slip a finger into the tight forbidden closure, while working her quim with his tongue and the fingers of his other hand. Her body responded by sucking at him like a mouth, drawing him deeper still.

Circling the little bud again and again, he could feel the waves of pleasure building inside Felicia, each scintillating spasm echoing the passion he felt in his own body. He knew what she liked and took her again and again to the very brink of release, stopping and starting, varying the touch and the intensity of his attentions, until he could sense that she could take no more. Drawing her clitoris between his lips he renewed his attentions, feeling the surges tightening in her sex like the waves of a storm tide.

'Jack,' she screamed, tearing at his hair as if she were demented. 'Oh, my God. You little bastard, you're just so good at this.' Her words were punctuated with breathy moans.

Around his fingers, he felt her whole body convulsing. The awesome glittering pulse, spreading out from her sex, felt as if it might sweep him away with its power.

Before the last wave had rolled through her slim frame, he slipped his cock from his trousers and slid it deep inside the still throbbing confines of her sex. Her body sucked him in gratefully, closing around him like a tight fist.

She let out a throaty roar and wrapped her legs up around his waist, dragging him deeper. He brushed his pelvis against hers, making her whimper.

'Oh Jack,' she purred, and looked up into his eyes.

Her lips sought his, as if she was hungry to share the taste of her own excitement. Her tongue worked around his mouth, lapping and sucking as if it was another quim she was kissing.

The thought ripped away the last vestiges of control. Now the chase was his, he plunged into her again and again, relishing the wetness of her kisses, the scent of her sex, the soft; enticing magic of her body as it welcomed him in - and knew he was lost.

The first silvery pulse hit him, followed almost instantly by another and then another, until every atom of his body was suffused with pleasure.

At the very last second, when nothing could have stopped him riding the wild ride out towards oblivion, he saw Jessica Harper standing in the shadows of the barn.

Her face was ashen, her eyes glowing in the gloom, though the shadows didn't hide the desire in her expression - and Jack Healy realised, as the waves of pleasure closed over him, that he would give his soul for it to have been her writhing beneath him.

Jessica hurried back into the drawing room. Since she had been gone, Alice seemed to have finally established some order out of the chaos. Seeing the clothes all neatly arranged with shoes and hats, Jessica realised how long she had been out looking for Jack.

'Did you get the whip?' said Alice, getting to her feet.

Jessica shook her head.

'No, no I didn't,' she said quickly. 'Jack was busy. Sorry.'

Alice moaned. 'Damn it. Never mind, I'll ask him when he comes in to be fitted for his costume. Are you all right? You look very pale. Why don't you go and stand by the fire and warm up.' She stretched. 'I'm just about done here now, though it'll be mayhem once everyone comes in to try their things on. I was going to ring and ask for a tray of coffee, maybe that will warm us up.'

Jessica huddled by the hearth, rubbing her hands together. Her shivering had nothing to do with the weather, but what she had seen in the stables. She could hardly believe her eyes.

She knew Jack had seen her and wondered how on earth she could face him again. The sense of shock at discovering him with the woman in the barn had been rapidly displaced by the same hungry need she had woken up with. What perturbed her was the intensity of what she felt. Had it been so long since she had felt a man buried deep inside her? She realised with a start that it had been years - and that she ached to be touched.

As Jack had plunged into the woman amongst the tumble of hay, she had felt her own sex contract instinctively, almost as if his cock was throbbing deep inside her. She could imagine his weight, the heat of his breath on her naked skin—

Jessica shivered again and huddled closer to the coals. What was it about Jack Healy that was so compelling? Or was it just that she had been alone too long? The thought brought a flurry of pain up in her throat and she struggled to hold back the tears that threatened to engulf her.

Before she had time to compose herself, the door to the drawing room burst open. Bunty Redknap came in, red-faced and sweating profusely.

'Are you ready for the animals yet, poppet?' he said to Alice. 'They're all champing at the bit to jump into their frocks.'

Alice snorted. 'I did say twelve, Bunty.'

Miranda scurried in, in Bunty's wake.

'But I've finished my read through.' She did a twirl. 'Of course I will marry you, Prince Charming,' she purred in a voice like liquid silk, fluttering her impossibly long eyelashes in a great show of virginal innocence.

Jessica stared at her and wondered if there was ever a Cinderella who oozed so much blatant sexuality. The pretence of innocence added a strange, erotic charge.

Bunty looked heavenwards.

'Sorry, Alice. I had to bring her with me; she just can't keep her hands off Buttons. And Prince Charming is getting a little piqued about it.'

Alice snorted. 'Miranda, darling, you are supposed to fall deeply, madly in love with Prince Charming. That's the whole point of the pantomime.'

Miranda pouted like a petulant schoolgirl. 'I do know that, but I don't like girls. I can't see why Helen has to play Prince Charming in the first place, and when she kisses me she keeps trying to ram her tongue halfway down my throat.' Miranda pulled a face. 'Besides, I never did like redheads.'

Jessica had an intense image of the red-headed woman writhing beneath Jack's body, matching him stroke for stroke as they fought their way towards release. She had no doubt that Helen, Miranda's Prince Charming, was the same stunning creature. Hadn't Jack said he thought she had a penchant for female flesh?

Beside her, Alice sighed and pulled a costume off the rails. 'If you insist, Bunty, but how you can rehearse Cinderella with her in here, is beyond me. Here, Miranda, try your rags on.'

Without a hint of self-consciousness, Miranda hauled her dress up over her head. Underneath she was wearing a tiny peach silk camisole top and French knickers. Her nipples hardened instantly in the cold. Jessica looked away just as Miranda tugged off her top. Her breasts were pert and tiny, the nipples disproportionately large, like saucers, each tipped with a hard pink bud.

Before Miranda had time to take the off-the-shoulder ragged costume Alice was holding for her, the doors to the dining room opened again and Jack Heally walked in. He absorbed the tableau in an instant and grinned.

'I always have had a good sense of good timing,' he said with a wry grin.

Miranda giggled and cupped her breasts in her hands, making a half-hearted attempt to cover herself. If anything, the effect seemed to accentuate her exposure.

'You're so naughty,' she said, with a giggle. 'I'm playing Cinderella.'

Jack snorted. 'Then all I can say is, my compliments to our costume designer.'

He noticed Jessica standing by the hearth and smiled.

'I see we meet again, Miss Harper. It rather appears that when there's something on show you're there to take in the sights.'

Jessica was so stunned that she couldn't move.

'I...' she began. Even as she opened her mouth she knew there were no words that she could possibly say. She felt herself blushing furiously and was angry for letting Jack disarm her so efficiently.

He moved closer, while Miranda slithered into her costume.

'Or is it,' he whispered, in an undertone, 'that you are afraid to experience the pleasures for yourself? Are you afraid, Jessica?'

She looked up into his dark eyes, unable to say a word. Her heart beat out a frantic rhythm and she felt so hot that she wondered fleetingly if she might faint.

'Well,' he said in a low voice. 'Are you afraid?'

Jessica tried hard to break away from the hold of his gaze.

She squared her shoulders. Surely she was stronger than this?

'No,' she said, in a soft voice. 'I'm not afraid. Or at least, I didn't used to be.'

Before Jack could reply, Alice's voice interrupted the intense hold his eyes had on Jessica.

'What do you fancy being then, Jack? There's plenty here to choose from. I've brought the most wonderful highwayman's costume with me.'

Jack spun round, releasing Jessica. She felt dizzy. 'Where is it?'

Alice held up a hanger with a frock coat and breeches on it. She grinned. 'Why don't you try it on? I'm sure it will suit you.'

Jack's eyes worked along the rails. 'Have you got any more spare costumes?'

Alice nodded. 'Dozens. I like to be prepared and besides, you did say you'd cover the cost of shipping and handling.'

Jack snorted and then took the hanger out of her fingers, eyes still moving along the clothes.

'How many costumes do you think you've got that aren't being used?'

Alice shrugged. 'I'm not sure, twenty, thirty, maybe more.'

'In that case, as I've paid for them to be delivered, why don't we have a fancy dress party? What do you think?'

Miranda, now transformed into a ragged, waif-like Cinderella, clapped her hands in delight.

'What a super idea. I know exactly what I can wear. I adore dressing up.' She spun round in a perfect pirouette. 'And you could be a naughty highwayman, Jack, come to steal my virtue.'

Bunty Redknap, who had been watching the proceedings with a world-weary eye, snorted and mopped his brow with a large handkerchief.

'A little late for that, Miranda, my dear. If you'll excuse me, I must be getting back to the mob. Shall I tell them that we're planning a fancy dress party as well as everything else?'

Jack picked up a tricorn hat, dropped it onto his head and nodded.

'Yes, on Christmas Eve, I think, if Alice doesn't mind everyone using the costumes. All my guests should be here by then.'

Alice lifted up her hands in surrender. 'If that's what you'd like, you're paying the piper.'

'There's your answer,' said Jack to Bunty, who nodded and left.

Jack turned back to Jessica, his intense expression returning. 'What about you? What would you like to come as?'

Jessica held his gaze.

'What do you suggest?' she said lightly, struggling to project a confidence she didn't quite feel. 'What about a top hat and veil? It did look rather fetching this morning.'

Jack threw back his head and laughed. 'Perhaps I've misjudged you,' he said, the humour lingering in his tone.

Jessica bit her lip. 'Perhaps.'

Jack moved closer and caught hold of her hand. 'You're fascinating, I'm very tempted to say I want you.'

Jessica jerked her hand away.

'Really?' she said, edging across the hearth. 'Is that supposed to be some kind of compliment? From what I've seen of you so far, you appear to already have everything you want.'

The mischievous sparkle didn't leave his eyes. 'And there was me thinking you were such a mouse,' he said in a gently mocking voice.

Jessica smiled. 'Perhaps it's just that I'm just out of practise.'

Behind them there was an explosion of noise as the rest of the theatrical troupe poured into the dining room like a river.

Alice leapt to her feet, arms spread wide to stop them helping themselves.

'Haven't any of you got a watch on? It's nowhere near twelve yet,' she snapped angrily.

Jessica slid past Jack.

'If you'll excuse me, I think Alice could do with a hand.'

Chapter 4

The Christmas Tree

Lunch was served at one o'clock in the dining room. Jessica couldn't help but smile as she took her seat at the table. Some of the actors stayed in costume, others had changed back to their normal day clothes, while others had settled on a compromise, mixing cavalry twills with a doublet, or in the case of Helen, the red-headed Prince Charming, embroidered jodhpurs and thigh boots with a Fair Isle twinset and pearls. It was a noisy affair, and Jessica was relieved to see that Jack had decided to absent himself from the mayhem.

She needed time to work out exactly what it was she felt. Across the table, Alice couldn't resist the temptation to fiddle with Dandinni's epaulets. The twins, Rupert and Bobby Haywood, argued about who was going to wear what, while Bunty Redknap, happy in his role as an ugly sister, ploughed through a plate of sausages wearing a bouffant cream wig.

Jessica sprinkled her lunch with salt, wondering what the staff at St Winifred's academy for young ladies would think if they could see her now. Familiar faces and names bubbled up in her mind. She wasn't sure exactly how she had ended up in such a safe academic backwater.

In some ways she had used her job as a sanctuary. It had given her a home, an occupation, something to fill her mind since Robert had been killed. The name of her fiancé sent a tiny flutter of well worn grief down her spine.

She looked up at Alice. They had both been engaged. Alice's lover, Ludo, had died in the Great War too, along with countless brothers and fathers and... She stopped the train of thought.

Perhaps it was time to let the memories heal. Moving on didn't mean that she had to forget. Robert had loved her too much to want her to spend the rest of her life in mourning.

Across the table, Alice lifted a glass in toast.

'Here's to a very jolly Christmas,' she said brightly, glancing round the assembled company. 'It's wonderful to see you all again.' Her gaze rested for a second or two on Jessica. 'Old friends,' she said quietly and drained the glass.

Jessica wondered if by some alchemy Alice had read her mind.

'Hear, hear,' said Bunty enthusiastically. 'Now, enough of this rampant sentimentality. After lunch I want everybody back to work, that's everybody. I want—'

'Look, look!' said one of the twins, cutting Bunty short as he clambered to his feet. He waved everyone over to the window. Outside, slowly wending their way across the windswept lawn, two men were struggling under the weight of an enormous pine tree.

Miranda's face lit up. 'Oh, the Christmas tree. I wonder if Jack's already arranged to dress it? I'm going to ask him if I can do it. Oh, I love Christmas.' Leaving her lunch she hurried out into the hall.

Bunty grimaced. 'Saints preserves us, that damned girl! Why on earth did you invite her, Alice?' he snapped in exasperation. 'Not to mention giving her the lead.'

Prince Charming, resplendent in her twinset and jodhpurs, smiled indulgently. 'She's very sweet,' she said.

Alice sighed. 'You know what Miranda's like. She'll be word perfect for the performance. She can learn lines as she breathes in. Don't worry, Bunty. I'll have a word with her. She's just excited, that's all.'

Bunty looked heavenwards and returned to his sausages.

Jessica watched the progress of men and tree. It was going to be a very strange Christmas.

Jack Healy sat in his study, looking down on the gardens. The tree was a gift from Felicia and George. It would look wonderful in the hall, decked and alight with candles. He poured himself a small post-luncheon brandy and then stretched back into his chair, his mind returning again and again to the matter of Jessica Harper. In the drawing room she had seemed less diffident. Her eyes had met his boldly and she had smiled with those full red lips.

He imagined her lips closed tight around his cock. The thought made the little trickle of desire boil in his belly and the fantasy rapidly took on a life of its own. When she had caressed him to hardness with her mouth, she would climb up onto his hips. Straddled across him, he imagined seeing the open wet lips of her quim blush pink amongst a sea of dark curled hair.

He could imagine the sensation of her breasts brushing his chest as she lowered herself slowly, delicately onto his shaft. He would gasp as her tightness closed around him, feeling the heat and the moisture engulf him like a silken glove.

Jack refilled his brandy glass. When he had looked into Jessica's eyes in the barn, he had sensed her hunger. His cock ached now, swollen and constricted inside his jodhpurs.

A knock at the door made him aware of where he was. Quickly buttoning his jacket, he went to answer it.

'Hello,' said Miranda, in her little girl lost voice. 'I hope I'm not disturbing you. Alice said I ought to come up and talk to you.'

Jack waved her in, thinking about the impression she had made on him in the drawing room.

'Not at all. How can I help you?'

Miranda smiled. 'They're just delivering the tree,' she said breathlessly. 'And I wondered if you'd let me help decorate it? I love all those pretty little baubles and things.'

She paused, glancing down at the not inconsiderable bulge in his riding breeches. Her face coloured a little. She glanced around the room as if she half expected to see someone else there.

'Are you sure I'm not disturbing you?' she said, in breathy little whisper, eyes slowly returning to the outline of his cock.

Jack guessed that Prince Charming had already told everyone about their mutual passion over his desk - or perhaps, he thought with a wry smile, it had been Jessica who had let the cat out of the bag. Whichever, Miranda's glance was as welcome as a kiss, or the application of a knowing pair of hands. He felt the ache in his groin growing stronger.

Miranda shifted position, tipping one bare shoulder forward slightly. She was still wearing the ragged Cinderella costume and looked quite divine. In places, the dress was ripped to mid-thigh and as she moved he could see the silky fabric of her French knickers underneath. Barefoot and ragged, she had a touching air of vulnerability.

'Perhaps,' she said, eyes glittering, 'there is something I could do for you in return?'

Jack grinned - her invitation was unambiguous.

'Perhaps there is,' he said. 'What have you got in mind?'

She ran a hand down over her shoulder, down to her tiny breasts, where the fingers lingered on her rapidly hardening nipples.

'Oh, I don't know,' she said casually. Her hand snaked lower still, gathering up the ragged skirt.

Jack let out a long, low hiss of admiration, as she stroked at the lips of her quim where they pressed against the silk of her drawers. Her finger slid back and forth, brushing the front of her knickers. He could almost feel the liquid heat.

'Why don't you suggest something?' she said huskily. 'I'm very good at doing what I'm told.'

Jack coughed to clear his throat and his mind.

'In that case, why don't you come over here and let me do that for you?' he said thickly.

Miranda smiled, her eyes darkening as her fingers worked slowly on and on. 'I like a man to tell me what to do,' she said, creeping closer.

'Stop touching yourself then,' he said, letting an authoritative edge creep into his voice. Her hand fluttered away like a tiny bird.

'Take off your knickers and let me look at you,' he said, feeling his cock throbbing in his jodhpurs.

The girl shimmied out of her drawers, holding the skirt up so that he could examine her. Her sex was plump, like a ripe peach, trimmed with a ruff of palest mink.

She flexed her hips so the lips parted a fraction, revealing the moist crimson treasures within. Jack swallowed hard and then groaned aloud as there was another knock on the door. Miranda, to his surprise, didn't move, but remained still, holding up her skirt as if she had been frozen to the spot.

Shaking his head in disbelief, Jack opened the door a fraction and was surprised to see Felicia Gudgeon standing on the landing, still dressed in her riding habit.

'George has gone out. I just don't believe it,' she snapped crossly, pushing past him. 'Not so much as a word, not even a little note. It's so unlike him. I see the tree arrived—'

The words dried in her throat as she saw Miranda standing in front of Jack's desk. She lifted an eyebrow.

'No wonder you didn't throw the door open and welcome me in. Is this one of your precious little theatricals?'

Jack nodded. 'This is Miranda. She is trading a little light relief for the chance to decorate your precious tree.'

Felicia smiled. 'Oh Jack, and there was me thinking I was the only woman in your life.' She laughed. 'What a terrible shame you haven't got a title or oodles of money. If you had, I could leave George and stay here with you all the time. What you really need is a wife to take you in hand.' As she spoke she let her eyes move down slowly to his angry cock, leaving him in no doubt what she meant. Jack reddened.

Beside them, Miranda shivered. Felicia smiled again. 'Don't let me keep you from your fun.' She eyed the girl's body speculatively. 'Or perhaps you'd prefer it if I joined in? Would you like that?'

Jack was about to speak when Miranda said softly, 'I'm not awfully keen on girls.'

Felicia pulled off her little top hat and veil and threw them onto Jack's desk.

'Oh, don't let that worry you, poppet. Just think of me as another of your endless string of admirers. Besides, it's my tree.' She dropped to her knees, and planted a moist kiss on the fragrant folds of the girl's quim. Jack stared at Felicia with a mixture of astonishment and delight.

Miranda let out a little squeal of pleasure as Felicia ran her tongue along the sensitive, peachy, lush lips. Miranda's reluctance vanished in an instant, and Jack moved closer, watching with delight as the girl writhed and giggled in response to Felicia's busy tongue.

He found it impossible to simply be an observer; he'd been excited before Miranda arrived. Felicia's joining them and her reaction had been completely unexpected - but certainly not unwelcome. Dropping to his knees he lifted Felicia's full skirt, running an appreciative hand over her rounded buttocks.

She responded by dropping her hips, giving him greater access. It took him seconds to slide aside her panties, still wet and hot from his earlier attentions. She moaned at his caresses, pressing her mouth to Miranda's gaping quim as he brushed the swollen ridge of her clitoris.

'Oh please, just fuck me, Jack,' she murmured against the girl's compliant body. 'I'll teach George to go out without telling me.'

Jack, finally unleashing his hungry anxious cock, couldn't help but smile.

Felicia was furious and that, quite simply, was the explanation for her behaviour. She was seducing Miranda out of pure spite. Miranda really didn't mind either. She was very quickly reaching the point of no return. Slipping the shoulder strap of her costume down, her fingers were working at the hard engorged peaks of her huge nipples.

Jack guided his cock inside the familiar contours of Felicia's body, letting her anger and her need draw him deeper. Her heat embraced him and like a handshake she teased him by nipping the muscles of her quim tight around him. It was a sensation that always took his breath away - and now was no exception. She started to move, contracting her sex as a rhythmic counterpoint to the thrusts of her hips.

He knew he couldn't hold out long, and fought to bring her with him, struggling to keep up a steady circling motion on her little pleasure bud. It seemed that her fury acted as an aphrodisiac. The rhythm of her hips rapidly became ragged and instinctive.

Bucking beneath him, Felicia let out a little shriek of pleasure, while above them, Miranda echoed Felicia's delight with a throaty gasp of satisfaction. Seeing the women's shared orgasm, Jack was tipped over into the raging sea along with them.

No sooner had the last wave passed than Felicia got to her feet, went across to the sideboard and poured herself a stiff brandy. When she turned round, her face was impassive. She looked at the tray on Jack's desk.

'Eating alone? With all these cheerful souls in the house? Shame on you, Jack. Or is it that you just can't make up your mind which one to savour next?' She pulled a sliver of chicken off the bone on his plate and popped it between the lips that had so recently been feasting on Miranda's fragrant sex.

Miranda, her skin flushed, eyes alight, tidied her skirt and pulled her shoulder strap back up so the bodice covered her breasts. 'Can I deck the tree then?' she said cheerfully.

Jack, still on his knees, shook his head in disbelief, wondering how they could walk away as if nothing had happened. He nodded towards Miranda.

'Once the tree is set up I'll have the servants bring down the baubles for you.' The girl's face shone with delight. 'And as for you, Felicia, would you like me to order you a sandwich or would you prefer me to send my groom over to Tideacre to see if George is back yet?'

Felicia pulled a face. 'No, I'm going to stay out very late now, just to spite him.' She looked Miranda up and down. 'Maybe I'll help your little friend here to deck the tree.'

Jack shrugged. Who could figure the workings of the female mind?

'I think I'd better send the groom anyway so that George won't worry.'

Felicia pouted angrily. 'But I want him to worry.' She turned away. 'Do whatever you think is best. I'm off with—' she paused, tipping her head towards Miranda in mute enquiry.

The girl smiled her most beatific smile. 'Miranda de la Belle, I'm an actress,' she said breathlessly.

'Exactly, Miss Belle. I'm off with Miss Belle to sort the tree out.' She plucked the top hat off his desk. 'And if you'd like to arrange a sandwich as well, I'd be grateful, but not chicken. I really hate chicken.'

Jack smiled. 'Whatever you say, Felicia.'

Jessica hung the last of the ugly sisters' petticoats back on the rail and turned to look at Alice, who was brushing Bunty Redknap's wig. Outside it was already dark. The drawing room was bright with gas lamps and a fire burnt cheerfully in the grate.

Alice sighed and dropped the brush back onto a little side table. 'He's got gravy on this, would you believe it?' She leant closer and picked at the thick horsehair. 'And this looks remarkably like a smidgen of Lincolnshire pork sausage. If he weren't such a good director I'd be angry with him.' She stretched, pressing her hands to the small of her back. 'Actually, I might be angry with him anyway. He splashed red wine all down the front of his frock at lunch. God knows how I'm going to get the stain out.'

She looked across at Jessica. 'Pass me a glass of the same, will you? I've hidden a bottle of claret over there by the potted palm, or whatever that monstrosity is.' She grinned and pulled up a chair by the fireplace. 'You know, I think you unnerve Jack.'

Jessica, handing her friend a glass from the tray secreted in the foliage, looked up in surprise.

'I unnerve him?' she snorted, pulling the cork out of the bottle and filling both glasses. 'You must be joking. Every time I see the man, he is buried up to the hilt in some woman.'

Alice burst into laughter, choking as she inhaled a mouthful of wine.

'Don't exaggerate. You've only seen him with Helen, our dear lusty Prince Charming, surely that hardly counts as every time.'

Jessica blushed, taking a long pull on her wine glass. 'I haven't told you about this morning in the barn yet,' she said thickly.

Alice giggled, pressing her hand to her mouth. 'Oh no, not again? You're making it up.'

Jessica shook her head, feeling the wine working mischief in her stomach.

'It's true. This time he was with some snooty woman in a top hat and not very much else.'

Alice leant across and lifted her glass. 'Well, in that case, why don't we drink a toast to ladies in top hats?'

Jessica giggled and refilled her glass. 'All joking aside, I still think I ought to leave.'

Alice pulled a face. 'Oh, come on. Don't say that, Jessica. I need you here, you've seen what they're like. It would be like a menagerie if it weren't for you and me.'

Jessica held up a hand to silence her.

'That's the problem. I'm just not used to mixing with people like Jack, or Miranda or Bunty.' She paused. 'Or you, really. I have to tell you, Alice, I saw the photos of you and Charlie at your flat.'

Alice pulled a face. 'Really? Actually, that happened because of Jack as well.'

Jessica coloured. 'He wasn't the other man, was he?' she began.

'No, for God's sake, no,' snapped Alice defensively. 'I was really down on my luck. I was walking down Shaftesbury Avenue and there was Jack, all bright eyed and bushy tailed. He introduced me to a chap running a little revue club. Jack used to pop in to see me whenever he was in town.' She swirled the wine around in her glass. 'It was a nice job really; I was working as stage manager, wardrobe mistress, jack of all trades. The manager asked if I'd like to make a little extra money and that, as they say, was it. I'm not ashamed of the photographs. They paid the bills and helped me to pay for the lease on my flat.' She giggled. 'Though I would prefer it if my mother didn't find them.'

Jessica looked at her. 'And you met Charlie as well?' Alice giggled again. 'I should have said it was a mixed blessing.'

Jessica sat back on her heels, staring into the coals. 'We're just such different people now, Alice. Our lives are so far apart.' She looked up into her friend's eyes. 'It's an awfully long time since we shared a room at St Faith's.' Alice smiled and leaned forward, pressing a kiss to Jessica's forehead.

'I know, darling. It's funny, I was just thinking, sitting here, how much this seems like the senior common room. You and me snuggled up by the fire, only this time we've got claret, not cocoa.'

Jessica shivered. 'You never kissed me then,' she said, turning the wine glass round in her fingers.

Alice smiled. 'We were all far too chaste then, darling.' Their eyes met and Jessica felt a little glow of tenderness deep inside. Even now some part of her loved Alice and always would. Quickly she looked away, not wanting to contemplate the consequences.

'I keep thinking about Jack Heally,' she said quickly.

'Who wouldn't,' Alice snorted. 'I was going to say you hadn't seen his good side, but perhaps you have.'

'He makes me feel things I haven't felt for years. They're feelings that I thought had died since Robert was killed.'

Alice stared at her. 'And that's why you want to leave Malestone?'

Jessica shook her head. 'I don't know. I suppose I thought I'd never feel like that again. I only had to look at Robert and my whole body ached for him.' She drained her glass with an air of finality. 'Maybe I've lived too long without a man in my life. I feel like some silly schoolgirl with a crush. Jack Heally just makes me go weak at the knees. Ridiculous really, he's a complete rake and a womaniser. And what's worse is that being here, with all your worldly-wise cronies, I feel like some sort of simpering, narrow-minded schoolgirl, while at work I'm respected and in control. Silly, isn't it?'

Alice caught hold of her friend's hands. 'No, I don't think so, not really. Please don't go. Jack just isn't used to being around women like you. I'd really like you to stay. You've always been so special to me.'

Jessica's heart missed a beat. She and Alice were so close she could pick out the tiny freckles on her friend's nose. The wine had softened her fear. It was so tempting just to lean a little closer and kiss Alice. The thought was so unexpected that Jessica gasped and jumped to her feet.

'What is it?' said Alice, anxiously. 'Are you all right?'

Jessica blushed. 'I think I heard the gong for dinner,' she lied.

Alice looked up at the clock on the mantelpiece. 'It's barely seven. Mind you, perhaps we ought to go and change. Jack likes to eat promptly at eight and I feel so grimy. I just hope Bunty hasn't stolen all the bathwater. I'm not quite sure what he does in the bath.' She got stiffly to her feet. 'Will you help me turn the lamps down?'

Jessica nodded and hurried across the room. With her back to Alice, she wondered where the rogue desire had come from.

Upstairs, as Jessica dressed for dinner, she stared into the dressing table mirror. Coming to Malestone House seemed to have unbottled a wellspring of feelings that she had kept in check. In fact, she had controlled them so long that she had forgotten they existed.

Her head ached - it would be easy to blame the wine, but she knew it wasn't that. She imagined Alice leaning towards her in front of the hearth. It wouldn't have taken much for her to have kissed Alice - and from the dark invitation in Alice's stormy grey eyes she knew her advance wouldn't have been unwelcome. What was happening to her?

She slipped off her dressing gown, almost unconsciously, and stared at her body. It had a creamy glow to it, a certain air of ripeness that was unmistakable. Her breasts were small but full, with the palest pink nipples. Below, her narrow waist swelled provocatively into broad womanly hips, which in turn framed the dark triangle of her sex.

She felt a shiver of sadness - she had neglected her physical needs for so long that it almost felt as if they had come back to haunt her. Tentatively she stroked at the buds of her nipples. They hardened under her fingertips and as she circled them, seeking comfort, her body cried out for more.

Almost without thought, while one hand worked on her nipples, she brushed her fingers down over her ribs and belly, relishing the sensation the touch lit - as if the caress ignited a trail of flares in its wake.

In the mirror she watched her fingers outline the lips of her sex and sensed the rich heat within, creamy and soft. How could she have forgotten how good this felt? A single finger slipped inside, sensations of heat and wetness engulfing her. Under her fingertip was the little pulsing bud, seat of all pleasure. She threw back her head and closed her eyes. Relinquishing reality, she let her mind wander free, imagining Jack Heally crouching between her legs, his tongue playing a symphony on her clitoris, while behind her, Alice cupped and circled her breasts with knowing fingers, pressing the soft triangle of her own quim against Jessica's spine.

She imagined Jack's fingers working deep inside her and then sliding back between her open legs, to explore Alice's tight sopping quim. His caresses mingled their juices in an erotic cocktail of pleasure, while between her legs, Jessica felt his tongue lapping on and on.

The images were too much. Jessica felt the waves of pleasure gathering low down in her belly, followed by another and another. It was like riding a white, roaring explosion, made all the more stunning because it had been dammed up for so long. The sensations took her breath away. Her fantasy was so vivid that she could almost hear Alice gasping behind her.

When she opened her eyes as the last of the tremors passed, Jessica was almost surprised to find herself still standing in front of the mirror. The eyes that looked back at her were dark and glittering. She leant forward to look at her own familiar features. Tiny diamonds of sweat had lifted on her top lip, her skin was flushed and glowing with energy. She swallowed hard - it really had been too long since she had felt like this.

From downstairs she heard the doleful clang of the gong announcing dinner and hurried to get dressed. Just before opening the door, she took one final look in the mirror.

The dark eyes had returned to normal, her glowing skin just made her look alarmingly wholesome and healthy. Jessica smiled at her reflection. Perhaps she ought to stay at Malestone after all.

Chapter 5

Bunty's Cabaret

As Jessica reached the landing, the noise from the hall bubbled up towards her. Looking over the banister, she was surprised to see Miranda giggling and talking with the woman she had seen earlier in the day with Jack in the barn. Between them was a table, littered with tinsel, holly and glass balls. A huge sheet had been suspended from the landing, masking the Christmas tree, though Jessica could look down on it as she descended the stairs.

Bunches of holly and ivy, bound together with lavish red ribbon bows, had been hung all around the room. Miranda and her friend had obviously been busy - the whole room had a festive air.

The theatre troupe were standing in small groups, gossiping and sipping aperitifs. Jack Heally was handing out cocktails with the help of a footman and looked up as Jessica made her way down the stairs towards him.

'Good evening,' he said pleasantly. 'May I interest you in a little drink before we have dinner?'

Jessica nodded, aware that the tiny knot of tension had reappeared in her stomach. He handed her a glass, the drink inside topped off with a slice of lemon and a cherry.

'Try one of these, they're absolutely wonderful. Bunty gave me his special recipe.' As he spoke, his gaze moved slowly down over her body. She felt herself colour under his undisguised examination and was angry that he could have such an effect on her. She straightened up and looked him in the eye.

'Your friend isn't wearing her top hat this evening?' she said, nodding towards Miranda and the woman in a riding habit.

Jack smiled. 'Her name is Felicia Gudgeon. She is married to one of my oldest and dearest friends, Sir George Gudgeon.'

Jessica lifted her glass in salute. 'You obviously take friendship very seriously.'

Jack grinned. 'Well, of course. I'm extremely loyal, obliging and very, very discreet. Ask Felicia if you don't believe me.' He turned to the tray behind him and took a glass for himself. 'Perhaps we ought to drink a toast to friendship.' He looked across the room, following the progress of Alice Fallon towards them.

Jessica felt her colour intensify. Had he guessed how she felt about Alice and if so, how? She sipped her drink, hoping he wouldn't notice her discomfort. Alice, looking wonderful in a grey silk evening dress, eased her way between the press of people and pulled a rueful face.

'I really can't believe it. Bunty is still wallowing in the bathtub - and he's taken all the hot water.'

Jack poured her a drink. 'I'm afraid the plumbing at Malestone is rather antiquated. My father thought too many creature comforts made a man soft.'

Alice waved his apology away. 'Oh, it's all right. I'm not complaining. It's like home from home, except that in London it's Charlie who hogs all the water.' She took a long pull from her glass and eyed the contents appreciatively. 'Gosh, this is delicious. What's Miranda got planned for the tree?'

Jack smiled. 'A grand unveiling after we've eaten, I think. It was Felicia's idea.'

Jessica pointed the diminutive Felicia out to Alice. 'That's Felicia over there, she's the one without the top hat.'

Alice smothered a giggle with the back of her hand and then looked at Jessica. 'You decided to stay, then?'

Jessica nodded. 'I think so.' She glanced back at Jack who was mixing another jug of cocktails. 'I think maybe I've been overreacting. You may just have saved me from a life as a crusty old maid at St Winifred's.'

Alice grinned. 'Could be.'

On the far side of the hall servants opened double doors into the dining room. It appeared that Miranda and Felicia had been at work there, too. The panelling was hung with swags of luxuriant greenery and ribbons, while the centre of the table was dominated by a row of ornate candelabra, all alight and decked out with glass baubles. The effect was magical.

Jack smiled as the group fell silent.

'Miranda, Felicia, I think you've achieved the impossible and shut everyone up. It looks marvellous.'

Miranda turned round, blushing with delight. 'It is lovely, isn't it? Just wait until you see the tree.'

The silence didn't last long. Everyone seemed to begin talking at once and headed in to eat. Jack offered Alice and Jessica an arm each. 'Shall we dine, ladies?' he said.

Alice smiled and slipped her arm through his.

'You're so very gallant, Jack Heally,' she said with a grin. 'I'd quite forgotten how much I enjoy your company.'

Jessica was a little more reluctant. As her hand touched his, she felt a little *frisson* of excitement. Jack, as if he felt it too, turned towards her.

'I'd be honoured if you'd both sit next to me,' he said, in an undertone. 'I have always preferred the company of beautiful women.'

Jessica lifted an eyebrow.

'You surprise me,' she said with a smile. 'What about your friend, Felicia? Won't she be miffed that you haven't offered her your arm?'

'Oh, don't worry about Felicia. She is quite entranced with Miranda at the moment. She won't even notice.' Ahead of them the footmen were pulling out chairs for the diners.

Guided by Jack, Jessica sat on his right, Alice on his left. 'Alice, I'd like to run through what we've got planned for the next few days.' Jack shook a linen napkin out on his lap as he spoke, while around them the servants began to serve the soup.

Alice smiled. 'I knew I should have brought my notebook.' She glanced down the length of the table. 'Bunty isn't here yet, that's odd.'

Jack smiled. 'I have an idea he is up to something, don't worry. I'll organise for whatever it is he misses to be put aside for him. Now, tell me again what you've got planned.' Alice looked up, as if trying to pluck thoughts out of thin air. 'Right, all your guests will be here by the twenty-second? Yes?'

Jack nodded. 'That's right. Some will be arriving tomorrow, but most of them are coming down on Friday.'

'We'll be rehearsing until then. We've got a little revue planned for the twenty-second, lots of songs, jokes - you know the kind of thing. Then there's the Pantomime on the twenty-third. Your fancy dress ball on Christmas Eve.' She grinned, counting the events off on her fingers. 'Then carols around the tree on Christmas Day and that, my dear, is about it.'

Jack picked up his spoon. 'Sounds fine. Let's eat the soup while it's hot. Now about...'

Jessica wasn't quite sure whether she was relieved or frustrated that the main topic of conversation revolved around what Alice had planned for the festivities, and who was doing what.

Bunty Redknap, resplendent in a spotty bowtie, plus-fours and Norfolk jacket, arrived along with the main course. Settling himself down, he amused everyone by standing a bowl of soup beside his plate, alternating between the two. When Alice asked him where he had been, he tapped his nose and winked.

The food and wine were plentiful and after a glass or two Jessica felt herself relaxing.

Jack was a wonderful host, making jokes, talking intelligently about a dozen different things - maybe she had misjudged him after all.

'You are going to sing too, aren't you?' said one of the Haywood twins who was seated next to Jessica. 'Alice says you've got a lovely voice.'

Jessica was about to answer, not certain whether she was speaking to Rupert or Bobby, when she felt a hand brush her leg. For a second, she thought she had imagined it.

'I'm a bit rusty,' she began. As she spoke, the hand moved delicately up over her thigh, stroking tentatively. She felt the heat rising in the pit of her stomach and looked, red-faced, at Jack. He appeared to be deep in conversation with Alice about how best to arrange the stage curtains.

The twin, meanwhile, refilled Jessica's wine glass.

'Oh, come on,' he said. 'No room for false modesty here. What are you? Contralto, soprano?'

Jessica tried very hard to concentrate on his voice, while in her lap, the touch of the unseen hand was compelling and totally unnerving. She took a deep breath. The fingers began to stroke at the soft folds of fabric covering her sex. As casually as she could, Jessica glanced down. Jack's hand rested innocently on her thigh. She pulled her napkin up over it, then turned her attention back to the twin on her left.

'Contralto,' she said softly. 'I'm a contralto.'

The twin clapped his hands. 'I knew it. Do you know the contralto part for "Silent Night"? It's one of my favourites, I...'

Under cover of the linen napkin, Jack's hand moved stealthily across the rise of Jessica's sex, trying to persuade her to open her legs. She glared at him, wanting him to catch her eye so she could make him stop. She froze as the thought formed. Did she really want him to stop?

As if he could read her mind, Jack slowly began to gather up her skirt with his fingertips, pulling the material higher and higher. She didn't resist him, struggling instead to keep her concentration on what her fellow diners were saying.

Beside her, Jack shifted position, apparently enraptured by Alice's conversation about wings, and tabs, and spotlights, but Jessica knew it was to give him greater access. Almost without thinking, as he brushed the silken folds of her knickers, she opened her legs a fraction. His expression did not betray the fact that he was so close to the prize, if anything he seemed even more engrossed in Alice's suggestions.

His caresses were soft but persistent. He seemed to know exactly where to touch her. A single finger eased under the moist fabric of her knickers, trying hard to find a way in.

Jessica slipped a little lower in the chair and was instantly rewarded by Jack's finger sliding inside her.

She felt her colour deepen as he began to explore the sensitive folds. She glanced around the table at the faces of her fellow guests. They seemed totally oblivious to the seduction being played out under the table. Beside her, the Haywood twin was still cataloguing his favourite carols.

This couldn't really be happening. Glancing down, she could see her nipples hardening through the fabric of her dress and wondered where on earth this was going to lead. She didn't dare contemplate the idea that Jack's tender invasion might bring her to the point of no return. It was unthinkable.

Suddenly, Jack swung round to face her, eyes alight with mischief and desire. Inside her knickers, his fingers wriggled provocatively, sending a shuddering bolt of pleasure through her.

'A contralto, eh?' he said conversationally. 'You really are full of surprises, aren't you, Jessica?'

She stared at him, trying hard to maintain her composure. 'I'm a little out of practice. It's been several years since I last performed,' she said carefully, suppressing a shiver as his thumb brushed down over her throbbing clitoris.

He refilled her glass. 'Oh, don't worry,' he said pleasantly. 'I'm sure it will all come flooding back to you, if only you'd let it. What you need is a little more confidence in your own abilities. Relax a little more.'

Jessica didn't know whether to be furious or to laugh.

Meanwhile, Jack stared into her eyes, obviously expecting a reply, while his devilish fingers slipped in and out of her sopping quim.

She coughed and looked down, breaking the hold of his gaze.

'What do you suggest?' she said, glancing up at him from under her lashes.

Jack grinned, hand slithering out from inside her, leaving her feeling unfulfilled and empty.

'Oh, lots of practice, I'd say,' he said mischievously. 'They do say practice makes perfect.'

'That's right,' said the twin sitting beside her. 'I wouldn't mind helping you, if you've got a mind to practise. I play the piano jolly well. I'm singing my usual set in the review, I know that inside out and I'm just a guest at Prince Charming's ball, so I've got plenty of time to put you through your paces, if you fancy the idea.'

Jack pressed his fingers together in front of his face and leant forward, breathing deeply.

Jessica shivered, knowing he would be able to smell her excitement.

'There we are then,' he said with delight. 'A volunteer, what more could you want?'

Jessica smiled at the twin. 'That's very kind of you.' She looked back at Jack, eyes alight. 'Presumably you don't need any practice.'

Jack grinned, lifting a wine glass to his lips.

'Oh, I never practise,' he said in a low voice. 'I'm a natural.'

Jessica struggled not to blush but found it impossible. Fortunately, the tension was broken by the arrival of dessert. Bunty's ecstatic whoop of delight, when they gave him a huge dish full of steamed treacle sponge and custard, made everyone laugh.

As the drawing room was full of costumes, coffee and liqueurs were served in the hall. While a footman handed out cigars to the gentlemen, Felicia and Miranda scurried back and forth, in preparation for the unveiling of the tree.

At some prearranged signal the lights in the hall were lowered and Bunty Redknap, on the piano, played a triumphant flurry of chords in the gloom.

Jessica had spent most of her time with Alice since dinner, pointedly avoiding Jack, who seemed happy to circulate, chatting to the other members of the troupe. Occasionally he would glance up and catch her eyes, his expression alight with mischief.

As Bunty's spectacular piano solo came to a close, Felicia waved towards the two footmen positioned on the balcony. On the count of three, they released the ropes holding the huge cotton sheet. As it fluttered to the ground the tree was exposed. It was beautiful, decked out with glittering golden and silver baubles and a wealth of tinsel and shiny parcels which glittered in the light from the fire.

A flurry of spontaneous applause broke out amongst the little group. As it faded, Bunty began to pick out another tune on the piano. It sounded Arabian, and within seconds of it beginning, one of the other players picked up a clarinet to add a sensuous counter rhythm.

Jessica glanced round, trying to work out what was happening. On the bottom of the stairs, someone lit two lamps, so that the flight of steps was illuminated in

41

a makeshift spotlight.

Beside her, Alice giggled.

'This must have been why Bunty was late for dinner.' Open-mouthed, Jessica watched as a figure slowly descended the stairs, dressed as an Arab slave boy, complete with sheer silk trousers, a jewel in his navel and a tiny cropped waistcoat. It took her a few seconds to realise it was one of the Haywood twins who she had been talking to at dinner. His blonde hair was slicked back, eyes outlined with kohl. He moved sensuously, circling his hips in time to the hypnotic music of the clarinet and piano.

'So that's where my Aladdin costume went to,' Alice hissed crossly.

The boy's movements were erotically charged, though his eyes were focused on the middle distance. His pelvis circled slowly, hips gyrating in time to Bunty Redknap's accompaniment. After a few seconds, another figure shimmied in from the shadows to join him. Dressed as a sultan, Helen, Prince Charming, crossed her arms over her heavy breasts and beckoned the slave boy towards her. Her handsome face was stern and forbidding. The boy danced towards her, his light movements a stark contrast to the woman beside him. She mimed her disapproval and then indicated he ought to fetch something. Head bowed, the boy danced off into the shadows, whilst the female sultan slowly began to unfasten her waistcoat.

Jessica was stunned, hypnotised by the figures in the spotlight. She was uncertain whether what she felt was excitement or shock.

The boy reappeared, carrying a huge towel and an ornate jug. She beckoned him closer. He dipped his hands into the jug and then began to undress her with the deference of a terrified slave. His hands slid up under her waistcoat, pushing it back off her broad shoulders so that her heavy breasts were exposed. His fingers, presumably oiled, left a shimmering trail to mark his progress. There was a murmur of approval from the audience as the boy's hands lingered over her nipples.

When he finally took them away, Jessica could see that the tip of each breast was encrusted with gems and an ornate ring hung from each. The boy, worshipping his mistress, pressed a respectful kiss to each heavy ring, before snaking around behind her. His hands worked at the tie of the woman's harem pants, pulling the string back and forth, hands sliding between her muscular legs. The woman flexed her knees, allowing him to slither beneath her, planting kisses on her mount of Venus, which jutted forward like a clenched fist.

The atmosphere created by the dancers was electrifying. Every eye in the room was firmly on the makeshift stage. Jessica, hardly able to believe her eyes, felt every pulse of the music vibrate through her, making her mouth water and her body hum.

On stage, the boy artfully removed his mistress's trousers and at the very last second, just before she was exposed - wrapped her in the folds of the towel.

The woman, holding the corners of the towel out like wings, shimmied towards him, obscuring the audience's view of her voluptuous frame. The boy aped fear and then surrender. Jessica glanced down at his harem trousers and saw, to her surprise, the jutting outline of his cock pressing against the thin fabric.

This wasn't acting or miming, the boy was genuinely aroused by the woman's gyrations.

Jessica felt heat rising in her stomach, as the tempo of the music subtly changed so that it began to throb like an excited heartbeat.

Suddenly, the woman turned to face her audience, jiggling her rounded hips in a mesmerising display of eastern dancing. The hair around her sex was clipped close to the skin so that every thrust, every shimmy, revealed a little more of the moist folds within. She bent her knees - head thrown back - while the slave boy crept closer and closer.

Jessica realised she was holding her breath.

On stage, the boy pulled down the waistband of his trousers and cradled his throbbing cock between his fingers.

Jessica stared in astonishment - his shaft was oiled and glinted like smooth silk in the lamp light, but more surprising still was the silver ring which hung from his foreskin.

Undulating towards her, the ring shimmering like a cut diamond, he guided his arched cock deep inside his sultan queen - who rewarded him with a moan of pure pleasure.

Jessica felt her sex contract as the boy slid home. She could almost feel his bulk, and the heat where he pressed up against the woman's body. She closed her eyes, imagining the cool silver ring nestled tight up inside her, its cold kiss a stunning contrast to the heat and wetness.

The idea took her breath away and made her shiver. She felt heady, knowing there was nothing that would distract her until the performance on stage had reached its obvious conclusion.

The couple began to move together. Jessica couldn't believe that their movements were choreographed, but it seemed as if they were still dancing. The boy bent over backwards towards the audience, forcing himself deeper, while the woman supported him by grasping his waist. A glisten of sweat rose between her heavy breasts, and trickled down like a kiss towards the junction of their two bodies.

Out in the shadows, seamlessly woven in and out of the dance, Jessica was aware of music driving the lovers on towards release. She heard the tempo quicken again and knew, without a doubt, that the slave boy and his sultan queen were lost.

The boy shuddered, grabbing the woman around the hips and to Jessica's surprise, at the very point of release they began to turn around. The effect was startling. On and on they moved until finally, exhausted, they both stepped out into the shadows.

There was a split second's silence and then a thunderous burst of applause. The slave boy, trousers now back in place and the sultan queen wrapped up in her towel, stepped back into the spotlight to take a long slow bow to renewed applause and whistles of approval.

Jessica turned away, letting out a long held breath. She had never witnessed anything like the exhibition on the stage and couldn't believe the sensations the dancers had lit inside her. Trembling she looked up, straight into the dark glittering eyes of Jack Heally.

He grinned. 'Perhaps our little friend is the perfect partner for you to practise with after all,' he said in a low voice. 'He certainly has an awful lot of style.'

Jessica drained the glass she was holding.

'I'm not sure whether it was him or his twin,' she said flatly, trying hard to keep the emotion out of her voice. 'It's very difficult to tell them apart.'

Jack snorted. 'Perhaps you ought to try both of them. If they're both as good as that, it seems a terrible shame to miss out on the opportunity.'

The light in the hall grew brighter. He took her glass and then turned to Alice.

'Would you like a refill, too?' he asked. 'I must say, I have to compliment you on the calibre of performers you've brought down with you. They're quite stunning.'

Alice snorted. 'Don't thank me, thank Bunty. He insisted I invite the Haywood boys. This little performance was undoubtedly his idea. He adores them both, he just can't make up his mind which one he loves best. I'm surprised he didn't have them both up there performing. Helen would have lapped it up.' She grinned. 'Literally and metaphorically. And, yes, if it's another of Bunty's cocktails you're offering me, fill it up.'

Jack turned back to Jessica, who really hadn't recovered from the effects of the performance. 'And what about you, Jessica, what would you like?'

The expression on his face suggested it wasn't just a drink that was on offer.

'A cocktail would be fine for me, too,' she said lightly, refusing to be drawn into another word game with him.

Jack lifted an eyebrow. 'Wouldn't you prefer to sample something a little stronger? I'm sure I could find something that you'd enjoy.' As he spoke he lifted a finger to his mouth and sucked it.

Jessica stared at him, feeling an unnerving ripple of excitement. His lips worked greedily at the finger he had slipped inside her. She didn't know what to say and stared at him, feeling a strange tight sensation growing stronger in her stomach.

Unexpectedly, Felicia Gudgeon came to her rescue. Hurrying across the room, face flushed with delight, she caught hold of Jack's arm.

'My God, Jack, that was absolutely wonderful. I really wish George had been here to see it. He'd have loved your little floor show.' She glanced up at the long case clock near the hall stand.

'I expect he's home by now. Did you do the right thing and send a groom over to tell him that I was here?'

Jack nodded. 'Of course, I said you had stayed to help deck the tree and would be home after dinner.'

Felicia pouted. 'So now I'm supposed to leave, am I?'

Jack smiled. 'You could always give him a ring and tell him you're staying a little longer. I'm not sure what else Bunty and Alice have in store for us.'

Alice shrugged. 'Don't look at me, darling. I'd planned on an early night.'

'No, no, you're right,' Felicia said briskly. 'I really ought to be off. Is there any chance either you or one of your thespian friends could run me home in a motor? It's a bit dark to ride back on Topper.'

Jack nodded. 'I've already had him stabled. Give me a minute or two and I'll arrange a driver for you. Why don't you have another cocktail while you wait?'

Felicia sighed theatrically. 'Oh, all right, if you insist,' she said. 'I'm sure I could force another one down. Let me go and find Miranda.'

Chapter 6

Alice's Midnight Feast

Anything that followed the entertainment arranged by Bunty Redknap would seem anticlimactic, but it didn't stop the actors and dancers gathering round the piano and then the gramophone to sing and dance. Jessica was reminded of Alice's comment about her live-in lover, Charlie. 'He'd tap dance under a streetlight, if you let him.' It seemed all theatricals were made of the same stuff.

Everyone clamoured for the chance to shine, including Felicia Gudgeon, who joined Miranda at the piano to sing a breathy rendition of '*My Sweetheart's Sweet Blue Eyes*'.

Felicia seemed quite put out when Jack announced his driver was ready to take her home, finally leaving with promises to return early the next day.

While everyone else posed and preened by the piano, Jessica stayed close to Alice, and wasn't altogether sorry when her friend announced that she was planning an early night. They climbed the stairs together, after wishing everyone sweet dreams. Jessica made certain that she didn't catch Jack's eye and hurried along the landing to her room.

The jollity and noise downstairs had disguised the winter storm blowing up outside. Jessica glanced out of her bedroom window before pulling the curtains closed. Outside it was raining hard and a fierce north-easterly gale was roaring between the chimneys.

Even with the little fire stoked up in the grate, the room seemed chilly. The impression was accentuated by the noises of the wind outside. She snuggled up under the eiderdown, trying hard to ignore the ferocious gusts and sounds of rain lashing at the casement windows.

Sleep eluded her. Every time she closed her eyes all she could see was a stream of erotic images: Jack Heally, fingers pressed up tight inside her, eyes alight with desire at the dinner table. The sultan queen and her slave boy, locked in a wild frenzied dance of passion, Jack with Felicia Gudgeon in the stables, Jack with Prince Charming.

Jessica huddled miserably under the covers and listened to the other revellers making their way to bed. Time seemed to pass very slowly. She tossed and turned from side to side. Though her body was exhausted her mind refused to be still. She could still feel the unfulfilled heat of desire inside her and cursed Jack Heally for fanning the flames.

Outside, the rain continued to pour, wind roaring like an angry lion. Frustrated, she sat up and peered into the dying coals. On her bedside table was a book she had brought with her, perhaps she just ought to get up, turn on the lamp, make up the fire, and resign herself to a sleepless night.

A quiet tap-tap-tap at the door made her jump.

'Who's there?' she hissed nervously into the darkness. Faces and names raced through her mind. What if it was Jack? Or one of the twins? She wasn't sure whether to reply or pretend to be asleep.

'It's me,' hissed Alice. 'Are you still awake?'

Jessica laughed and clambered out of bed feeling the tension trickle away.

'No, I'm sound asleep,' she said with a grin, opening the door just a fraction.

Outside on the landing, wrapped up in an oversized dressing gown, Alice Fallon was holding a butler's tray.

'So much for my early night,' Alice said ruefully. 'I can't sleep in this storm, so I've been downstairs and made a jug of cocoa. Can I interest you in joining me?'

Jessica waved her inside. In the light from the landing, Jessica could see there was a steaming jug of cocoa, two mugs and a bowl on the tray.

'What were you going to do if I was asleep?'

Alice grinned. 'I'd just have had to drink it all by myself. Turn the lamp up, will you. I've filched half a fruit cake as well, it's in my pocket.'

Jessica pulled the fireside chair and small table closer to the hearth and dropped a few more lumps of coal into the grate.

'Did the rain keep you awake?'

Alice rolled her eyes heavenwards. 'The rain, the wind, and the hail. You're more sheltered on this side of the house, in my room the windows have blown open twice.' She shivered. 'It's cold in here too. Instead of stoking the fire up, why don't we have this in bed? Move the table closer, I'll be mother.'

Jessica grinned. 'Are you sure?'

But Alice had already put the tray on the bedside cabinet and was slithering down under the bedclothes.

'God, my feet are frozen,' she said miserably. 'Come on, bring the table over here and I'll carve up the cake.'

Jessica sighed and pulled the little table up alongside the bed.

'Don't get crumbs in the bedclothes,' she said, as Alice produced a great wedge of cake wrapped in grease-proof paper from her dressing gown pocket.

'As if I would,' giggled Alice. 'Now hurry up and get in before you get frozen too. Jack did say his father didn't go much for creature comforts. I can see what he means now. This house is so draughty.' She patted the mattress, inviting Jessica to join her. 'Oh, and I found some cream in the pantry, so I brought a pot-full up to put in the cocoa. This is going to be delicious.'

Jessica climbed into bed. It seemed an impossibly long time since she had shared a bed with anyone - and she had never shared one with a woman before.

Alice gave the cocoa a good stir, filled the two mugs and then topped each one off with a huge blob of cream.

'Perfection,' she whispered and handed Jessica her drink. 'I'll just serve up the cake; sorry I didn't remember to bring my plates.'

There was a split second when Alice's fingertips brushed Jessica's wrist. Her touch was fleeting, but so soft, so unthreatening, that it made Jessica shiver.

Alice stared at her. 'Are you cold?' She draped her arm around her friend's shoulder and pulled her closer. Jessica was so surprised that she gasped. Alice smiled.

'Let's just have this cake and then we can snuggle down. You don't mind me if I stay in here with you, do you?'

Jessica shook her head. She didn't mind at all. Though some part of her was afraid of what might happen she was too embarrassed to put the thoughts into words.

Alice was sipping her cocoa. Disentangling her arm from Jessica, she broke the fruit cake into two huge wedges.

'Here we are, darling, comfort food. It may rain, it may blow, but the old girls of St Faith's Academy will survive the Norfolk night. Oh, hang on a minute. I'd forgotten, I pinched something else as well.'

Slithering a hand back under the bedclothes, she pulled a small bottle of brandy out from her dressing gown and before Jessica could protest, she unscrewed the top and poured a healthy slug into each mug.

'There, that will warm us up,' she said, lifting her mug in salute. 'Cheers, bottoms up, and all that. Here's to a glorious Christmas in cold, wet, windswept Norfolk.' She took a long pull on the cocoa. 'Gosh, this tastes lovely.' She ran her tongue around her lips, lapping away a chocolate and cream moustache. 'Try it. See what you think.'

Jessica took a mouthful. She had to agree, it did taste marvellous. She took another mouthful, letting the rich taste soothe away her fears. Alice leant back against the headboard.

'You know, I realised, being with you today, just how much I've missed your company. We were always such good friends when we were at school. I'm so used to being with all these theatrical people, all ego and look at me, me, me. I'd quite forgotten what real people, real friends, are like. Bunty, Miranda, Helen, the twins; they're just like children.' She pulled a face and mimicked Miranda's breathy lisp. 'Look at me, dress me, I want my costume now!'

Jessica giggled and then looked into the top of the mug accusingly. There must have been more brandy in it than she'd thought, or maybe it was working with the remains of Bunty's cocktails.

'Bunty is amazing,' Jessica said and then giggled again. 'Actually you all are. I can't believe the things you get up to. Is it like this all the time?'

Alice snorted and poured a little more brandy into each of their mugs. 'Oh Jessie, darling, I really have missed you so much. We ought to have got together years ago, or at the very least, seen a lot more of each other. I could have stopped you from getting all prissy and you could have kept me sane.' As she spoke, she leant forward and kissed Jessica full on the lips.

Jessica froze, totally stunned. A white-hot flash of panic roared through her, followed by a lightening strike of desire. Gasping, she wriggled across the bed, more afraid of what she felt than what Alice had done.

Alice stared at her. 'What's the matter?'

In the soft lamplight and the glow from the hearth, Jessica could see the outline of Alice's breasts through her nightdress. They peeped provocatively through the thin fabric, framed by the heavy lines of her dressing gown. Seeing them switched on a battery of senses which Jessica had been struggling to ignore. She realised she could smell Alice's body - a soft sensuous perfume that lifted goose bumps on her skin. Jessica tried to swallow, aware that her pulse was racing. Alice was still no more than a heartbeat away, smiling.

'Don't worry,' she said and stroked Jessica's cheek with a fingertip. Her expression intensified. 'I do understand how you feel,' she said in an undertone. 'I can see it in your eyes.'

Jessica looked away. 'I've never touched a woman,' she said thickly. 'I'm not sure that I can or that I want to.' Alice caught hold of Jessica's hand and guided it up under her breasts. Jessica shivered, stunned by how delicate and soft Alice's skin felt.

'See,' purred Alice, 'it really isn't so terrible, is it? I feel just like you. It's just like touching yourself.' She paused, holding Jessica's hand tight up against her. Alice smiled, eyes twinkling. 'But don't let me force you; I don't want you to do anything you're not happy with.'

Jessica groaned, feeling Alice's nipples harden under her fingertips. She shook her head, instinctively circling the taut little peaks with her thumbs.

'It isn't that I don't want to,' she whispered unsteadily. 'I just can't believe I can feel this way about another woman.'

Alice grinned. 'But you do, don't you? Why fight it? What harm are we doing to anyone? You're lonely and all I've got is the awful Charlie waiting for me at home. He wouldn't understand mutual need, or gentleness, or sensitivity if it ran up and bit him.'

She giggled and slipped her dressing gown off, throwing it onto the floor, then lifted the bedclothes.

'Why don't we just snuggle down and ride the storm out together?' She lifted Jessica's hand away, and with a smooth movement pulled her nightdress up over her head. Her body looked golden in the lamplight, stomach muscles taut, breasts pert and uptilted.

Jessica felt the desire shivering through her again. Male or female, it would be very difficult to resist such an exquisite body. In the soft shadows, between her thighs, Jessica could see the dark triangle of Alice's sex. As she stared at her friend's beautiful sensuous body, she felt a wave of tenderness mingle with raw desire.

She knew she wanted nothing more than to take Alice in her arms and feel those soft tender curves pressed against her. The knowledge was like a revelation. She stood her mug down on the bedside table and tugged at the hem of her own nightdress.

'Here, let me help you,' said Alice. Her fingers gathered up the fabric and slipped it over Jessica's head.

'Gosh, you are so beautiful,' Alice whispered, her eyes moving appreciatively over Jessica's blushing, chilly frame. Jessica's colour intensified as she felt her nipples hardening in the cold.

Alice leaned forward and pressed a single kiss on one tight little bud and then the other. Jessica shivered, the longing to respond only held back by a sense of fear. Alice smiled up at her and ran her tongue around one of the tight peaks. Jessica felt as if she couldn't move, while a frantic pulse beat a tattoo in her ears.

'It feels good, doesn't it?' Alice whispered. Jessica nodded, unable to find the words to answer her. Almost without thinking, she reached out to pull Alice closer. The woman crept into her arms, her lips returning to Jessica's throbbing nipples.

Alice sucked and lapped, sending wave after wave of pleasure through Jessica's stunned mind. Every sensation was tinged with a mixture of reluctance and fear. Alice wriggled closer and slipped a hand between Jessica's thighs. Jessica stiffened.

'It's all right, let me touch you,' Alice said softly. 'Why don't we lie down? It's so cold.'

As if to emphasise Alice's invitation, a huge gust of wind rattled the casements, making Jessica jump.

'I'm afraid,' she murmured, almost to herself.

Alice put a hand on her shoulder and guided her under the bedclothes, silencing her words with a kiss.

'There's really no need to be,' Alice said, as she pulled the eiderdown over her shoulders. She was so close that all Jessica could see in the gloom were her friend's dark glittering eyes. Feeling the brush of Alice's breasts against her was almost more than she could bear.

Why should she fight the raw hunger that was bubbling up inside her? Earlier in the day, when they'd sat in the dining room, hadn't she considered kissing Alice, hadn't she felt the same desire that obviously Alice felt for her?

'I don't know what to do,' she said, unsteadily.

Alice laughed. 'Of course you do. Don't tell me you've never touched yourself before.'

Jessica blushed. 'Yes,' she began.

Alice brushed a finger down over Jessica's belly.

'What feels good for you will feel good for me. Don't be afraid, just touch me. You'll know, just listen to how you feel. Let go, let your body tell you what it wants and what it has to give.'

Alice caressed the sensitive triangle of hair that framed Jessica's sex. Quelling her fear and reluctance, Jessica opened her legs and at once Alice slid a hand between her thighs, a single finger seeking entry. Alice groaned with delight and eased into the silvery moist passageway that lay within.

Jessica quietened her racing mind and instead listened to the frantic call of her body. Her hands lifted again to Alice's engorged nipples and she was rewarded by a murmur of approval.

The other woman's body felt like liquid silk. It was so enticing, so sensual, that Jessica couldn't resist the desire to explore. She moved closer, breathing in the compelling perfume of Alice's skin and planted a single tentative kiss on the woman's open lips.

Her friend's tongue touched hers, lapping gently, exploring the contours of Jessica's mouth. For an instant, Jessica imagined the same tongue working its way up between her thighs, eagerly kissing the folds of her quim. She knew then that there was no going back.

Alice's fingers brushed the stormy bud of her clitoris, sending a plume of pleasure up through Jessica's belly. Jessica kissed Alice hard, imagining the wetness and the heat her friend would have discovered.

Cupping Alice's breasts, Jessica stroked the full curves, relishing their softness, while her hips moved unconsciously against Alice's busy, knowing fingers.

One of Alice's hands locked in Jessica's hair, guiding her lips down towards her breasts. Jessica trickled a fanfare of kisses down over Alice's shoulders, lapping at the throbbing pulse in her throat, kissing the rise and swell of her friend's beautiful breasts. A nipple brushed her cheek and without thinking, she sucked it deep into her mouth, already knowing how it would make Alice feel. Alice let out a throaty sob of enjoyment and caught hold of Jessica's hand, pressing it down towards her belly.

'Touch me,' she murmured. 'I want you to touch me. I'm so wet. I need to feel your fingers inside me - please.'

The delicate curls around Alice's quim, tickling and soft, didn't prepare Jessica for the raw heat that glowed below. Without thinking, she slid a finger between the engorged lips of her friend's quim and gasped at the wetness that engulfed her. Alice's sex nibbled at her fingers, begging her to go deeper. As she slid two fingers home, Alice's sex tightened around her like a hungry mouth.

It was like making love to herself. Jessica could imagine every sensation, every touch. She started to circle the swollen bud, nestling like a ripe cherry between the outer lips of Alice's quim.

Alice groaned excitedly, opening her legs, offering herself up like a sacrifice to Jessica's exploring hands. As she lifted her hips, Alice's attention to Jessica's clitoris intensified so that Jessica hadn't time to gather her thoughts.

On and on the spiral went - every time Jessica's fingers moved, Alice's echoed the caress deep inside the soft folds of her body. It was an addictive game. Jessica's pulse was racing. Oblivious to the storm raging outside, no longer cold, diamonds of sweat began to lift on her face and in the valley between her breasts. Her breath came in feverish gasps, pleasure rolling out from her quim like flashes of sheet lightning.

Just as she thought she couldn't take any more, and she sensed Alice was no more than an instant away from release, her friend wriggled away.

Jessica let out a ragged sobbing breath.

'Please,' she begged, 'don't stop now,' but before she could continue her protest, Alice slithered down under the bedclothes, until she was crouched between Jessica's open thighs. Grinning, she pressed a tentative kiss to the rise of Jessica's sex.

Jessica was astonished. 'Alice—' she snorted, but too late. Alice spread the lips of Jessica's sex with her tongue and nibbled eagerly at her clitoris, lapping up and down like a hungry kitten.

The sensations were electric and so intense that they took Jessica's breath away, making her tremble. Gasping, she tried to turn round, struggling to find a way to caress her friend, desperate to share the pleasure. Alice glanced up at her with a sly excited expression. Her lips were slick with Jessica's silky juices.

'Please, let me touch you,' Jessica murmured.

Alice shimmied round so that they lay side by side.

'Are you sure you want to do this?' she whispered.

Jessica shivered, aware of the smell of her own body on her friend's fingers and face. In some ways she didn't want Alice to ask. It was so much easier when she listened to her body's quiet but insistent voice. She nodded and didn't resist as Alice moved again. This time her friend turned in the bed so that her hips were level with Jessica's face. The invitation was silent but implicit.

Jessica took a deep breath. In her wildest, most feverish dreams she had never imagined making love to a woman, but now, inches from her face, Alice's fragrant quim drew her like a bee to an orchid. The perfume was hypnotic - irresistible.

She pressed a single uncertain kiss to the inside of Alice's thigh. Alice rewarded her with a soft mewl of joy and a split second later, Jessica felt a similar fluttering kiss on her own thigh.

Jessica's first few kisses were anxious and tinged with reluctance, as she prepared herself for the caress that would open up the way into Alice's soft fragrant wetness.

She ran her tongue along the ridge where Alice's outer lips met, tasting the subtle ocean flavours of her juices. The smell and the taste made her mind reel. It was so like her own scent but subtly different - like a tone of the same colour. As she slipped her tongue deeper, Alice did the same between Jessica's legs.

It felt like a competition - one kiss, one caress, was followed by another and another. It seemed like an erotic game of follow the leader. Sometimes Alice took the lead, sometimes Jessica, in some unspoken telepathic connectedness that drove Jessica out beyond fear, beyond reluctance, beyond logic, into an intense white plain of pleasure, so pure and all engulfing that she thought she might cry from the sheer intensity of what she felt.

When the last of the tremors had passed, Alice turned round and gathered Jessica up into her arms.

'I love you so much,' Alice purred, on an outward breath. 'I always have. I'm so glad you came to Malestone.'

Jessica lay in the other woman's arms, trembling. Some part of her was glad they had made love, too, but she was stunned that the release her body demanded had been provided by one of her oldest and dearest girlfriends.

Outside, the storm had faded and the wind dropped, as if nature was echoing their exhausted passion. Jessica could feel sleep calling her, making her limbs ache and her eyes heavy. Alice turned over, curling up against Jessica's belly. She wriggled until she was comfortable, each tiny brush of her body reigniting little sparks of pleasure in Jessica's tired mind.

'If nothing else, it's a great cure for insomnia,' whispered Alice, sleepily.

Jessica smiled and slipped her arm around her friend's waist. 'I thought that was the brandy,' she said with a grin.

Alice's reply was a sleepy laugh.

When Jessica was woken by winter sunlight pushing its way between the curtains, her mind was flooded by memories of a vivid dream. The images made her blush. She and Alice had... she stopped, as the woman curled up beside her moaned softly and stretched sleepily.

On the bedside table stood an empty cocoa mug and the remains of a slice of fruit cake. It hadn't been a dream. She took a deep breath, unsure quite how she felt. Part of her was stunned and horrified, but another part was glad - almost relieved.

Alice stretched and ran a hand down over Jessica's spine. The caress was tender rather than passionate.

'Hello,' she whispered, voice still thick with sleep. 'Has the storm blown over?'

Jessica smiled. Certainly the weather had improved, but Jessica could feel a renewed flutter of desire, as intense as any storm, brewing inside her.

Alice pulled the blankets down a little and peered round at the new morning.

'God, it's still cold, and far too early for breakfast,' she moaned. 'Maybe we ought to just stay in bed.'

As Alice moved, Jessica could smell the perfume of her body - a delicate cocktail of perspiration and the subtle, more compelling odour of pleasure. For an instant, Jessica was afraid that their liaison might spoil the friendship that she and Alice had shared.

Alice grinned at her and tugged the eiderdown back up over her shoulders.

'What do you say? Shall we camp out up here and forget about waiting hand and foot on the theatrical mob?' Alice's light joking tone and expression reassured Jessica that nothing had changed between them.

'What?' Jessica said, slithering out of bed. 'And let them run amok amongst all your carefully sorted costumes? I don't know about you, but I'm going down to breakfast. I'm famished.'

Alice, eiderdown pulled up tight under her chin, snorted. 'You slave driver. If you're hungry I've still got a bit of cake left here.' She glanced towards the bedside cabinet.

The chill nipped at Jessica's naked body. As she looked around for her nightdress or robe she was aware Alice was watching her. Alice rolled over and pulled the bedclothes back.

'Instead of getting dressed, why don't you come back to bed for a little while? What time is it, anyway? Eight, half-past? Everyone had a late night; they won't be down for breakfast until at least nine.' Her eyes darkened. She patted the mattress beside her. 'Come back to bed and let me warm you up.'

Jessica stared at her. It was one thing to make love in the darkness, their intimate caresses hidden by shadows - she bit her lip, imagining Alice's breasts pressed against her and the soft creamy silk of her skin moving beneath her fingertips. The temptation was too much, without further protest she crept back into bed.

'You are frozen,' Alice whispered, slipping an arm around her. 'Come here, I'm really warm.'

Jessica sighed, engulfed by the sleepy heat from Alice's naked body. Outside the wind had faded to no more than a purr.

Chapter 7

December 20

Jessica and Alice were the last ones to arrive downstairs for breakfast. It seemed that Jack and Prince Charming had renewed their acquaintance during the night and sat at the end of the table, deep in conversation. As Jessica helped herself to bacon and eggs, Jack did nothing more than look up at her with a grin.

'Sleep well?' he said, slyly.

Jessica felt her colour rising, but was determined not to give herself away. He had no way of knowing that she had spent the night with Alice.

'The storm kept me awake,' she said casually, pulling out a chair between Bunty Redknap and Alice.

Jack sipped his cup of tea. 'Really? If you were frightened you should have come and found me, maybe I could have taken your mind off the weather.'

Beside him, Prince Charming grinned.

Across the table, one of the Haywood twins chirped, 'Are you two coming into town with us this morning?'

Alice and Jessica both looked up.

'Who is going into town?' said Alice sharply.

The twin grinned. 'Oh, everyone. We're going to King's Lynn. Last minute Christmas shopping and all that. We shouldn't be more than an hour or two.'

Alice glared at Bunty. 'What about rehearsals? I thought you were going to start straight after breakfast?'

Bunty lifted his hands in resignation. 'It is Christmas, darling. Besides, it's good for morale. They've all promised to work really hard when they get back.'

Alice snorted. 'What about you Jack, are you going too?'

Their host smiled and patted his lips with a napkin. 'I'm afraid not, duty calls. Besides, Felicia said she'd be coming over with George and I'm expecting the first of my guests to arrive some time this morning. Hardly good form for their host to be absent when they show up.'

Alice looked at Jessica. 'I was hoping to get everyone fitted for their costumes this morning.'

Jessica smiled. 'We pinned a lot of the costumes up yesterday, we could do those, couldn't we?'

Alice looked heavenwards, as Miranda began to reel off a list of things she couldn't live without that Jack promised her could be bought in King's Lynn.

'All right, all right,' said Alice, after a second or two. 'Just make sure you're all back by lunchtime.'

Bunty grinned. 'Of course, my dear, as if we'd let you down.' He clapped his hands. 'Righty-o chaps, you heard what Alice said. Chop, chop, we have to get a move on. Who wants to ride with me?'

Malestone seemed very empty without the noisy troupe singing and rehearsing in the music room. Jessica and Alice sat in the drawing room, in comfortable chairs, pulled up on either side of the hearth. On the mantelshelf the clock ticked away, the noise sounding unnaturally loud, as the two women tacked up dresses and adjusted seams so that the costumes would fit the players.

Jessica quite enjoyed the companionable silence. She glanced up from moving the buttons on Dandinni's jacket for the ball. On the other side of the hearth, Alice bit through a thread and dropped another costume onto the rapidly growing pile beside her.

Alice grinned. 'Actually, Bunty has probably done us a favour by taking them all into town. We'd never be able to get these done so quickly with everyone milling around insisting we do theirs first.' She stretched and yawned. 'I want to say, whatever else happens, I'm glad about last night.'

Jessica coloured and looked away.

Alice stared at her. 'You're not telling me you're sorry, are you?'

Jessica shook her head. 'No, it's just something I never imagined happening in a million years.'

Alice grinned. 'Well, it has now and I'm pleased.' She knelt beside Jessica. 'I don't think I've really loved anyone since Ludo died.' She stopped and took hold of Jessica's hand. 'I suppose in some ways we're the same, you and I. Life could have been so different for both of us - I just hope you don't hate me for seducing you.'

Jessica felt a tiny pain inside. 'Oh no—' she began, but before she could finish the sentence, the door to the drawing room swung open. Jack Healy, dressing in his riding habit, took in the scene beside the hearth and smiled knowingly.

'I just popped in to see that you had everything you want,' he said pleasantly.

Alice got to her feet. 'We're absolutely fine,' she said.

Jack nodded. 'I can see that.' He grinned at Jessica. 'I've obviously misjudged you, Jessica. I thought it was me you had taken a shine to, but perhaps it was Helen or maybe Felicia you were more interested in?'

Jessica blushed crimson. 'How dare you?' she hissed, clambering to her feet.

Jack lifted his hands in mock surrender.

'Gently, gently,' he murmured. 'It's all the same to me. I'm just glad you've found a way to relieve that awful yearning I saw in your eyes when you arrived. And you are in good hands. Helen, dear Prince Charming, assures me Alice is very, very talented when it comes to dealing with yearnings.'

Jessica swung round to look at Alice, who was hanging the costume she had been working on back onto the rail.

'Alice?' she whispered, in disbelief, feeling a brittle sense of hurt and betrayal.

Alice glared at Jack.

'You really are a complete and utter bastard, Jack Healy,' Alice snapped, turning round to face Jessica. 'Take no notice of him, Jess, he's just jealous and spiteful. I have always loved you, darling. You must know that. But Jack's right, you aren't the first woman I've made love to, but I...' she paused, expression softening. 'I wanted to be your first. Jack seemed to make you so nervous, I just wanted to show you that love, that touching, that - Oh I don't know, I suppose I wanted to show you that it's possible to have pleasure again. Do you understand?'

Jessica shivered. Between them, they had both set out to seduce her and it seemed that Alice had won. Jessica bit her lip, trying hard to retain some shred of dignity.

'Is that why you invited me to Malestone, to seduce me? Or was it just to humiliate me?'

Alice's colour drained. 'Oh no, how could you possibly think that? No, I really do need you here and I certainly didn't intend to humiliate you.'

Jessica looked first at Jack and then Alice, not quite sure what she felt or what to believe. Finally, she sighed and sat down in the armchair beside the fire. What was done couldn't be changed and there was no denying the pleasure Alice had given her. She shook her head and then looked up at Jack, whose expression was impassive.

'I thought you were busy this morning?' she hissed. 'Or did you take time off to come in here and upset me?'

Jack looked hurt. 'Certainly not,' he said defensively. 'I thought you must already know about Alice.' He tugged his jacket straight, gathering up his composure. 'Actually, I came in to invite you both to join me for coffee in the sitting room. Some of my friends have just arrived from London and I thought you'd like to meet them.'

Jessica lifted an eyebrow. 'And I suppose you have already told them about

Alice and me?'

Jack looked even more wounded. 'Good God, no.' He sighed. 'Would you like to join us for coffee or not?'

Jessica stood up. 'Why not?' she said wearily.

She wasn't sure she wanted to be alone with Alice at the moment - or Jack Heally.

Alice slipped off her blouse and then glared at Jack. 'Why did you have to upset Jessica this morning?'

Jack smiled, leaning forward to press a moist kiss to each of her pert dark nipples as they presented themselves. It was late afternoon and they were upstairs in Jack's bedroom. The room was lit by candles. Outside, the darkness pressing at the windows made it seem as if they were alone in the world.

'A little jealous, maybe?' Jack said, admiring her lithe figure. 'Why should you have first pickings of all the succulent morsels on offer? Where is Jessica now, anyway?'

Alice shivered her skirt down over her slim hips.

'She said your friend, Harry Stolworthy, had invited her to play Nap before dinner. I'm surprised you asked me up here at all after this morning's little fiasco. You make me so cross sometimes. Aren't you supposed to be downstairs, busy playing host?'

Jack grinned. 'Maybe you're right, but Harry and the others can amuse themselves for a little while.' He pulled her closer, pressing his lips to hers, tangling his fingers in her hair so that she had no choice but to kiss him in return.

'I just couldn't resist the temptation to kiss the lips that had kissed Jessica's. What did you do? Did you snake that pretty little tongue of yours up inside her pussy, lap at her quim until she begged you to stop?'

Alice pulled away, gasping, eyes fire-bright.

'You really are a complete bastard, Jack.' She grinned. 'I thought you'd got a liaison with Felicia planned today as well - or am I first substitute?'

Jack snorted. 'George rang earlier to say that they had to go to lunch with the Henshaws.' He grinned. 'Felicia will love that, she'll be bored senseless, so I asked George if they'd like to join us for dinner.'

He slid a hand between her thighs, cradling the swell of her sex. 'My, my, Miss Fallon, you are so wet. Is it something to do with me or have you been thinking about Jessica Harper's tight little cunt all day?'

Alice rubbed herself provocatively against him. 'You really are obsessed with her, aren't you? It's not very flattering for me to be here when I know your mind is elsewhere.'

Jack turned slightly and took a riding crop off his bedside table. 'Jessica mentioned over coffee you needed one of these for your coachman.'

Alice eyed the thin leather rod appreciatively. 'She's got a good memory.'

Jack, eyes dancing with mischief, flexed the crop. 'Amongst other things. I thought you might like to test it out before you take it away with you?'

Alice, eyes still firmly fixed on the shaft of the whip, nodded. 'Why not?' she whispered, and then looked up into Jack's stormy eyes. 'What had you got in mind?'

Jack indicated the chair in front of the dressing table. 'Why don't you bend over there and point your sweet little backside up in the air. You can even see what I've got planned for you in the mirror.'

Alice nodded. 'Sounds like one of your better ideas. Would you like me to take these off?' She stroked a single finger across the front of her knickers.

Jack nodded, letting his eyes explore her ripe body. For an instant, as she bent over, exposing the lips of her fur-trimmed pussy, wet and slick between her legs, he imagined her with Jessica Harper. In his mind he saw the two women, pressed breast to breast, in a passionate embrace. He could almost see Alice's long fingers making their way down to Jessica's hungry sex.

He shivered and flexed the whip once again. Before Jessica's visit was over he would ensure he had her, he would take her - make her realise that only a man could truly give her what she needed. She was wasted on Alice.

Between his legs he could feel the heavy throb in his swollen cock. At the moment he would bestow his pleasure on Alice Fallon, but very soon it would be Jessica writhing over the stool, plump buttocks turned towards him, waiting for his attentions. The thought made him smile wolfishly.

Over the chair, Alice was waiting. He could see the throb of the pulse in her throat and the way her breasts trembled in anticipation. It wasn't polite to keep a lady waiting. He drew the crop back and brought it down with a resounding crack across Alice's creamy skin. She let out a little shriek of pain. An instant later a single red weal lifted on her plump cheeks. He swung the whip again. Six strokes, and then he would slip his raging shaft between those fragrant lips.

He saw her stiffen, bracing herself for the next stroke. In the mirror, he could see her eyes had darkened and her face and breasts were flushed with expectation. He grinned and brought the crop down again. Alice dropped her hips, revealing a tantalising sliver of the crimson interior of her sex. Four more strokes and then he would fill her to the hilt, imagining it was Jessica Harper who writhed appreciatively beneath him.

Downstairs in the sitting room, Harry Stolworthy refilled Jessica's teacup.

'So what do you teach?' he said pleasantly. Jessica sorted out the hand that he had just dealt her and looked up into his grey-green eyes. He was very blond, with strong, sharply defined features. His complexion and his manner were as light as Jack Heally's were dark, she thought, tucking an ace in beside a queen of the same suit.

'English,' she said, smiling, while beside her, Bunty Redknap puffed thoughtfully over his new hand. On Jessica's right, Miranda pouted, running her tongue over her teeth as she stared down at her cards.

Harry glanced at Miranda. 'So what's your bid?'

The tall blonde screwed up her nose thoughtfully. They had been playing for most of the afternoon, but even so Miranda still hadn't quite grasped the rules.

Jessica had been relieved when Jack had led her and Alice into the sitting room to meet his newly arrived guests. It had taken her mind off the scene they had played out in the drawing room. She had tried very hard not to think about the things that had been said.

Jack, stepping back into his role as convivial host, had introduced Alice and Jessica to the five newly arrived men. It appeared that four had travelled down as a group, while the fifth had taken a cab from the station. The fifth guest - Harry Stolworthy - didn't seem to know the others very well.

Jessica knew exactly how he felt. He looked extremely uncomfortable. Dressed in an expensive, obviously new, country style suit, he stared around the room, turning his coffee cup nervously between long thin fingers. He looked almost as ill at ease as Jessica felt.

'Are you one of Jack's infamous theatricals?' he said, as the footman served her with coffee.

Jessica shook her head. 'No, I'm here as a help-mate for Alice Fallon. What about you?'

Harry sniffed. 'Old friend of Jack's. We used to know each other in London before the war.' He smiled disarmingly. 'You know how these things are. We've kept in contact, cards and such like. I was rather touched when he asked me to come down for Christmas.' He paused and looked over at Alice and Jack, who were talking to the rest of the group. It was obvious from the laughter and the way the conversation was flowing that it wasn't the first time that Alice had met them.

Harry turned towards Jessica. 'I wasn't sure whether to come or not, really, I don't know many of the people here.'

Jessica smiled at him. He smiled back at her, looking extremely boyish and touchingly vulnerable.

'What about you?' he said.

Jessica laughed. 'I'm in exactly the same boat. Alice invited me. I don't really know anyone here either.'

Harry grinned and lifted his cup in salute.

'In that case perhaps we two outsiders ought to stick together.'

At that moment, the doors to the sitting room opened, and the rest of Alice's group came in, all laughing, all talking, still laden down with bags and boxes and coats.

Jessica could almost feel Harry take a step back, as if he were intimidated by the arrival of the noisy troupe of actors. Across the room Jack began another round of introductions.

Jessica glanced at Harry's cup.

'Would you like another one of those?' she said conversationally. It seemed to take Harry a minute or two to make up his mind and then he nodded.

'Whereabouts do you come from?' she said, making an effort to draw him into conversation. He seemed even shyer than she was.

He seemed relieved that she hadn't abandoned him and insisted that he accompany her to lunch, and afterwards suggested perhaps they could meet up for a game of cards later in the day.

Bunty had offered to join them and Miranda - terrified of being left out of anything - had agreed to make up a four, though Jessica now realised the beautiful blonde had had no idea what she was agreeing to.

Fortunately, the return of Bunty and the rest of the troupe meant that Alice and Jessica had no time to talk. A steady flow of people trickled in and out of the drawing room all afternoon for fittings.

When the costumes had been sorted out and Bunty announced rehearsals were over for the day, Harry had met Jessica at the drawing room door. He had had someone set up a card table close to the fire in the sitting room and they had played cards for most of the afternoon.

Outside it was blustery and wet. For the first time since she had arrived Jessica felt totally at ease. She took another look at her hand and then glanced expectantly at Miranda.

Bunty was glaring at Miranda in exasperation. 'Will you please make a bid, darling? One, two, three, four, or five tricks, or none at all.'

Miranda pouted again. 'What are the names of the tricks again?'

Bunty sighed. 'It really doesn't matter what you call them, just tell us how many you intend to win.'

'I'm getting awfully bored with this,' Miranda said. 'Isn't it time we went to change for dinner? I bought the most gorgeous little dress in town, pale blue...'

For Bunty it was the final straw. He slapped his cards down onto the baize. 'Will you damned well call the tricks, Miranda, for God's sake.'

Harry glanced up at Jessica and looked heavenwards. 'Maybe Miranda's right. Perhaps we just ought to play this hand and then stop,' he said chivalrously.

Miranda was still staring at her hand. 'All right, all right. I'll go Nap.'

Bunty snatched the cards out of her hands and snorted. 'How the hell can you call Nap with these cards?'

Miranda glared at him. 'You asked me to make my call,' she snapped furiously, and got to her feet. 'I've had enough of this. I already said I was bored. I'm going upstairs to get changed.' She saved a sickly smile for Harry and Jessica. 'Thank you for the game. Perhaps Bunty would like to play my hand as he seems to know so much about it.' With a flounce she headed off towards the doors.

Bunty lifted his hand in apology.

'Sorry,' he said, getting to his feet. 'My fault, I think; she is just such a child. We spent all morning trailing round after her while she looked in every last shop. I suppose I had better go and smooth her ruffled feathers.'

He gathered up the discarded cards into a neat pile.

Harry looked at Jessica. 'Looks like there's just us two left, then. Would you care for a hand of something else or are you bored too? Perhaps we could just talk?'

Jessica smiled. 'I really don't mind.'

Harry shuffled the pack and then smiled up at her. 'You know you're awfully easy to be with. May I ask you if you're engaged or seeing someone?' He reddened slightly as he spoke and then blustered, 'Not that I'm prying, of course. I don't mean to be too personal or anything.'

Jessica smiled, he sounded almost coy. 'No, I'm not seeing anyone at the moment. I was engaged, but my fiancé was killed in Flanders.'

Harry's colour intensified. 'Oh gosh, I'm so sorry, I didn't mean—'

Jessica held up a hand to silence him. 'No really, it's all right. Please don't apologise. It's an awfully long time ago now and we were all terribly young. I was barely twenty.' She stared out into the darkening day. 'Sometimes it seems as if I was another person then, as if it all happened to someone else.' Realising she was making Harry uncomfortable, she looked round and smiled. 'It's over four years ago now - a long time. Hard to imagine really where all that time has gone. What about you? Have you got a sweetheart?'

Harry shrugged, still blushing. 'No one special at the moment. It's been hard to find the time. My parents died in a boating accident a couple of years ago and I've been sorting out their affairs.' He smiled. 'You know how longwinded these things are.'

Jessica stared at him. He looked like a little boy lost. She got to her feet. 'Would you like me to ring for some more tea?'

Harry nodded and then stood up. Before she could protest he took hold of her hand and lifted it to his lips. Jessica stared at him in astonishment. He smiled shyly.

'I hope you won't think me too forward, Jessica,' he said, as he pressed a kiss to her fingertips. 'I'm so glad that I accepted Jack's invitation. I hadn't realised how lonely my life had become. I'd quite forgotten how much I missed convivial female company.'

Jessica was totally disarmed by his chivalry, so very different from the raw lustful advances of Alice and Jack. She shivered, frozen to the spot. Harry was still holding her hand. She glanced at the bell pull.

'Would you like me to ring for that tea?' she whispered.

Harry's grey eyes flashed. 'Perhaps we ought to go and get changed for dinner after all,' he said, reddening furiously. 'I'm not sure if I can be responsible for my actions if I stay here alone with you.' He stepped closer and pressed a chaste kiss to her cheek. 'Perhaps you would do me the honour of sitting next to me at dinner?'

Jessica smiled graciously. 'I would be delighted, Harry.'

He tugged at his tie, looking slightly uneasy. 'Good show. Look, if you'll excuse me, I think perhaps I ought to go.'

After he closed the door, Jessica sat back at the little table and stacked the cards back in their shoe. She found it impossible to suppress a smile of delight. Harry Stolworthy was wonderful, a stark contrast to the other house guests. And he was right; they really ought to stick together.

She touched her cheek, as if she could trap his kiss against her skin. What a gentleman, she thought. She got up and headed upstairs. If Alice tapped on her door tonight, she would pretend to be asleep.

Upstairs, in Jack's bedroom, Alice rolled off the bed. Her buttocks were crisscrossed with a series of angry red stripes and Jack could see a glistening smear of his seed trickling down onto her thighs.

He watched with delight as she collected her clothes. She was completely unselfconscious of her nakedness.

'You're very keen to be off,' he said, lying at full stretch on the bed, arms folded behind his neck.

Alice looked over her shoulder. 'The last thing I want is for Jessica to discover me coming out of your bedroom.'

Jack rolled over onto his belly, grinning. 'She doesn't know where my bedroom is - yet. I thought we might try for a replay before dinner.' She glanced at the bedside clock. 'We've got plenty of time yet.'

Alice snorted and sat down to pull on her stockings. 'I'm hoping to get into the bathroom before Bunty.' She bent down and picked the riding crop off the carpet. 'Besides,' she said, waving the whip, 'I've got what I came for.'

Jack grinned, clutching his chest theatrically. 'You only want me for one thing.'

Alice laughed and cracked the whip down through the air. 'Maybe you're right, perhaps one of these days you'd like to try being on the receiving end for a change.'

Jack pulled a face, delighted by the way Alice looked. She was framed by the ornate fireplace behind her, naked except for her stockings. Legs spread, clutching the crop across her breasts, she looked quite stunning.

'No thanks,' he said. 'But should you ever want to do any more photographs, I think you may have found the perfect pose. Miss Alice Fallon, corrective training given to very naughty boys.'

Alice giggled and cracked the whip again.

'What a splendid idea. Maybe I ought to think about it. Last year I had the most terrible run of bad luck with jobs. At least a little horse whipping would pay the rent.' She turned to admire her reflection in the dressing table mirror. Jack crept up behind her and slipped his arms round her torso, cupping her breasts and nibbling at the curve of her neck.

In the mirror, Alice pouted. 'Of course, I'd have to get rid of Charlie, or perhaps I could rent a little room somewhere.'

Jack grinned, biting her shoulder. 'I think whatever you decide, you'd be better off getting rid of Charlie. You could invite one of your delightful lady friends to live with you instead. Then, when you weren't tanning the arse of some judge or other, you could lick pussy as a sort of antidote. In fact, you could make money out of that too. Lots of my friends would be very happy to pay for a little demonstration.'

Alice pushed him away. 'Just let me get dressed, Jack. I'll never get to the bathroom before Bunty if I keep listening to you. But if I ever need an agent, I'll bear you in mind.' As she spoke, she pulled on her blouse and skirt, gathering up her knickers into a ball.

Chapter 8

Passion in the Library

'So what have you got planned for us tonight?' said Felicia Gudgeon, later that evening as she took her place at the dinner table.

Bunty Redknap grinned and tapped the side of his nose. Sitting beside Felicia, George Gudgeon poured himself a large glass of wine and settled himself down to enjoy a hearty meal.

Jack, at the head of the table, flanked by Alice and Helen, watched with amusement as Harry Stolworthy helped Jessica into her seat. It seemed that she was avoiding him, and certainly Harry was an attentive alternative.

Jack stared at her - she had paid extra attention to her appearance, presumably for Stolworthy's benefit, and looked quite stunning in a delicate blue evening dress. Her dark hair was as sleek and shiny as a cat's pelt. The shoestring straps of her dress accentuated her slim shoulders and beneath the slippery fabric, Jack could see her breasts moving like liquid as she took her place at the table. As he watched Jessica's face and the way Stolworthy looked at her, his amusement was rapidly displaced by something darker and far less attractive.

George Gudgeon adjusted his monocle, as Harry pulled out the chair beside Jessica.

'Don't I know you?' the old man said, in his slow ponderous voice.

Harry coloured slightly. 'Er, no, sir. I don't think we've met before. I'm Harry Stolworthy.' He offered George his hand across the linen and silver.

George shook it and then sniffed imperiously.

'I never forget a face, not so good on names these days, but I'm certain we've met before...' He screwed up his nose, concentrating on dragging some distant memory to the surface. 'Let me think. What about the Reef Club, have you ever been there? Or what about Dougy Phelps, do you know him?'

Harry shook his head; his colour had intensified as everyone at the table turned to listen to George's booming voice.

George peered into the bowl of soup the footman had set in front of him and then back up at Harry.

'It'll come back to me, don't you worry,' he said, plucking up the napkin from beside his plate and tucking it into his collar. He smiled, revealing a set of gnarled yellowed teeth. 'It may take me a while, but it'll be in there somewhere.' He tapped the side of his head, then turned his attention to his dinner.

Harry, looking relieved to be let off the hook, smiled at Jessica and then began to eat.

Dinner was a pleasant, if noisy affair. Despite the convivial company, Jack's attention was drawn time and again to the centre of the table, where Harry and Jessica seemed to be deep in conversation. Their voices were so low that he couldn't pick up what they were saying. He was annoyed and jealous by degrees.

He jumped as he felt something sharp being pressed against his arm. Looking round, he saw that Alice Fallon had poked him with her dessert fork.

'You haven't been listening to a word I said, have you? Stop staring at our young lovers,' she hissed in an undertone.

He glared at her.

Alice smiled ruefully. 'You really can't blame Jessica, she's been hounded by you and she thinks I've betrayed our friendship. Hardly surprising she's looking elsewhere for company.'

Alice was right, of course, but it did nothing to lighten, Jack's mood. He had heard young Stolworthy was down on his luck, lost both parents and - realising they had hardly seen each other in years - invited him to spend Christmas at Malestone in a moment of sympathy. And now here was Harry turning the full weight of his charms on Jessica Harper. Jack stabbed miserably at his pudding.

As if to deliberately darken his mood, Jessica threw back her head and laughed at something young Stolworthy had said. Jack sniffed and turned towards Alice.

'Has Bunty got something planned for after dinner?' he said.

Alice nodded. 'I'd be very surprised if he hadn't. I think he prefers burlesque to theatre any day.'

Jack sucked his teeth and pushed his plate away. Along the table, Jessica was totally oblivious to his state of mind. Jack threw down his napkin and went in search of coffee and brandy. He was in no mood for one of Bunty's infamous frothy cocktails.

Jessica didn't resist as Harry Stolworthy slipped his arm through hers and guided her out into the hall. He smiled at her.

'I have to say it again, Jessica, you really do look absolutely stunning in that dress. Blue is your colour.'

Jessica blushed and thanked him. She wasn't used to so much flattery and although it was quite pleasant, another part of her was very slightly embarrassed by Harry's eager attentions. She glanced around the hall. The only saving grace was that Harry was taking her mind off Jack and Alice. She couldn't help wondering if all his attention was genuine. Despite her doubts, Harry's rather courtly manner and deferential air made him a refreshing change from the rest of the people staying at Malestone.

He handed her a coffee from the side table and glanced around the room.

'So what happens now? Do we all congregate around the piano? Play more cards? Or do the gentlemen retire for a game of billiards and a glass of port, leaving you ladies to chat?'

Jessica coloured slightly, remembering vividly Bunty's show from the night before. She had already seen Felicia and George making their way to one of the sofas; presumably this was so they had a front row seat for whatever was to follow.

'Last night they put on a little show,' she said uncomfortably.

Harry lifted an eyebrow. 'Really? What, singing and that kind of thing? Sounds like great fun.'

Jessica pulled a face. 'Not exactly singing.' She struggled to find some kind of reasonable description of what had happened but couldn't.

Right on cue, Bunty Redknap played a flurry of chords on the piano. Behind him, two other members of the group joined in on a trumpet and a snare drum. A third settled himself behind a double bass. Jessica glanced round uneasily, wondering what would follow.

'I'm not really sure if you want to watch this,' she began, as Bunty played the introduction to one of the new racy American jazz tunes. From the shadows of the drawing room door she watched the Haywood twins, accompanied by three of the male dancers, shimmy out into the centre of the room. What was most startling was that they were all dressed as women. Each wore a tight cocktail dress, and a cloche hat. They looked quite perfect, even down to their shoes and long dangling beads. Their boyish faces were skilfully painted with rouge and lipstick, and the twins had matching beauty spots painted on opposite cheeks.

Jessica swallowed hard as Harry stared in amazement at the boys dancing in perfect time. His mouth fell open and for an instant, Jessica wished the floor would do the same and swallow her whole. He took a deep breath and flushed crimson before turning to Jessica.

'Dash me,' he said in astonishment. 'This is rather a rum show.'

Jessica swallowed. 'Bunty's entertainment is a little raunchy for my tastes.'

Harry nodded. 'I can see why.' He smiled as if he could sense her discomfort. 'Would you rather we went and found a quiet spot and talked? I really wouldn't object to missing Mr Redknap's exhibition. There's a fire in the library, we could drink our coffee there.'

Jessica felt immeasurably grateful, putting aside her reservations about Harry's motives.

'That would be wonderful,' she said softly. By now the dance had begun to degenerate. The twins' hips moved with more and more accentuated thrusts, while every eye in the hall, with the exception of Harry's and Jessica's, watched and waited for what was to follow.

Harry slipped his arm through Jessica's.

'Come on, no one will even notice we've gone,' he said quietly.

Jack Heally watched Bunty's show with a mixture of excitement and distaste. He had never been particularly enamoured of male flesh, but the dancers, so lithe and so subtle, crossed the boundaries into androgyny. The twins in particular, with their heavily made up eyes and thrusting hips, were quite mesmerising.

Like mirror images of each other they began to stroke and touch themselves, fondling padded breasts, slipping their fingers up under their narrow skirts. All the time, every movement was accentuated by the throbbing jungle beat of the jazz music. The twins stood at either end of the row, like book ends framing the three other dancers. Jack wondered what would happen next.

Their cavorting seemed a dull show by comparison to the Arabian queen and her attentive slave boy. Just as he considered turning away, four young men in evening dress tap danced their way across the room, each one complete with top hat and cane, standing with their backs to the audience.

After another two bars, they spun round in perfect formation and revealed they were, in fact, four of the girls, Miranda and Helen included.

Now the tempo quickened. Each girl, with her pencilled moustache and monocle, began to pay court to the boys on either side of them. The boys feigned embarrassment and coyness - but it didn't last. From their jacket pockets the girls produced five-pound notes, which were quickly distributed amongst the boys. With great show they secreted their money down their cleavages or tucked them into stocking tops.

Jack couldn't help but grin. The mime was perfect. He glanced around the room, trying to spot Jessica and Harry, interested to see what they made of the exhibition. He couldn't see them, but then again the crowd was obscuring a lot of the other members of the audience.

When Jack looked back, the first of the twins had lifted his skirt to reveal a thick arching cock jutting out towards Miranda. She screwed her monocle tighter into her eye, as if to examine what was on offer and then unbuttoned her trousers. Bending forward, taking the twin's throbbing shaft between her perfectly painted little lips, her trousers dropped down, revealing her exquisite, rounded backside. The next boy in line feigned shock and then, with an almost imperceptible tilt of his hips, lifted his skirt and slipped an equally engorged cock into her quim. A little gasp of delight echoed through the audience as he pressed home.

Beside him, Helen turned to the next man and gave him a knowing wink. Coyly he lifted his skirt, she smiled and ran a finger along his thick shaft, unbuttoned her trousers, bent over and guided him deep inside her. As she did so, she slipped a hand between the legs of the man buried to the hilt in Miranda, cradling his ample balls. Within seconds all the dancers were linked by mouth, hand or sex. The effect was quite astonishing. Bunty subtly altered the beat of the music until each dancer was sucking or thrusting or stroking in time to a heady beat.

Their climax when it came was like a chain reaction. Jack could hardly believe his eyes as he saw the first shudder convulse through one of the twins, echoed over and over and over between all the members of the chorus line.

As the last heady shiver died away, George Gudgeon got to his feet to lead a thunderous round of applause. He swung round to look across the faces of the assembled crowd. Finding Jack with his eyes, he said, 'Wonderful, old chap. Absolutely first class. Oh, and I remember now where I saw that chap.'

Jack stared at him. 'Sorry?'

George waved his words away. 'The chap who sat opposite me at dinner.' He pulled a face. 'What was his name?'

Alice came to his rescue. 'Stolworthy, Harry Stolworthy.'

'Yes, that's him,' said George, taking a hefty tug on his cigar. 'I met him up at Ushers, last year some time. He was all done up to the nines—'

Jack stared at him. 'Ushers?'

George nodded.

Alice had appeared at Jack's elbow. 'Ushers?' she repeated.

George Gudgeon frowned. 'Are you all deaf, or something? Surely you must have heard of Ushers? It's full of bohemian types. Chaps dressed up as women, women in suits—' He snorted and then grinned. 'You never know who you're going to find beside you in the gents. Your Mr Stolworthy is a nancy-boy. I saw him at Ushers with his little friend.' He paused and blew out a long plume of smoke, staring into the shadows. 'Can't remember his friend's name, but it'll come to me. It's all up here somewhere.' He tapped the side of his forehead and then looked around for his glass, oblivious to the impact his words had had on Alice and Jack.

Jack stared at Alice. 'Where are they?'

'Harry and Jessica? God only knows. We really ought to say something to her,' Alice said.

'What do you suggest? Do you imagine for one instant that she's going to believe anything we say?'

Alice pulled a face. 'Perhaps George made a mistake - or maybe Harry likes men and women.' She paused. 'I mean, it's not uncommon, is it? And he is being so charming to her.'

Jack looked sceptical. 'It doesn't seem right to me.' He looked around the room. 'Let's face it, there's enough totty and tail on offer here that he wouldn't have to worry about someone like Jessica, unless of course he wanted something else.'

Alice glared at him. 'A challenge, you mean? Aren't you rather biased, Jack? After all, aren't you the one who has been trying to seduce her since she arrived?'

Jack sipped his brandy, his eyes scanning the faces of his guests.

Harry Stolworthy dropped a few more lumps of coal onto the fire in the library and turned back to Jessica, who was sitting on a stool by the hearth.

'Warm enough?' he said pleasantly, settling himself down beside her.

Jessica nodded. The huge room was in complete darkness except for one tiny lamp and the fire. The book-lined walls seemed to deaden any noise and so, sitting in the gloom, the sounds of the revels in the hall were no more than distant whispers.

Jessica looked across at Harry, who was watching the flames in the grate. Since he arrived, they seemed to have done nothing but talk. They had talked about family and friends, their homes, her job, his estate, and touched fleetingly on the power of grief and sadness.

It had been a long time since she'd met a man she could talk to or go beyond the social niceties with. Harry leant back on his haunches. The way he looked at her made her shiver inside.

'Would you care for another brandy? I saw a tray over by the door.' As he spoke, he extended a hand and stroked the curve of the wrist that held her glass.

His touch was gentle but insistent. She stared up at him. His eyes had darkened to pinpricks and she could sense his desire. For a second or two she tensed, wondering if perhaps his shy, little-boy-lost nature was an act. The eyes that held hers were confident. She turned slightly, slipping her glass between his fingers.

'I'd love one, please,' she said softly, trying to defuse the atmosphere between them. He smiled, set the glass down, and moved towards her, kissing her gently on the lips. His kiss was delicate, a tantalising suggestion of what he could offer her. She moaned without thinking and to her astonishment, felt Harry's hand brush across her breast.

His touch made her pulse quicken. He kissed her again, this time it was less gentle, his tongue seeking entry between her closed lips. She shivered, fighting to catch her breath as his fingers stroked her rapidly hardening nipples.

The need inside her bubbled up like a wellspring. She wasn't sure whether she was more perturbed by Harry or the insistent animal hunger in her body. While his kisses lit flares in her mind, his hands lifted to the straps of her dress, sliding them down over her shoulders. She felt powerless to resist, as if her desire had a will of its own that overcame every shred of reason. Harry groaned as his fingers found her naked breasts, cupping and stroking. Every tiny caress seemed to work its way down into the pit of her belly, where it glowed like a white fire.

He kissed her throat, the sensitive tips of her earlobes, her shoulders. It was like a fusillade of sensations, each one driving the capacity for rational thought further and further away.

When his lips closed around her erect nipples, she decided to stop thinking and let her body take control. Between her legs the sensation of heat was growing. Wetness trickled out from deep inside her like strands of white silk. She felt his fingers working at the hem of her skirt and shivered, watching his progress in her mind's eye, feeling his fingertips brush her thighs.

Harry's touch was both exciting and strangely soothing. As he found the rise of her sex she let out a long sigh of pleasure. He pulled back a little and smiled at her. The nervous man she had seen in the sitting-room had vanished, a more self assured Harry Stolworthy looked down at her with bright, confident eyes.

'God, you feel wonderful,' he murmured, eyes drinking in her exposure. 'I'd forgotten just how good a woman feels.' He ran a finger down over one of her breasts, circling the sensitive peak of her nipples. 'So many soft curves and such beautiful, beautiful skin.'

She shivered under his undisguised admiration. He kissed one nipple and then the other, letting his tongue trace their contours. It was a tiny act of worship that made her skin tingle with anticipation.

His hands slid over her body, pushing her dress lower, and caught hold of the waistband of her knickers. Almost without thinking, Jessica lifted her hips and he slid her dress and panties off, tugging them gently over her thighs and off over her feet. As he lifted each foot in turn, his face was almost level with the dark triangle of her sex. He looked up triumphantly, eyes flashing, and nuzzled the dark hair, lapping at the folds, seeking a way inside. His tongue, like an arrowhead, found the hard engorged ridge of her clitoris, making Jessica gasp.

He kissed it again, circling artfully around the throbbing peak. As he lapped and sucked, his fingers slid deep inside her. Her body closed around him, drawing him deeper, while his fingers set up a heady counter rhythm to the attentions of his tongue.

It felt as if every thought, every sensation, from breathing to sight, was centred on that one tiny spot. She heard Harry moan with pleasure as she started to move with him. Mesmerised by his caresses, she let go of any lingering scraps of doubt and fear. He seemed to sense her relaxing and increasing his efforts, drove her on and on towards release.

As Harry's tongue worked harder, she locked her fingers in his hair, pulling him close to her, surrendering to his every touch, every kiss. Wave after wave of pleasure built deep inside her, growing in intensity like a spring being wound tighter and tighter.

Just as she felt the final flurries building, seconds before the sensations would explode inside her head, Harry pulled away. She groaned in pure frustration.

'Turn over,' Harry whispered thickly.

She was so close to release she could hardly believe he had spoken. 'Please,' she whispered. 'Don't stop now.'

'Trust me,' he murmured. 'Just turn over.'

She could barely move she was trembling so much, but didn't resist as his steady hands helped her onto all fours. He slid his hands back up over her waist and she heard him let out a long appreciative moan.

Jessica reddened in spite of her excitement, imagining the picture she presented to him. Legs apart, her sex would be totally exposed, framed by the rounded orbs of her buttocks. It seemed to be an age before he touched her again, so long in fact, that she almost cried out when he ran a hand over her backside and then slid a finger inside her.

'My God, you're so tight,' he hissed, 'and so wet.'

She whimpered, feeling the brush of his thumb across her already glowing clitoris. There were a few seconds when he seemed to hesitate and she was afraid he would deny her the pleasure her body demanded. She heard him fumbling with his clothes and then let out a sigh of relief as she felt the brush of his cock against her inner thigh. It was a soft nuzzling request for entry. She closed her eyes, and slid a hand between her legs to guide him home.

His shaft was thick and meaty, totally at odds with his slim, aesthetic frame. It had been so long since Jessica had touched a man that she had forgotten how hard and threatening a cock could feel. It seemed alive in her palm. She wondered fleetingly how her body could accept something so powerful and unyielding, drawing it into the delicate depths that lay between her thighs.

Slowly, almost nervously, she guided him into her, aware of the tightness and the way he filled her to the very brim. Her excitement, creamy and thick, sealed him into her, easing his way fully home. The sensation of him inside her was breath-stopping. Her body seemed to absorb him, pulling him deeper and deeper.

As he began to move she moaned in apprehension, his cock felt like a huge warm piston, easing in and out, making every nerve-ending in her body glow.

His fingers returned to her clitoris, his other hand seeking out her breasts. He delicately nipped at the buds, tightening his thumb and forefinger on the sensitive swollen flesh. The sheer intensity of his caresses drove her fear away and she began to move with him, welcoming his weight and the heat of his body against her back. The whisper of his breath on her naked back was electrifying. He licked along her spine, nibbling and kissing, murmuring words of encouragement as she drove her hips up to meet his. The feelings were all absorbing.

She felt the waves of pleasure rekindle, intensify and then rise up inside her like a sheet of white hot flame. Deep inside, she felt her sex sucking at Harry's shaft, closing again and again around it and then the first stunning throb of his climax, hot on the heels of her own.

At that moment it felt as if she was inside his head and he in hers. She couldn't work out where one body began and the other ended. On and on the pleasure went, until, exhausted, she collapsed down onto the floor.

Harry slipped out from behind her, panting hard.

'My God,' he murmured, 'I'd completely forgotten how good that felt.'

She rolled over, picking up her dress to cover her exposed body. He grinned down at her, and kissed each naked, blushing breast in turn before helping her slip the dress back over her shoulders.

For a moment, she wished he would say something tender or reassuring. Almost as if he could read her mind, he cradled her face in his hands and kissed her fiercely. 'You are quite perfect, Jessica,' he said. 'I really can't believe it was pure chance that brought us together.'

He knelt back on his heels and she noticed him slide something off his exhausted shaft. She looked up at him in surprise as he dropped a rubber sheath onto the low fire.

He smiled at her unasked question. 'I think most chaps come prepared,' he said, reddening furiously. 'I didn't mean to embarrass you. I'm sure it's from being in the army.' Avoiding her eyes, he picked up the brandy balloon from the hearth. 'Would you care for that drink now?'

Jessica nodded, trying hard to order her muddled thoughts.

Harry offered her his hand. 'Shall we have this drink and then go back to the others? I think, by the sound of it, their little cabaret must be over and done with. Perhaps we ought to put in an appearance.'

As Jessica got to her feet he pressed a chaste kiss to her cheek. 'You know, you really are quite amazing.'

Chapter 9

21 December

Jack Heally woke up the next morning, still feeling drunk and with a hangover. He groaned theatrically as he stumbled across his bedroom towards the bathroom. His mouth felt like wet cardboard and every step he took sent pain ricocheting up through his throbbing skull.

Glancing back at the tangle of sheets on the bed, he wondered whether he had managed to persuade anyone to share it with him. A flicker of movement amongst the bedclothes suggested he had - and he wracked his brain to try and remember who it was.

It certainly wasn't likely to have been Jessica Harper. Her name sent up another spark of pain through his brandy-addled mind. She and Harry Stolworthy had reappeared just as Felicia had stepped up to the piano to sing.

Jack turned the tap on in the sink and filled the basin with icy water, then eyed it speculatively, wondering if his skull might explode if he plunged his face into it.

Harry and Jessica had stood side by side in the shadows, near the corridor that led into the rest of the house. They tried to make it appear as if they had been there all along, but Jack wasn't at all convinced by their little charade. When he'd caught Jessica's eye, she had blushed furiously and Stolworthy had slipped a proprietorial arm around her waist.

The way she looked, the way Stolworthy moved, left Jack in no doubt that they had slipped away to make love in some quiet little backwater, while everyone else was watching Bunty's preposterous show.

He had looked round for Alice Fallon, only to discover she was tucked up in an alcove with her arm around Prince Charming. Feeling neglected and disproportionately miserable, he had made his way over to the cocktail cabinet and poured himself another brandy - and then another and another.

Jack grimaced at his reflection in the mirror above the sink. His skin had an unhealthy yellowish tinge and his eyes looked decidedly bloodshot. Through the open bathroom door, he could see his unidentified bedmate rolling over, wrapping themselves up in the eiderdown. He ran his tongue over his teeth, trying to work out who it might be.

After a few more seconds, a tumble of blonde hair appeared and then Alice Fallon pulled the bedclothes down and peered at him over her naked shoulder. She grinned at his dishevelled appearance.

'Morning, darling. Headache?' she said brightly.

Jack would have rolled his eyes, except that he doubted his brain would stand it. She wriggled across the bed, still wrapped up in the sheets. Between his legs he was aware of the press of a raging, drink-induced erection. Seeing Alice's plump pink breasts made him groan.

He ran his fingers through his hair, trying to ignore the throb in his groin. As his fingers met his scalp, he winced. Every hair follicle appeared to have a small explosive charge attached to the end of it.

On the bed, Alice smiled indulgently.

'You rather went to town last night, didn't you? I can't believe how much you drank. Helen and I had to help you get undressed and then we put you to bed. How are you feeling?'

Jack indicated the bed. 'Did we - er, you know?'

Alice grinned. 'A jolly threesome? Not exactly, though you were quite keen on the idea before you passed out. We tossed up for who would stay here to keep an eye on you. You were in a pretty bad way.'

Jack snorted and instantly regretted it.

Alice's eyes travelled down to the bulge in the front of his pyjamas. 'Mind you, I can think of a way you could make it up to me.'

Jack glanced back at the sink full of icy cold water and decided, on balance, there were far more pleasant ways to clear an aching head. He pulled the plug and picked up his toothbrush.

'Give me a minute,' he said, forcing a grin. 'And I'll see what I can do.'

Alice rolled over onto her belly and lifted her legs up in the air. 'Can you remember anything at all about last night?'

Jack shook his head, sending up a plume of pain-tinged stars somewhere behind his eyes.

She giggled, face alight with mischief. She rolled over again and ran a hand across her pert breasts and taut belly, her fingers outlining the lips of her quim.

'How terrible. So, you don't remember stripping off and dancing on the sideboard, then?'

Jack managed to raise an eyebrow.

In the little bedroom on the floor below, Jessica Harper stretched and then snuggled back under the bedclothes. Beside her, Harry Stolworthy looked up and blinked, as if he couldn't quite work out where he was.

Focusing on her face, he finally smiled.

'Good morning, Jessica,' he said in a low voice. 'How are you this morning?'

Jessica felt a ripple of amusement. He sounded as if they had just been introduced at a formal social function. Her amusement was quickly replaced by surprise. He had barely finished the sentence before he clambered out of bed, and started collecting his clothes together.

'I really shouldn't have stayed all night,' he mumbled unhappily, pulling on his trousers. 'I do apologise. I'll try and make sure no one sees me leave.' He looked embarrassed. 'I really didn't mean to stay...'

Jessica stared at him, feeling like some cheap whore.

'Pardon?' she said, trying hard to retain some scrap of dignity.

He turned round, blushing furiously.

'What I meant to say is, what if anyone sees me leaving your room? Or finds out that I've not spent the night in mine? I—' he stopped abruptly. 'I'm concerned about your reputation, Jessica. It's hardly very chivalrous of me to compromise your reputation when we barely know each other.'

Jessica fought to suppress a giggle and wondered what he meant by knowing each other. There was hardly a square inch of each other's flesh that they hadn't touched or kissed in the few hours they had been together.

'Harry,' she said as evenly as she could, 'Malestone is full of people engaged in all sorts of sexual high jinx. Most of them would feel compromised if they weren't caught leaving someone else's bedroom.'

Harry did not look convinced.

'I think,' he said, after a few seconds, 'that perhaps Malestone isn't really a very good place for you to stay. Perhaps there's a hotel locally where we could find you more suitable accommodation? I suppose you are committed to helping Alice? Perhaps we can arrange for a car to bring you here each day to give her a hand? I'm sure no one would object.'

She stared at him. 'Sorry?' she said, wondering if it was possible she had misunderstood him.

Harry carried on buttoning his shirt.

'The whole atmosphere in this house is morally unsound. I'm rather surprised you've stayed as long as you have. I wouldn't have thought Bunty Redknap and his crowd were your sort of people at all.'

Jessica stared at him in complete astonishment. She had had the same doubts and fears herself, but hearing Harry voice them made her feel quite indignant.

'Harry, as you said yourself, I barely know you.' Her words were spoken in a carefully controlled voice. 'I only met you yesterday and I met you because I was here at Malestone. Neither of us is really in any position to take the moral high ground.'

Harry looked very uncomfortable. He glanced up at her with his grey eyes.

'We can always tell people that we met in London, at a dance or something,' he said quietly.

Jessica stared at him. 'People?' she repeated.

Harry nodded, unable to quite meet her gaze.

'I suppose, Jessica, what I'm trying to say is that we've rather been thrown together - and for that I'm extremely grateful - but I would like it very much if, after we leave here, we could begin again—' He stopped and began to pick nervously at the piping on the eiderdown.

Jessica felt an odd mixture of elation and apprehension. 'What exactly are you saying, Harry?' she asked in a low voice.

His colour deepened. 'I was rather hoping that you'd consider going out with me once we get back to normal life. I don't live that far away from Somerset that we can't see each other from time to time. In some ways, you and I have a lot in common. The years go by so quickly.' His words came out in a tumbled rush. 'I mean, I haven't got an awful lot to offer you, but perhaps...' he paused, turning to look into her eyes. 'I suppose, Jessica, what I'm asking is, would you consider marrying me?'

Jessica gasped. 'Oh, Harry.' She quickly tried to gather her thoughts. Of all the things she thought Harry might suggest, she certainly hadn't expected a proposal. 'I'm very flattered, but we hardly know each other,' she spluttered.

Harry held up his hands. 'I'm not saying we have to get married immediately - of course not. But I want to make you understand that my interest in you is something long lasting, not just a wild fling.'

He sat down on the bed and kissed her gently on the lips. Jessica shivered.

'I'll talk to Jack today about finding a hotel in the village,' he continued.

Jessica still hadn't quite recovered from Harry's suggestion, but even so managed to shake her head.

'No, Harry. We're only here for a few more days and Alice really does need me here.'

It surprised her that she used the word we. Everything was happening far too fast. Coming to Malestone had thrown every aspect of her life into total confusion. She pulled the bedclothes up around her shoulders, feeling totally muddled.

'I need time to think,' she said, almost to herself. Harry's hand slid down under the bedclothes and stroked her sleep-warm skin.

'You feel quite divine,' he purred, sliding back onto the bed beside her. 'I never want to let you go again.'

His hand moved towards the warm junction between her thighs. She groaned and lay back amongst the pillows, revelling in the sensation his touch lit in her. Would it be so terrible to be with a man who made her feel this way? She struggled to maintain some sense of balance, but her body's needs silenced the rational voice.

Harry's touch was like gossamer, trailing into the soft wet folds of her quim, brushing down against the bud of her clitoris. Instinctively, she opened her legs to let him have greater access.

He chuckled as he pressed kisses to her collar bones. 'Perhaps my getting dressed so quickly was a little premature, after all,' he whispered. 'I was worried that I might compromise you.' His fingers dipped into the silky pool of moisture, trailing her juices out onto the sensitive skin of her thighs.

She shivered, lifting herself up so that his fingers could work deeper and deeper.

'I was rather hoping that you might consider compromising me again,' she said, with a smile.

He moved away from her and began to undo his shirt. 'If you insist,' he whispered, eyes darkening with desire.

When he climbed into bed beside her, she pulled him down into her arms. No longer reticent, hungry only for the satisfaction his caresses promised, she relinquished all control and gave herself over entirely to the call of her instincts.

Harry moaned, rolling over on his back, dragging her with him. He reached up to caress her breasts, his fingers rolling her engorged nipples between thumb and finger. She straddled his waist, eagerly guiding his shaft into her.

He froze, as his cock brushed against the heat and wetness of her quim.

'Wait,' he said softly and leant over the edge of the bed to rescue his jacket. She sat back on her heels, suddenly conscious of her nakedness and the way his eyes moved over the contours of her body, as he unrolled a sheath over his cock.

The expression on his face was one of elation and something, she realised with surprise, that was almost triumphant.

He pressed his cock up against her belly.

'Marry me, Jessica,' he whispered. 'Please say you'll marry me.'

She lifted herself a fraction, which was all her body needed to draw him inside. Wasn't he supposed to say that he loved her? That he would love her forever? She glanced down into his eyes and wondered if perhaps he was confusing love with lust. She shivered as her body opened up to accept him, excited by the way his shaft felt inside her. Whether this was lust or love, she was as addicted as he was.

'I told you,' she said, gasping as her sex closed tight around him. 'It's all much too fast. I need time to think.'

He thrust so fiercely that he took her breath away.

'Rubbish,' he murmured between gritted teeth. 'Why waste time thinking? Haven't you already wasted too many years already?'

His words stung her, but before Jessica could think of a reply, his fingers brushed over her clitoris and his hips followed hard behind, sending a cascade of pleasure tumbling through her mind.

She moved with him, matching him stroke for stroke, leaving behind everything except for the chase towards release. He lunged up, holding her tight. As she let out a throaty cry of delight, he closed his teeth around her nipple, nipping and biting, tongue lapping at the pinpricks of pain as they exploded inside her.

His fingers tightened on her hips, dragging her down onto his engorged angry cock. His fury and his passion were breathtaking and for an instant she almost felt as if she would be burnt up in his heat.

On and on he pushed, until she imagined she could see their excitement, like the tail of a comet, stretching out behind them, intense and glowing. An instant later, the sensations exploded through her, sending glittering crystal shards of pleasure out to every last cell, every last hair, every fingertip. Sobbing, she collapsed down on Harry's chest, the sweat trickling down her face.

'Marry me,' he hissed, as one last shudder convulsed through them both. 'Just say you will marry me. Please, Jessica, say yes.'

'Yes,' Jessica whispered, hardly able to believe she was answering him. 'Yes.'

He tightened his embrace. 'Oh, my dear,' he purred, 'that's just what I needed to hear.' Gently he rolled her off him and cradled her in the crook of his arm. 'I'm so glad I accepted Jack's invitation. I think coming to Malestone may have solved everything.'

It seemed an odd thing to say. Jessica glanced across at Harry and realised he was falling asleep. Safe in his arms she wondered what he meant. 'Solved everything' seemed a strange way to describe finding a woman you wanted to marry. Or was she just being oversensitive? Logic and reason were rapidly replacing the wild voice of passion.

Seeing Harry's face in profile, eyes closed, thick lashes resting on his sharp cheekbones, she felt a flurry of tenderness. Perhaps everything was happening too fast, but hadn't he already said they could meet up once she went back to St Winifred's, that they could begin again and this time take their courtship more slowly, a step at a time?

Jessica smiled, feeling his sleepiness seeping into her mind. She had always been sensible, she wouldn't let Harry sweep her reserve away on his grand passion - however tempting the prospect. She closed her eyes, fantasising about what would happen in the months to come.

Once they were away from Malestone he would court her, take her out to dinner, take her dancing. After a month or two, if they still felt the same, she would take him home to meet her parents.

Gradually, Malestone and this frantic passionate beginning would be forgotten, tidied away in the gentle familiarity of a real love affair. She smiled, concentrating on the feelings of sexual satisfaction that lingered in her mind like wisps of smoke. It might not be possible to forget everything - her body demanded too much to be content with a return to chaste kisses and holding hands, but as long as they were discreet, what would it matter?

For a moment, she imagined sneaking Harry into her rooms at St Winifred's and smiled again. She imagined them creeping up the stairs on tiptoe, Harry with his hand sliding provocatively up under the matronly clothes she wore for school. Sharing her hard single bed. Perhaps not.

She snuggled up against Harry's slim frame and surrendered to the call of sleep.

Jessica and Harry were last ones down for breakfast, which rather undermined all Harry's good intentions - not that he seemed to care now. His previously nervous disposition appeared to have evaporated since she had accepted his proposal of marriage.

Catching hold of her elbow as they got to the doors of the dining room, he spun her round into his arms.

'God, Jessica you've made me so happy,' he said with a grin and kissed her fiercely.

Jessica wriggled away.

'Steady,' she said, good humouredly. 'We've got lots of time. I still need time to think, and then we have to arrange what happens after we leave Malestone. I...'

Harry lifted a finger to her lips to silence her.

'It's all very, very simple,' he said brightly. 'We just get married. It shouldn't take more than a few days to arrange.' He tugged at his jacket, puffing up his chest. 'We could be Mr and Mrs Stolworthy by the New Year. We ought to make an announcement and let everyone know.'

Jessica stared at him, feeling a huge bubble of panic rising up in her chest. 'No, Harry,' she began. 'Not yet. I thought you understood.'

He spun round, looking totally crestfallen. 'What do you mean, no? You haven't changed your mind, have you? I really couldn't bear it.'

Jessica shook her head in disbelief.

'Harry, we can't just get married. We need time to get to know each other properly - and do things properly. My parents are in New York at the moment, you'll have to meet them, and do all the social, ordinary things people do together. I don't even know what you like to eat—'

He grinned and leaned forward, so his mouth was level with her ear. 'I've developed rather a taste for pussy,' he whispered.

Jessica blushed crimson, while beside her Harry opened the dining room doors.

As they walked in only Alice Fallon and Jack Heally looked up. Their expressions, thought Jessica, with an uncharacteristic sense of satisfaction, were disapproving. They couldn't have her themselves and were furious that someone else had. She let Harry pull out her chair for her and didn't protest when he suggested he get breakfast for them both.

Her doubts about Harry's eagerness and her anxiety that things were moving too fast were put to one side, as she enjoyed Jack and Alice's obvious jealousy. It might not be a very mature attitude, she thought, accepting a cup of tea from Harry, but it felt rather good.

Bunty clapped his hands and announced that he expected everyone in the theatre troupe to go straight to rehearsals as soon as breakfast was over. Jack, looking decidedly peaky, invited his other guests to join him for a tour of the estate. Alice looked up and whispered to Jessica, 'We need to start sorting out the props and curtains. With a bit of luck Bunty will be ready for the first dress rehearsal this afternoon.'

Jessica nodded and then turned her attention back to Harry Stolworthy. He smiled at her and lifted a cup in silent salute. In spite of everything, having him there beside her and so obviously smitten was tremendously flattering. Even the way he looked at her made a tremor of desire flicker in her belly. Let Jack and Alice think what they like.

At the very least, Harry Stolworthy satisfied the need she had neglected so long. Whether or not the lust she felt could grow into love strong enough to sustain a marriage was another matter. She smiled at him - it was very tempting just to say yes to his enthusiastic courtship. When they had a chance to be alone, she would have to explain that she really did need time to think. Explain that her reluctance had nothing to do with what she felt at that moment. After all, if this wasn't just a mad infatuation, their chance meeting could lead to a lifetime together. Whatever his fears, they really did have plenty of time.

She touched his hand affectionately; surely she would be able to make him understand. For an instant, Jessica wondered if she could really love him, day in day out. Wasn't love supposed to come before falling into bed with someone?

Her touch made Harry smile broadly. He looked so content and relaxed sitting beside her - perhaps love could grow out of lust after all. At least she had the chance to find out.

Jack Healy waited out in the hall for Alice to leave the dining room. He had had to excuse himself from the table, leaving the latecomers - the love birds - to enjoy their breakfast. Their obvious infatuation had made him feel physically sick. He could barely bring himself to look at them.

As Alice crossed the hall towards the drawing room Jack hurried after her and grabbed hold of her arm. She jumped.

'Oh Jack, it's you. You frightened me. What do you want?'

'I need to talk about bloody Harry Stolworthy and Jessica. We have to do something about it.'

Alice laughed, as around them a steady stream of people headed off towards rehearsals.

'Jack, you really are the limit. We had plenty of time to discuss this, this morning, but you didn't seem so keen to talk about it then. What's the matter? Does seeing Jessica so happy put your nose out of joint?'

Jack frowned. Alice's assessment of the situation was far too close to the mark.

'There's something not right about that chap. You heard what George Gudgeon said last night.'

Alice looked heavenwards. 'Your friend George was three parts cut, and he could very easily have been mistaken about Harry. Anyway, even if it is true, what does it matter? You shouldn't underestimate Jessica, perhaps she already knows about Harry's sexual preferences.'

Jack pulled a face. 'Don't be such a fool,' he hissed. 'She is a complete innocent. Christ, she couldn't even work you out.'

Alice's expression hardened. 'No, you're right. But she'd certainly got the measure of you, hadn't she, Jack Healy?' She poked him furiously. 'This is just a matter of jealousy. Harry Stolworthy's got her and you haven't - it's as simple as that. Look, try and get this into some sort of perspective. Four more days and it will all be over. Jessica will go home to her teaching job at St Winifred's, Harry Stolworthy will go back to wherever it is he hails from, and you can get on with your life.'

Jack groaned miserably. If only it really were that simple. Every time he looked at Jessica he got this unexpected ache, some sort of longing that he couldn't quite define.

'Will you at least talk to Jessica?' he said, with a hint of appeal in his voice.

'And say what?' Alice asked.

His pained expression made her smile.

'Oh, all right, but don't expect any results. But I'll be damned lucky if she speaks to me at all after your revelations about my liking a little female flesh from time to time.'

Jack coloured. 'Thank you,' he said softly, wishing there was something more he could say or do.

From behind them in the dining room, he heard Jessica Harper laugh and fought the temptation to march straight in and wring young Stolworthy's neck.

Chapter 10

22 December

Jack dragged his coat up tight round his ears and struggled to keep his mind on his guests and their conversation, as they toured the estate. Norman Marlow, Bob Fields, Robin Welsh and Jim Randal, who were walking with him, had all been in his house at school. On their left, Harry Stolworthy, excluded by a steady stream of bawdy, good-humoured recollections and shared memories, was talking to Jack's groom.

Harry had been pointedly ignoring Stolworthy ever since they'd left Malestone, which gave him a dark sense of satisfaction. As Norman began another story, aided and abetted by the others, Jack glanced across the paddock towards the main drive that led up to the house. Later that day everyone else would arrive and the house would be heaving with friends and acquaintances: the Greens, Tippy and Gena Foster, Iona Fontaine, Liza Frazier and her new beau... The list was long. In his mind's eye he ran through a crowd of familiar faces, while around him his old friends continued their small talk.

'Jack?'

Norman's voice disturbed his thoughts, making him aware that he was neglecting his role as host.

'Isn't that Felicia? The woman who was at dinner last night?' Norman pointed towards the rider of a chestnut horse, who was cantering across the frosty parkland towards them.

Jack screwed up his eyes against the winter sunlight and winced. The idea of being bounced about on the back of the headstrong mount made his skull thump in time with every stride of the huge horse. As she cleared the last hedge, Felicia lifted a hand in greeting.

'Morning all,' she said cheerfully, reining the huge animal in. 'How are you this morning? Beautiful day, isn't it?'

While everyone exchanged greetings, Jack had to smile as he caught Felicia eyeing his friends up like prize stock at a cattle auction.

She grinned at Jack. 'You're very quiet this morning. I'm rather surprised you're up and about. You certainly tied one on last night.'

Jack sighed. 'How very kind of you to remind me, Felicia. How are you?'

'Fine.' She slipped down off the sweating horse and handed the reins, without a word, to the groom. Jack struggled to suppress a grin as the man's eyes roamed across Felicia's body with easy familiarity.

'I just rode over to tell you we'd be along later on today. George was most impressed by last night's little exhibition. I don't think he was too keen on the idea of staying, until he saw what Bunty had in store for us.' She grinned. 'He couldn't keep his hands off me on the way home.'

She glanced up at Harry Stolworthy, who was listening to the conversation without comment. 'I must say, you look like the cat who's been at the cream. George says that he's met you before.'

Stolworthy reddened. 'I think he's mistaken,' he said quickly.

Felicia shrugged. 'I wouldn't have thought so. He may strike you as being an old duffer but he's as sharp as a razor.' She smiled ruefully and rubbed her thighs. 'And as horny as an old goat. Mind you, his performance is not so hot these days. All that frantic pawing and fumbling just leaves me baying for more.'

She eyed Norman up, batting her long eyelashes. 'It's terribly hard for someone like me to be saddled with someone *so old*.'

Jack laughed. 'And so rich. Leave poor Norman alone. I thought you were smitten with Miranda at the moment?'

Felicia pouted provocatively. 'Variety is the spice of life,' she said, slipping her arm first through Norman's and then Jack's. Her attention, however, was firmly on Norman. 'What do you do?' she said pleasantly. 'We never really got to talk to each other last night, did we?'

Norman grinned and turned to Jack. 'Do I really need to go through all this small talk?' He stood head and shoulders above the diminutive Felicia.

Jack smiled. 'Hardly. Speaking from experience I would suggest you find somewhere quiet and fuck her senseless, that's what she's really after. She's just being uncharacteristically coy this morning.'

Felicia feigned indignation. 'Jack, how could you?' she hissed. 'And in front of company too.'

Jack grinned. 'So, I'm wrong then? You have my most profound apologies, Felicia.'

'Not exactly, but I expected that you might exercise a little more tact,' she said, with a sly grin. 'What will your friends think of me?'

'You really care?' he said lightly. 'No one will mind if you pair vanish into the undergrowth, but do be gentle with him, Felicia, and find somewhere out of this wind. Norman's not used to all this bracing country air.'

While the other men seemed to be amused by the exchange, Harry Stolworthy could barely mask his discomfort.

Jack glanced at him. 'Not to your taste, eh, Stolworthy?' he said with a malicious grin.

Harry reddened. Jack, feeling a wave of anger, continued. 'Or perhaps you'd prefer it if you had Norman to yourself. Felicia might get in the way.' The venom in his own voice surprised him.

Harry Stolworthy stared at him, eyes bright with fury, while Norman leapt to Harry's defence.

'I say, Jack, that's a bit strong. Hardly the way to speak to old friends.'

Norman's good humour broke the icy look that locked Harry and Jack together.

Jack forced a grin. 'Perhaps you're right.' He glanced at Stolworthy, aware that unless he was very careful, his jealousy - if that was what it was - might easily spoil everyone's Christmas. He sighed, struggling to swallow the feeling that festered low down in his stomach. His annoyance and jealousy were irrational. He turned away and took a deep breath.

'I should know by my age not to mix grape and grain. Sorry about that, I think this damned hangover has boiled my brain.' He was careful to look at Norman when he spoke - his apology didn't extend to Harry Stolworthy.

Norman, meanwhile, turned, lifted Felicia's hand and kissed her fingertips.

'What had you got in mind then, Mrs Gudgeon? May I call you Mrs Gudgeon?'

Felicia smiled and performed a deep curtsy. 'Actually, it's Lady Gudgeon,' she said with a purr. 'And Jack's right, it's far too cold for passion in the great outdoors.' Her eyes twinkled mischievously as she looked from man to man.

Jack could see the flush rising in her cheeks as some plan formulated behind those delicate blue eyes. She glanced over her shoulders toward the copse that backed onto the paddock.

'Over in the trees is the Old Lodge cottage.' She disentangled herself from the two men. 'What about a little game of chase?' Her voice was alight with laughter. 'Perhaps I've misjudged Norman, maybe he isn't the one for me after all.' As she spoke she spun around and made a break across the rough grass. 'Perhaps it ought to be whoever catches me. Give me a minute or two's head start.' There was an edge of excitement in her tone.

Jack smiled. He'd played this game with Felicia before. He knew her delicate appearance belied her stamina. She was as strong and quick as a yearling and by the time the men set off to trail her, she would be hidden in the trees - but not so well hidden that some one, or maybe two would overlook her.

Norman looked at Jack for his approval.

'Do you mind?' he said, slipping off his jacket as Felicia vanished out of sight.

Jack shook his head. 'Hardly. You heard the lady, be my guest. Just save a little for me.'

Robin, Bob and Jim followed Norman's example and seconds later, sloughing off their heavy overcoats, headed off towards the dark stand of trees. They whooped as they broke into a run. Jack could sense their excitement - the thrill of the chase would make the prize all the sweeter. Beside him, Harry Stolworthy stared after the running men.

Jack smiled ruefully. 'Not your style?'

Stolworthy sniffed. 'I prefer my women to be a little less obvious.'

Jack rolled his eyes heavenwards and chose to say nothing. He glanced at his groom, still leading Felicia's gelding, and held out a hand. The man passed Jack the reins without a word and Jack climbed up into the saddle.

'If you'll excuse me, Harry, I've got an obvious woman to hunt down. I'll see you back up at the house.'

He kicked the horse firmly and careered off across the field, where his friends were already hot on the heels of Lady Gudgeon. He had been right, riding a horse with a hangover was not a very bright move, but even so he kicked the horse on. As he passed the front runner - Norman - he grinned as they shouted their good natured disapproval. Breaking through the trees, he slowed the horse so that he could listen to the sounds of the forest, still and crisp after the roar of the wind.

Unlike the other men, Jack knew his quarry well. Felicia wanted to be caught, but she would still make them work for their prize. Picking his way along one of the main paths he heard Norman, Bob, Jim and Robin enter the wood behind him. Their voices sounded strange and distorted as they echoed between the trees. They would stand far less chance of finding Felicia if they stayed in a pack. Despite the good humoured nature of the chase he could already feel the adrenaline begin to pump in his veins. He dismounted, tied the horse to a fallen tree and then set off in earnest.

Creeping around, careful to keep well out of sight, he could feel his cock stirring inside his trousers. He smiled. Even if he wasn't the first to find Felicia, he would still have a little something to offer her. A flicker of movement between the trees caught his attention and he headed towards it, hoping it was not one of the many deer on the estate. Behind him everything was quiet. It seemed that his friends had read his mind and split up.

He was working around the paths in a long slow arc, doubling back so that he would come out almost where he had seen Felicia go into the wood. She preferred to make love in the warmth and he didn't think she would stray too far away from the Old Lodge cottage.

He saw another movement ahead of him and silently made his way between the curls of bracken and tumble of fallen trees. In spite of himself, Jack could feel the excitement building in his belly, like a spring that wound tighter and tighter with every passing minute. He approached the cottage slowly, as quietly as he could, until he reached a small steep bank, a hundred yards away.

At the base, sheltered from prying eyes, two figures were rolling around on a carpet of pine needles. He focused on them for a second, trying to make sense of the limbs and positions and then he realised with a start that Felicia was ahead of him, running along the rim of the bank being pursued by Norman.

Jack looked back down into the hollow. The two figures were obscured to all but him by a wall of holly and other evergreens. As he watched, he realised with a stomach-wrenching certainty that one of the figures was Harry Stolworthy and the other was his groom. Unable to resist the pull of their frantic coupling he moved closer, stunned that all his suspicions and fears were being proved true so graphically.

Stolworthy had a hand between the cheeks of the groom's backside, stroking the man's thick engorged shaft. His expression was deadpan. His other hand was guiding his own cock into the most secret places of the groom's body. The older man let out a low grunt as Stolworthy found his mark and then very slowly they began to move in tandem.

Even from his hiding place, Jack could sense the apprehension in the older man's body and hear Stolworthy's soft encouraging noises as he slid deeper inside the man crouching amongst the pine needles.

Jack was stunned, he couldn't imagine what lever, what ploy Stolworthy had used to persuade his man to cooperate. As the unlikely lovers began to move more instinctively, the groom threw back his head and howled like a wolf, sweat trickling down his swarthy face. Above him, Stolworthy's face was impassive, eyes fixed in the middle distance as he rode his way out to release.

The contrast of their clothes, stance and demeanour was unsettling. It was all Jack could do to stop himself from dashing across the clearing like some misguided knight in shining armour to rescue his employee.

Suddenly, Stolworthy's expression changed to something akin to ecstasy. Jack's treacherous mind reminded him that this was the man that had slept with Jessica. She would already know what his face looked like as his climax roared through them both. Beneath Stolworthy, the groom collapsed down in a breathless heap amongst the pine needles, but not before Jack saw a spurt of glistening semen explode from his cock.

Jack realised he had been holding his breath and inhaled with a long snorting gasp. Up on the top of the bank, Felicia was being brought to ground by the excited advances of Norman Marlow.

Jack tore his attention away from Stolworthy and his companion. Without looking back, he began a slow circle that would bring him up to the Old Lodge cottage. He wanted to have the images from the clearing wiped out by an impassioned hour or so in Felicia's company. Breaking through the undergrowth, he met Bob, Robin and Jim - apparently everyone had the same idea. He was certain Felicia wouldn't object.

In the drawing room of Malestone House there was an uneasy silence that had lasted for most of the morning. Even the constant to-ing and fro-ing of the actors, dancers and singers hadn't quite melted the icy atmosphere between Jessica Harper and Alice Fallon.

Finally, a footman came in to announce that coffee was being served in the hall. As Jessica stretched and looked up from her work, Alice's eyes met hers.

'We have to talk,' Alice said flatly, laying aside an embroidered frock coat she had been repairing. 'I can't stand this not talking to each other.'

Jessica sighed, feeling the mixture of pain and hurt receding under her friend's open and deeply troubled expression.

Alice moved closer. 'I'm really sorry that you think I've used you. Nothing could be further from the truth. Jack can be very spiteful when he wants - he was just jealous of me, of us.'

Jessica nodded. 'I know,' she said, with genuine relief that they were finally speaking again. All morning her stomach had been tying itself into tighter and tighter knots. 'But it doesn't matter now,' she said. 'Everything has changed.'

Alice stared at her. 'What do you mean? You're not talking about Harry

Stolworthy, are you?'

Jessica took a deep breath, wondering how she could possibly explain about Harry. The easiest way seemed to just say it.

'Harry has asked me to marry him,' she said quietly, looking down at the floor so that Alice couldn't read her expression. 'And I have said yes.'

She heard Alice gasp and looked up into her friend's incredulous eyes.

'You said yes? How could you?' Alice gasped. 'For God's sake, Jessica, you hardly know the man.'

Jessica felt her colour deepen. Alice had quoted her protest to Harry almost word for word.

'Not at once, of course,' she said quickly. 'I mean, we both need more time to be sure of what we feel about each other.'

Alice got to her feet. 'But you've already said yes? I can't believe you've done that. Going to bed with someone doesn't mean you're in love with them.' She stopped, reddening violently. 'You need to think this over.'

Jessica bit her lip. 'I've more or less told Harry the same thing, but he's quite insistent. He said I'd wasted too many years thinking already.' She paused, feeling tears forming behind her eyes. 'I suppose in some ways he's right. It's been so lonely since Robert died—' A thick sob bubbled up in her throat. In seconds Alice was beside her, holding her close.

'Oh, Jessica, please don't cry. I understand, I really do, but being lonely is no reason to marry the first man that comes along. For God's sake, it's not as if you're not attractive. You practically had to beat Jack off with a stick. The sea is full of happy little fish looking for a mate. Why Stolworthy, of all people?'

Jessica swallowed hard, trying to keep her tears and sadness under control but failing miserably.

'It's all easy for you to say. You live a life where there are men around all the time. Trust me, they aren't so thick on the ground in an all-girls school.'

Alice stared at her. 'Are you saying you think that Harry is your only choice? Your last chance? If you think that then you're mad. God, you're beautiful, Jessica. If you set your mind to it you could have any one of the men who is here. Jack is totally bloody obsessed with you.'

Jessica laughed mirthlessly. 'He just wants to make love to me. I'm sure if I went round this house I'd find a trophy room full of stuffed mounted animal heads. He just wants to add me to his collection.'

Alice shook her head. 'It would be a lie to say that there wasn't something in that. I suppose you're right; Jack takes pride in his undisputed aim to have us all, but in another way I think you're wrong. He is completely and utterly besotted by you.'

'Only because I've had the gall to turn him down.'

'Never mind about Jack, what about Harry? What do you know about him?'

Jessica blushed furiously. 'He makes me feel wonderful. I've never known anyone who is so attentive or so kind.'

Alice looked incredulous. 'You've known him two days, barely that. Have you thought it could be an act? I feel responsible for you. If I hadn't invited you to Malestone...'

Jessica felt a blaze of fury.

'Are you saying I'm so inexperienced I wouldn't know the difference? I'm not some poor pathetic maiden aunt who you've got to take care of, you know. I've already told you I'm not going to rush into marrying Harry. I'll give it time. And you're right; I was flattered to be asked. It was like a breath of fresh air to meet someone who was normal after having you and Jack argue over me like dogs over a bone.' She stopped, struggling to regain her composure.

'If it doesn't work out what have I lost? He makes me feel so wonderful. When he touches me—' she stopped, reddening again, and sat down heavily in the fireside chair. 'You are right. It's foolish and not like me at all. But for once in my life I want to be reckless. It's all happened so fast that I've barely had time to think. Maybe I will get hurt, but that's no reason not to try, is it?'

Alice leant forward and kissed her gently on the forehead. 'Of course, you're right. It really is none of my business. I'm just worried about you. I don't want to see you get hurt. Harry Stolworthy seems too good to be true. There's something about him that I don't like - and because I'm your friend I have to say something. I think there are things he isn't telling you.' She took a deep breath. 'George Gudgeon thinks he has seen him at Ushers.'

Jessica shook her head. 'I don't understand. What's that?'

Alice looked heavenwards. 'It's a club. A very select club.' She stopped, as if she hoped Jessica would be able to guess whatever was on her mind.

'I still don't know what you're trying to say,' Jessica said.

Alice sighed. 'It's a club for men who prefer the company of other men - and women who are the same.' She stared at Jessica. 'Now do you understand what I mean?'

Jessica tried hard to fix the idea in her mind.

'That can't be true,' she said in a whisper. 'I don't believe it.'

But even as she spoke, something struck her, something that Harry had said the night before. As they had made love in the library he'd whispered, 'I'd forgotten just how good a woman feels,' and ran a finger down over one of her breasts, circling the tight dark peak of her nipples. 'So many soft curves and such beautiful skin.'

The memory made her breath catch in her throat. At the time she had assumed it was just so long since he had been with a woman, but what if it was because he preferred the company of men?

She stared at Alice, disturbed that her friend could have planted such a dark thought in her mind. Even so, the thought took root and grew like a weed. For some reason she couldn't bring herself to argue with Alice; she had to look away.

'Shall we go and have coffee?' she managed to say after a second or two.

Alice nodded. Without speaking, she slipped her arm through Jessica's, and pulled her close. Alice's gentle, caring touch made Jessica want to cry. The sensation of their skin touching dissolved the last shreds of anger that she had felt about Alice's exquisite seduction. For an instant, she looked into her friend's eyes and felt a tiny flame of desire rekindle. The intensity of the heat surprised her.

In the Old Lodge cottage, Felicia rolled over onto her hands and knees and presented her plump pink backside to the assembled audience. Glimmering in the folds of her open quim were the silvery remnants of the winner's pleasure. On the straw beside her, Norman, totally drained, lay back and closed his eyes.

Felicia's sex was swollen, engorged with sheer excitement. To Jack, it looked as inviting as a warm, fragrant nest. Naked, her heavy but firm breasts moved like water as she wriggled into position. She glanced back over her shoulder at Jack and grinned.

Watching her make love to Norman had fuelled the raw angry desire gnawing in his belly and he couldn't wait to feel her close around him. Her familiar body would be the perfect antidote to Stolworthy and the groom.

Behind him, Jim said thickly, 'Do we toss for who gets what?'

Felicia giggled. 'How terribly old school tie of you, Jim. No, you don't toss for it. I tell you what I want and then you have to provide it.' She giggled, glancing at the threatening bulge in the front of Jim's cavalry twill. 'I really think I'd like that in my mouth, where I can keep an eye on it. Or do you object?'

Jim groaned and shook his head. He stepped up to Felicia, who with expert hands freed his throbbing shaft. She ran her tongue and fingers along its impressive length and made a thick guttural sound of approval.

Still cradling Jim's cock in her hands, she turned back to look at Bob, Robin and Jack. 'I'd like to feel you pushed up deep inside me, Jack,' she whispered, running her tongue around her lips. 'I've never met anyone who moves like you - and you, Robin, I think I can give you a hand.' As her eyes moved on, Bob held up a hand to stop her going further.

'Not for me, my dear. I'd prefer to watch.'

Felicia feigned disappointment. 'Are you sure? I'm awfully good with my hands,' she said softly, tightening her grip on Jim's enraged shaft.

Bob smiled. 'Really, I do prefer to watch.'

Felicia dropped her hips, making the lips of her sex contract. Above them the dark little bud of her anus followed suit. 'Perhaps you prefer something a little darker?' she said slowly. 'I really don't mind, though you'll have to ask Jack to roll underneath.'

Jack glanced at his compatriot. Jack knew his tastes and could sense his enthusiasm for what was on offer.

'Are you sure you don't mind?' said Bob, first to Felicia, and then to Jack.

Felicia giggled. 'Mind? Good Lord, no,' she said mischievously. 'It's my pleasure.'

Jack rolled into the warm hay beneath Felicia, taking the time to kiss the wet mound of her quim and each breast in turn as he wriggled into position. She groaned deliciously and writhed as he sucked one hard nipple over his tongue.

Gently, he guided his cock into her quim, gasping as her heat engulfed him.

With all the women he had ever made love to, he had never quite got used to the stunning contrast of their skin and the tight, wet confines of their sex. He always shivered as the head of his cock opened up the tight, wet channel. Every woman's sex was subtly different - the scent, the taste - but each always struck him as almost oceanic, like a sea flower, its liquid petals opening wide to suck him deep aside.

Felicia pressed down towards him, a hand skimming his throbbing balls. Looking up, he was confronted by the sight of Felicia drawing Jim deeper and deeper into her mouth, his friend's great hairy balls swaying in time with Felicia's devilish mouth. With Jim helping to support her weight she curled her fingers around Robin and pulled him closer.

Bob joining the quartet was almost more than Jack could bear. Up against his own shaft, through the membrane that divided one gloriously tight orifice from another, he felt Bob's cock making slow steady progress. The sensation was electrifying.

As they began to move, Jack struggled to maintain his control, turning his attention to the swollen scarlet bud that peeked out from Felicia's dripping molten quim. As he rushed it lovingly, he heard her moaning, the sound diffused around Jim's wet shaft as if it was bubbling up from a deep erotic ocean. The sound made his head spin.

His head flooded with a searing show of images: Prince Charming with her naked breasts pressed to Alice's mouth, Miranda with Felicia, Felicia making love to Norman, phantom Arabian dancers, and finally as he felt the first waves of pleasure breaking over him, he saw Harry Stolworthy, hunched over a figure in the clearing, amongst the pine needles, impaling it again and again. As the images became more intense he realised with a start that in his imagination the figure was Jessica Harper.

Chapter 11

The Crystal Room

When Jack got back to Malestone with the others, it was his intention to find Jessica and talk to her. Walking up the drive he thought over what he wanted to say. Around him, Norman, Jim, Robin and Bobby seemed happy but subdued, exhausted after their encounter with Felicia, who had ridden off home with hardly a backward glance.

The butler met Jack at the front door.

'Excuse me, sir. The party from London has arrived and I've sent a car out to collect those who couldn't find taxis.'

When Jack stepped inside the whole of the hall seemed to be packed with people, familiar faces, cradling coffee cups and glasses, deep in animated conversation. Newly arrived guests and theatricals mixed merrily around the Christmas tree.

Jessica was standing at the foot of the stairs with Harry - who had apparently beaten him back to the house. Before Jack had time to attract Jessica's attention, he was caught up in a round of welcomes and introductions, and the overwhelming need he had had to speak to Jessica was lost as his guests demanded his attention.

He recognised everyone and had arranged the numbers, bedrooms and provisions with his staff weeks earlier, but hadn't quite appreciated how many people there would be in the flesh.

Bella Youngs, smelling of gardenias, pressed a kiss to his cheeks, Howard Gordon shook his hand and wished him the greetings of the season. Susie Parlett propositioned him before he'd even had a chance to say hello. Faces came and went, kissing him, shaking hands. All in all, despite his plan for a jolly Christmas he felt completely overwhelmed.

Alice Fallon sneaked up alongside him, cradling a cup of coffee.

'And there was me thinking that my theatricals would outnumber your guests,' she said with a grin. 'When you plan a Christmas junket you certainly go about it in style.'

Jack took the cup out of her hand and took a swig.

'Did you get a chance to talk to Jessica?' he said, eyes working around the groups of people.

Alice sniffed. 'I did, but I don't think you're going to like what I found out. Stolworthy has asked her to marry him.'

Jack stared at her in disbelief. Usually, like everyone else, when Jack heard about gossip or bad luck, it almost inevitably elicited a wry grin, but he felt no triumph or cynical delight in Jessica's misfortune, only a sense of pain and fury that Stolworthy was quite obviously making a fool of her.

'Bastard,' he hissed. 'What the bloody hell is he playing at? She hasn't accepted him, has she?'

Alice slipped her arm through his and rescued her cup. 'I'm rather afraid that she has, though she is insisting they have a decently long engagement.' She paused. 'Perhaps Harry really loves her, Jack, have you thought of that? We've got absolutely no proof that he is a rogue. Even given what George Gudgeon said, he could very easily have been mistaken. Perhaps Harry is on the level after all.'

Jack smiled without a shred of humour. 'I think we can trust George's memory. I discovered Stolworthy in the woods this morning, buggering my bloody groom.'

It was Alice's turn to stare at Jack.

'No,' she hissed. 'My God, Jessica thinks he's a perfect gentleman, all set to whisk her down the aisle. At the very least he's lying to her.' She stopped for a few seconds, collecting her thoughts. 'Some men do like both. Harry wouldn't be the first to sample fish and fowl by any stretch of the imagination.'

Jack nodded. 'I know. I don't care whether he prefers men or women, it's none of my business.' He nodded towards the people in the hall. 'Half the crowd here would say their tastes occasionally run to a little dalliance with their own sex. What worries me is not what Harry likes, or where he gets it, but what he's trying to do to Jessica. Something stinks about this whole affair. It's too slick, too smooth and far too quick for my liking.'

Across the room, Jessica and Harry Stolworthy stood hand in hand talking to Miranda. The very sight of the two together made Jack furious and he wondered whether it was too early for a glass of brandy.

Alice, as if reading his mind, said in an undertone, 'You better stay sober over lunch. I've already asked Jessica if he'll come and give me a hand with the backdrops for the pantomime this afternoon. It'll be just the two of us until at least four o'clock. After that, Bunty is going to provide us with some muscle to help shift the scenery for the review tonight. It might be a good idea if you dropped in and had a word with her yourself.'

Jack nodded. 'Do you think she'll listen to me?' he said grimly, trying to ignore Stolworthy's eager little eyes combing the room.

Alice lifted an eyebrow. 'Probably not, but when has that ever stopped you?' She grinned and pulled him closer. 'We have to try. Just think how awful you'll feel if you don't say anything to her. I thought I might try ringing round to find out what people know about your Mr Stolworthy. It'll be a bit of a job because of Christmas, but there's no harm in trying, is there?'

Jack nodded. No harm at all. He just wondered whether Jessica would believe the evidence even if Alice found any.

Slowly, as guests were shown to their rooms, the hall began to empty. With relief, Jack retired to his office and at contemplating the prospect of lunch, sitting opposite Jessica Harper and the man she would no doubt like everyone to consider as her fiancé. After half an hour, he rang for a footman and asked for his lunch to be brought on a tray. He told the servant to pass on his apologies but explain that he had to attend to estate business before everything closed down for Christmas.

'Jessica's not here,' snapped Alice, later that afternoon, as Jack arrived 'unexpectedly' in the ballroom to see how the stage was coming along. He had spent lunchtime going over the speech he intended to make to Jessica and was nonplussed to find Alice struggling to hang curtains by herself.

In the dimly lit room, Alice threw a long grey sheet onto the makeshift stage.

'And I've got no idea where she is. Bunty met up with some old school chum who you'd invited and they've been drinking steadily all afternoon.' She looked furious, her normally cool features flushed and angry. 'It's complete bloody chaos.'

Jack lifted an eyebrow. 'What's this, artistic temperament?'

Alice sniffed. 'I wish it were. If you see Jessica, please tell her, I really do need a hand here. We've got to have everything ready by six at the latest.'

Jack went back out into the hall. In the corner by the stairs, the Christmas tree glistened in the firelight. Despite the large number of people in the house, everywhere seemed very quiet. He smiled ruefully, wondering how much of his cellar had been consumed over the hearty lunch of pheasant casserole, home grown vegetables and treacle tart. No doubt most of the guests were upstairs having a post luncheon nap.

The long case clock ticked away noisily, emphasising the silence. Jack considered what to do. Harry had probably taken Jessica off somewhere. Jack frowned; he had declined Susie Parlett's generous offer of an hour or two of after-lunch relief in anticipation of talking to Jessica.

But Jack had the perfect excuse to go looking for the lovers - after all, Alice needed Jessica to help her, that was the reason she had been invited in the first place. But did he really want to find them together? Jack's expression hardened. He took a deep breath and wondered where to begin. Presumably Alice had already been to Jessica's room - and probably Stolworthy's - but he had to make a start somewhere.

Upstairs, Jessica giggled as Harry led her along a gloomy passageway. He lifted a finger to his lips.

'Sssh. It's just round this corner. Jack mentioned this room to me years ago. I found it yesterday when I was exploring. Apparently his father used to use it as a room to entertain his lady friends. It seems he isn't the first generation to enjoy a dalliance or two.'

Jessica blushed, wishing she had had a little less wine with lunch. Harry had been in high spirits as they had eaten and topped her glass up as soon as she had taken more than a sip. When she had explained to him, over dessert, that she had to help Alice after lunch, he pulled a face.

'Oh, come on, just a little fun first and then you can do exactly what you like. All work and no play makes Jessica a dull girl. Besides, I've got a surprise for you.' He looked at her intently. 'Please say yes.'

Jessica stared into his pale grey eyes. She found it hard to believe the things Alice had said about Harry when she was sitting there at his side - and even harder to refuse him.

He had lifted her fingers to his lips. 'It won't take long, I promise.'

His tone and touch had been so compelling that she found it impossible to resist and so now she was creeping through Malestone, holding his hand, feeling the mischievous effects of the wine glowing in her stomach and struggling to swallow the compulsion to giggle.

'What's wrong with going to my room?' she said, as Harry led her along another dark corridor.

He smiled. 'Nothing, nothing at all, but we don't want to be disturbed, do we?'

Jessica blushed. All through lunch she had been aware of his desire, glowing between them like a bright fire. Every time she moved she had felt his hand stroking her thigh or caressing her arm. When he had filled her wine glass she had seen the look in his eyes. The intensity in his expression had made her shiver and deep in the pit of her stomach she knew he wanted her. There was nothing she would deny him.

'Close your eyes,' he said as they reached a set of double doors.

Still fighting the desire to laugh, she let him lead her into the room beyond. She felt the warmth and smelt perfume as soon as they stepped inside.

'Open them now,' Harry purred.

Jessica gasped. He had led her into an ornate boudoir. The curtains were closed tight and the room was alight with candles. One wall was dominated by a huge, gilt-framed mirror that overlooked a four-poster bed. In another wall, a fire burnt in the grate. Every surface seemed to have at least one candelabra, hung with crystal droplets. Flickering firelight and candlelight reflected and refracted in the facets making everything glitter and shimmer.

She turned round to look at Harry, who was closing the doors behind them.

'It's so beautiful,' she whispered. 'Are you sure we are allowed in here?'

Harry tapped his jacket pocket.

'The butler will keep quiet about where we are; greasing a palm or two should ensure we're undisturbed. Besides,' he said, 'no one uses this part of Malestone any more. All the other guests are safely installed in the main house.'

He moved across to a side table and unstopped a crystal decanter. 'Would you care for a little more wine?'

Jessica shook her head. 'No, I think I've had quite enough, my head is spinning now.' She smiled at him, feeling the tiny flutter of desire growing. In the candlelight, Harry looked beautiful. He turned, as if he could read her thoughts, and lifted his glass in a toast.

'This is a room for lovers,' he murmured. 'A secret place where anything is possible.'

She shivered. 'What do you want?' she said in a whisper.

The atmosphere in the beautiful room was suddenly charged with sexual promise.

Harry smiled wolfishly. 'Oh, I want everything, my love. Every last part of you belongs to me. That's something I need you to understand.' His voice was low and even, almost hypnotic. His tone seemed to light a dark flare somewhere inside her.

She bit her lip.

Harry continued. 'All I ask is that you do what I tell you. It's so simple, so easy.' His eyes darkened. 'I can show you astonishing pleasures, things you've never imagined in your wildest dreams.'

She stared at him, trying to reconcile the image of this self-assured man with the shy, boyish creature she had been introduced to the day before. It seemed as if time had stretched, as if she had known him forever. Standing, with a glass in his hand, he seemed totally in command and confident that she would do whatever it was he asked.

For an instant Jessica wondered if Alice was right, perhaps he was tricking her.

The thought evaporated as his eyes met hers.

'Take off your clothes,' he said in a low voice. 'Let me see my salvation.'

'What do you mean?' she whispered nervously, feeling his eyes moving down over her body.

He smiled and sat down in the armchair beside the fire. 'You have no idea,' he said in an undertone, 'how very much I need you in my life. Now take off your clothes, let me see the treasure I've found.'

Jessica swallowed hard. His eyes moved up to her face. His expression was almost frightening in its intensity. She found herself undoing the buttons on her dress without really thinking. Slipping the fabric down over her shoulders, all she could think of was the way his eyes seemed to consume her, drinking her in like the glass of wine he was cradling in his fingers.

Her dress slipped to the floor. Harry indicated the mirror behind her.

'Why don't you turn around and see how glorious you look? I can watch your reflection.' He leaned forward. 'I can see everything, touch everything...' his voice trailed off as she moved.

Framed in the mirror, Jessica was transformed into an erotic masterpiece. Her eyes had darkened to glittering pools. Her pert nipples were defined by the thin silk of her chemise. Her skin had an inner glow, a kind of pagan ripeness that stunned her. She was drawn to the power of the reflected image like a magnet. Harry may have been the instigator and now the observer, but in that moment she began to undress for her own pleasure. She slipped the straps of her chemise down, revelling in the way the light accentuated the glow on her smooth skin.

Her body was lean but unmistakably female. As she moved, letting the fabric slide down over her ribs and then hips, her muscles and soft curves were thrown into relief by the candlelight.

She stared again into the mirror, running an exploratory finger down over her throat, tracing the rim of her collarbones and the ripe swell of her breasts. She felt the tiny sparks of pleasure exploding in her mind as she watched the progress of her caress.

Her breasts were small and upturned, their nipples like tight carmine buds. Her hands worked over her narrow waist, her flat stomach, the basin of her broad hips - each image, each part of the whole, was as compelling as the last.

She knew she was already wet, her sheer cream silk knickers clung to every damp excited fold of her sex. She stroked the dark triangle of hair between her legs. Her juices trickled down over her thighs, their progress as sweet as a lover's touch. It seemed as if every part of her could easily turn to liquid, flowing out like a tide to sweep them both away.

Behind her, Harry got to his feet and stood at her shoulder, his fingers joining hers. His touch seemed cool, abstracted and distant, and for a few seconds she wondered if this was a dream, from which she would awake unsatisfied, still hungry and alone, in the narrow bed at St Winifred's school.

'What do you see?' Harry whispered. His eyes were as dark as hers, a mirror to her own passion.

She didn't want to speak, she wanted to revel in the way she felt and the things she could see.

He asked again, his tone more authoritative, more assertive, and she surrendered, letting him guide her fingers and her mind along the path he had chosen. His fingers slipped under the waistband of her knickers and eased them down over her hips as she tried to put into words the abstract longing and desire she felt.

His hands moved to cradle each of her breasts, fingers working at the delicate flesh. His lips and teeth nibbled at her shoulders, causing sharp flares of sensation that contrasted with the lightness of his caress. Behind her, she could feel his cock pressing through the rough material of his trousers. His desire was as all-pervading as hers and their mutual need was framed and held in the cool mirror of the glass.

His eyes caught hers. 'You are my salvation,' he murmured.

'Oh, Harry,' she whispered and did not protest as he turned her in his arms and kissed her.

Jack had looked in the stables, the bedrooms, and every public room he could think of. He was growing increasingly frantic, wondering if Stolworthy had somehow managed to persuade Jessica to leave Malestone. Out beyond the confines of the estate, Jack had no say, no jurisdiction over what Stolworthy might or might not have in mind. At least if Jessica was still in the house, he had the chance to convince her that Harry Stolworthy was up to no good. He didn't dwell too long on his own motives.

In a strange way, he thought, as he finished the final search through the rooms on the ground floor, he had a desire to protect Jessica's innocence, which struck him as amusing in view of the fact that he had wanted to seduce her himself.

Over Christmas, Malestone would be awash with every sexual excess imaginable, but at least the other guests knew exactly what was to be expected and were happy to consent. Jessica was different.

Jack headed off towards the green baize door that separated the servants' quarters from the rest of the house.

The difference was, he realised with a start, that he actually cared about Jessica's welfare. He grinned ruefully - his concern was out of character. Perhaps Alice was right: he was obsessed with Jessica Harper. On the back stairs he met his butler who was carrying an empty silver salver.

Jack had inherited a great many of the household staff from his father, the butler amongst them. The old man looked at him with an imperious glance. It had only been in the last few years that the old man had stopped referring to him as Master Jack.

'How may I help you, sir?' he said, in his low, beautifully modulated voice.

Jack grimaced. 'I wonder if you have seen Miss Harper and Mr Stolworthy. Miss Harper—' He stopped, seeing a flash of comprehension in the butler's eyes.

'The young lady who is helping Miss Fallon?'

Jack nodded.

The old man allowed himself a tiny uncharacteristic smile. 'Her young man asked if there was somewhere they could be alone. He said you'd told him about the crystal room, so I gave him directions and had one of the maids go up and light a fire for them.'

Jack stared at the butler in disbelief. He had no recollection of telling Stolworthy about the room in the old part of the house and certainly hadn't given him permission to use it. Without a word, he turned and headed back into the main house. He knew all about the crystal room and its secrets - he wondered just how much Stolworthy knew.

Along the corridor from the crystal room was a small, insignificant door that appeared to lead into a linen cupboard. Those who knew the secret were aware that this in turn led into another room. The hidden room was dominated by a large sheet of glass - the back of the ornate mirror in the crystal room - which offered the viewer a portal into the room beyond.

It had been here that Jack had seen his first sexual performance. No more than a schoolboy, he had watched in awe as his father had seduced endless men and women. Now, the icy fury in his veins making him tremble, he opened the door into the linen cupboard and stepped inside.

After a few seconds, when his eyes had accustomed themselves to the gloom, he found the door that led into the viewing room beyond. He was not alone. In the comfortable chairs arranged around the mirror he could pick out at least half a dozen faces of the guests he had invited to Malestone. He took a deep breath and looked out beyond the glass.

What he saw made him gasp. He couldn't make a scene in front of his houseguests and wondered, furiously, when Stolworthy had invited them to observe Jessica's seduction. He doubted that Jessica knew what was going on and didn't want to contemplate how she would feel if she knew she had an audience.

Naked, except for her stockings and shoes, she was standing in front of the mirror - and looked magnificent. For an instant she appeared to catch his eye and Jack wondered fleetingly if she knew he was there. He dismissed the thought as it formed.

Picked out in candlelight, her naked body was as sleek as a wild cat. Behind her Stolworthy's eyes glinted with satisfaction as he had her turn this way and that, as if he wanted her to revel in her nakedness. In the tense atmosphere in the little room behind the glass, the select audience murmured their approval of the choice morsel on display.

Jessica's stunning nakedness was accentuated by Harry's being dressed. Jack watched with a mixture of indignation and envy as Stolworthy ran a proprietorial hand over his prize. His fingers worked over her breasts, sliding down over her plump quim, opening it to reveal a sliver of the moist folds within. Jessica curled and stretched against his touch, her whole body delighting in his attentions. Every time she attempted to move away from the mirror's cold eye, Harry artfully guided her back.

Jack realised Stolworthy must have already searched the room. As he stroked Jessica, he looked up towards the ceiling. Jack stiffened, knowing exactly what it was Harry was looking for. Set in the ceiling rose was a long bar, not unlike a trapeze, that was lowered and raised by a fine chain linked to the bed.

Harry, leaving Jessica entranced by her own reflection, unhooked the chain and lowered the bar. Hanging from it were sets of lined manacles, which Jack had seen his father use time and again. He saw Jessica turn with surprise as the chain rattled and then saw her stiffen anxiously.

'Harry?' Jessica said, in surprise.

Harry Stolworthy extended a hand in invitation. 'Come over here, my love,' he said quietly.

Jessica stared at the bar with its little leather cuffs. Her stomach contracted as she felt a mix of fear and surprise. 'I don't think I want to do this,' she murmured thickly.

Harry grinned. 'Why not?'

He traced a finger across the leather straps with the same tenderness and intimacy that seconds before he had used on her body. As if some part of her could still feel the caress, she shivered.

'I'm afraid.'

Harry shook his head. 'No need to be afraid. I won't hurt you, I promise. Just let me show you all the things that I have to share.'

He held out his hand again and she instinctively stepped closer. He took her wrist, and before she had time to think, he pulled the leather strap tight and fastened the buckle.

'Let go,' he murmured. 'Don't think, just trust me.'

Even as he spoke, he was tightening the second strap. She looked up at him, feeling the panic growing alongside the passion in her belly. As he stepped away to pull on the thin chain she realised she was completely helpless.

'Harry—' she began, panic rising inside her. Her fear seemed to wipe away the effects of the wine she had had at lunch. Cold sober she stared at him, wondering what would follow.

He looked over his shoulder as he fixed the chain back onto its hook. She saw the expression in his eyes as he took in the details of her exposure. The look was electrifying and silenced her protest. Harry slowly raised the chain a little more, until she was just able to stand comfortably, arms lifted high above her head. Every part of her was exposed and vulnerable.

Smiling, he turned back towards her. 'You look quite exquisite,' he murmured, running his hands over her breasts. 'Quite, quite lovely.'

Behind the glass, Jack held his breath, wondering what would happen next. Around him the invited guests murmured their approval.

The bar was set at an angle to the mirror so that the watchers could see every movement, every caress. Stolworthy began to kiss Jessica. Their kisses were intense and Jack realised with a start that Jessica was as eager as Harry was. The girl was relishing every touch, as Harry's hands moved over her body, exploring, dipping a finger into the wet folds of her quim. She writhed against him, seeking out his fingers.

Jack moved closer to the glass, mesmerised by Jessica's raw sexuality, as slowly Stolworthy's kisses worked lower and lower, nipping at her skin, lapping at her nipples, making her fight against her restraints in her pursuit of pleasure.

Finally, Stolworthy sank to his knees, two fingers spreading the lips of her quim. The scarlet bead of her clitoris jutted forward and she thrust out her hips, chasing his tongue. Stolworthy grinned, moving away, making her work and beg for every touch.

A trickle of sweat broke out between Jessica's breasts as she strained to reach out to him. Stolworthy's fingers slipped inside her as his lips closed around her quim.

Jessica's eyes snapped shut and she threw back her head, grinding her hips against his face.

Jack, the pulse hammering in his chest, could barely breathe. Jessica had given herself over to Harry Stolworthy, surrendering to his every whim, offering herself up for his pleasure.

As Jessica's excitement began to mount, Jack saw something moving in the corner of the room. Silently the doors to the crystal room opened and one of the Haywood twins made his way across the room. Unaware of what was going on behind her, Jessica writhed and gasped under Harry's ministrations. The twin slipped noiselessly out of his clothes and Jack held his breath as the boy, as lithe and beautiful as any woman, stepped across towards the mirror.

Jack sensed the instant when Jessica was aware of the boy behind her. She froze, eyes alight with fear. The boy stepped closer, his magnificent pierced cock jutting forward like a lance, and embraced her. Before she could protest, his hands circled her and cupped her breasts.

Stolworthy returned his attention to her sex, nuzzling deep inside, tongue licking and probing. Meanwhile, the twin murmured soft words of encouragement and rubbed his torso up against Jessica's naked back.

Jack could sense her reluctance being overwhelmed by the sheer wealth of sensations. With a single movement, the twin eased his cock between Jessica's legs and Jack saw Harry Stolworthy draw its engorged purple head into his mouth, lapping at the glittering silver ring that hung from his foreskin.

Every caress was shared by both Jessica and the twin. The tableau was stunning. The three lovers began to move in harmony. Jessica, eyes firmly closed, was close to her climax. Jack could see the tension in her face as her breasts heaved up and down. He wished that it was him bringing her closer and closer to that explosive, all-consuming moment. His own cock throbbed like an aching tooth.

Jessica began to sob, overcome by the sheer intensity of what she felt. Behind her, pressing against her back, the twin's flesh felt like molten gold. His cock brushed against the outer lips of her sex, Harry's tongue echoing and intensifying every thrust. Just as she thought she couldn't take any more, Harry stepped back.

She could have screamed.

'Please,' she begged. 'Please don't stop now.'

Behind her she could feel the twin was seconds away from joining her. Harry grinned slyly and undid the chain so that her arms were lowered.

She had been held up for so long that she fell forward. The twin caught hold of her around the waist, but not before his cock brushed up against her backside. Jessica gasped as she felt the crown of his shaft nuzzle at the forbidden closure between her buttocks.

Harry grabbed the bar and took her weight, bending her double, easing her onto all fours. The twin dipped his finger into her quim and then drew the thick juices back up towards her anus. She tried to wriggle away, but was caught by the unexpected pleasure his touch created. While her mind screamed out in protest her body opened like a flower to the twin's knowing touch.

In front of her, Harry undid his flies and freed his huge arcing cock. He let it brush her cheek and then guided it towards her mouth. Her instinct was to suck him deep inside. Her tongue caressed the delicate sheath of flesh that covered the head and he rewarded her with a long throaty moan.

Behind them, the twin continued his assault on the tight bud of her backside. His fingers brought more and more of her juices up to smooth his path. Each time he touched her she felt a shard of fear and excitement roar through her. His other hand circled her belly, moving lower, seeking out her clitoris.

As he found it, she pushed back against him and was stunned to feel his cock breech the tight, dark puckering above her sex. She gasped in astonishment, her fear coming out as a sob along the contours of Harry's shaft.

What she felt was overwhelming; the tightness and pressure was offset by an explosion of pleasure that ricocheted through her like a lightning strike. As they began to move the boy's fingers slid inside her sex and she felt it contract hungrily around him.

As if she had lit a fuse within each of the men, Harry suddenly strained forward, flooding her mouth with his seed and the twin let out a wild hungry sob and plunged deep inside her. Seconds later, she felt the compulsive throb of his orgasm and screamed out with a mixture of fear, and pain, and pure, white hot passion as he plunged deeper still with cock and fingers.

Falling forward, she thought she might lose consciousness as the final eddies of excitement rippled through her. Rolling over, letting the twin slip out from inside her, she glanced up at Harry and saw again the expression of triumph on his handsome, flushed features. To her surprise he leant across her and planted a delicate kiss on the twin's open mouth.

In the room beyond the mirror, Jack Healy shook his head in disbelief, still in the no man's land between anger and envy. Jessica Harper was stunning, her passion far in excess of anything he could ever have imagined. As a few more seconds passed, while Harry tenderly kissed the twin, the revelation was replaced by a renewed conviction that he had to find a way to get Jessica away from Harry Stolworthy.

Chapter 12

Harry's Discovery

Jessica excused herself from dinner that evening, saying she had a headache - in fact her whole body ached. Between her legs the tender flesh throbbed. The rest of the guests and performers were busy making last-minute arrangements for the late night cabaret. She doubted they would notice her absence.

Certain everyone else was in the dining room, she locked herself in the bathroom and ran a tub full of hot water.

Without Harry by her side it was easier to think more clearly - it was impossible when he was with her. He seemed to find a way to overwhelm her doubts. Jessica stepped into the tub and let the water soothe away the aches and the sense of violation that lingered alongside the excitement and satisfaction.

She ought to have apologised to Alice for not helping her with the stage, but surely Bunty or one of the others would have stepped into the breech?

Jessica settled back and closed her eyes. The day's events replayed themselves without any prompting. She sighed. Alice was right. She had seen the tenderness in Harry's eyes as he had reached out to embrace Rupert Haywood. There was no denying the look of sheer ecstasy on his face as his arms had closed around the muscular young man. Was it possible that she could marry Harry, knowing that he preferred male flesh to female - or had she been mistaken?

She struggled to work out what it was she felt. Was it possible to fall in love so soon? The feelings she had for Harry seemed nothing like the tender familiarity she had had for her fiancé.

Thinking of Robert, the soldier she had loved and lost, conjured up his face in her mind. It surprised her that she could still visualise him - it seemed so long since she had held him in her arms. For years she had only been able to picture him clearly in her dreams. She had been a virgin when they met and would have remained so until they married, if the war hadn't hastened their passion.

Eyes tightly closed, she could still see the way he had looked at her after the first time they made love. Tender and kind, he had kissed away her fears and held her in his arms, reassuring her that all was well. She had shivered.

As she moved in the bath water, she could still feel the glow of satisfaction lingering between her legs and the sharp soreness where Rupert Haywood had impaled her. The contrasts could not be more obvious.

What she felt for Harry Stolworthy was nothing like the emotions she had had for Robert. Robert's love was supportive and generous. He had been a loving, selfless man, who she knew - had he lived - would have made a wonderful husband and father. Their love had had many dimensions and she believed that as the years had gone on they would have found more and more to love about each other.

Harry, by contrast, had fed her body's need like someone piling wood onto a fading fire. He had stirred things inside her that she had never known existed.

Jessica sat upright, eyes snapping open, as the next thought hit her. Why? Why was Harry Stolworthy so intent on seducing her? The thoughts were like icy fingers on her spine.

She allowed herself a humourless grin. At least Jack Heally hadn't tried to seduce her with subterfuge. Or was she letting her imagination run away with her? Was she misjudging Harry?

Thoughts tumbled through her head, turning the fictitious headache into a reality. She winced and lay back amongst the bubbles.

Downstairs, everyone else was making their way into dinner.

'Good evening,' said Jack with icy formality, as Harry took his place at the table. 'Jessica not joining us this evening?'

Harry looked up. 'No, I'm afraid not. She's complaining of a headache. I'm not sure she will be feeling better in time for tonight's little performance. I do hope you'll accept her apologies.' He smiled and filled his glass from the decanter in front of him. 'I think she may have caught a chill. All this country air, I imagine.'

Jack's eyes narrowed. 'You and I ought to talk.'

Harry nodded. 'My pleasure. What had you got in mind? I was going to compliment you on the house. As you know, I recently inherited my parent's home. It's rather draughty, but it will be a wonderful place once I've completed the renovations.'

Jack sighed - Stolworthy was remarkably cocksure. Beside him, Miranda began a conversation about houses, the Haywood twins joined in and Jack lost the imperative. On his left, another of the guests asked about the plans for Christmas and Felicia and Bunty began to list the programme of events.

Only Alice Fallon, sitting at the far end of the enormous table, looked subdued and thoughtful. He had had no chance to speak to her in private and made up his mind that when dinner was over he would find a way to get her on her own before the night's show began.

The final guest to take his place at the table, Sir George Gudgeon, was helped into the chair beside Jack and immediately shook out his napkin.

'Sorry about that,' he puffed. 'Leg's playing me up a touch.' He adjusted his monocle and poured himself a hearty glass of wine. 'Shall have to be a little circumspect about what I eat,' he said cheerfully. 'The quack says it's gout, but I reckon it's shrapnel myself.' He turned to Jack. 'You might have told me you had a performance arranged in the crystal room this afternoon.' He grinned. 'Brings back memories of me and your father—'

Across the table, Jack saw Harry stiffen and glance in George's direction. Jack smiled, not giving Stolworthy the satisfaction of letting him catch his eye.

'Oh, that,' Jack said dismissively. 'That was arranged by Mr Stolworthy. The chap you saw at the Ushers club.'

George sniffed, oblivious to the fact that Harry was no more than three or four places away from him.

'Don't suppose I missed much then. Shifty little blighter, that one. To be honest, I'm surprised you invited him, Jack.'

Now Jack looked up, staring Stolworthy straight in the eyes.

'Strange you should say that, George,' he said evenly, 'I'd come to more or less the same conclusion myself.'

After dinner, Jack cornered Alice over coffee and suggested they found somewhere quiet to talk.

'We'll go upstairs to my office,' he said, guiding her away from the rest of the party.

Alice smiled as they climbed the stairs.

'That's the best offer I've had all evening, but I can't be very long.' She glanced at her watch. 'I've told everyone we're going to start in an hour, though this is really Bunty's baby, not mine. And aren't you supposed to be down there playing host?'

'I doubt they'll even notice I've gone. Have you heard what happened this afternoon in the crystal room?' Jack asked.

Alice turned and lifted an eyebrow.

'Darling, my crowd like nothing more than a bit of gossip. Little tales like that tend to spread like germs. No wonder Jessica didn't want to help me with the curtains.'

Jack opened his office door and showed her inside.

'I don't think she knew what was going to happen and I'm damned certain she didn't know she was performing for an invited audience.' He walked over to the sideboard and poured two stiff brandies.

Alice took the glass he offered her and stared into the rim.

'I hope,' she said with a wry smile as she took a mouthful, 'that you're not planning another drinking binge. I'm not sure I'll have the energy to put you to bed tonight. There's still an awful lot to do tonight, not to mention tomorrow night's performance.'

Jack indicated the armchairs that flanked the fire. 'I've only just got rid of last night's hangover,' he said grimly.

Alice grinned and instead of sitting in the chair, dropped to her knees beside him.

'All this fuss about Jessica is so unlike you,' she said mischievously. She wriggled forward, running a finger around her lips. 'I'm not used to the new public-spirited Jack Heally. What's happened to the old Jack we all know and love?'

Jack grinned. 'Oh, he's here as well. He's just taking it easy for a change.'

Alice tossed her head. 'Rather boring. You know Bunty has arranged the *grande finale* for tonight's show?'

Jack sighed. 'I didn't doubt it.'

Alice smiled. 'It's one of my favourites, actually. Usually he asks Helen and one of the other girls—' she stopped, eyes alight. 'But perhaps you'd prefer to come and see for yourself. It's really not like you to be so maudlin.' She crept closer. 'Do you want me to go and talk to Jessica again?'

Jack nodded. 'I think that would be a good idea.'

Alice smiled, running a hand over the front of his thigh. 'I could go later, after the show, if you like?'

Jack grinned. 'Very tempting, but I'd prefer if you went now, while Stolworthy is otherwise engaged. You could say you've come to see if she's going to take part in tonight's cabaret.'

Alice pouted. 'If you insist. What are you going to do?'

Jack nodded towards the door. 'I'd better go back downstairs. You have to try and ensure she knows that Stolworthy is up to no good.'

Alice sighed. 'We've got no proof of that, but if you insist. Do you want me to mention the crystal room?'

Jack felt his colour rising. 'Not if you can possibly help it.'

Alice downed her brandy and waved him away. 'Go on then, back downstairs. I'll come and tell you how I get on.' She grinned. 'Though I have to warn you, I intend to make you pay for all this do-gooding, you know.'

Jack smiled.

Jessica hadn't really meant to fall asleep after her bath, but the bed looked so tempting. Still warm from the foaming water, she had slipped off her towel and robe and slid between the sheets. Sleep came quickly, embracing her like an eager lover. Intense erotic images chased her through unconsciousness. Harry reached out to embrace her, only to be transformed at the last moment into Jack Heally. Amongst the tangle of images she dreamt that there was someone in her room and reached out to catch hold of them before they vanished into the ether.

At first she thought it was her fiancé, Robert, but her mind dismissed that as impossible, then it seemed like Jack Heally and finally, as she turned to stare into the gloom, eyes unfocused, she realised she couldn't make out her visitor's face.

In the darkness, she heard them whisper her name and reached out to hold them closer. In her dream, she longed to feel their arms around her and felt elated when the shadowy figure slipped into bed beside her.

Now, on the edge of sleep, she turned over and felt the brush of naked skin against her body. A cool hand slid over her belly, fingers tenderly exploring her. In her imagination, her unseen dream lover was a strange combination of hard and soft, dark and light.

At first she thought it might be Harry Stolworthy, but even as her mind formed his face she knew it wasn't him. The touch was too tender and generous. The knowing caresses made her body hum with anticipation. Instinctively, she opened her legs, letting a smooth hand slide between her thighs to find the secrets that lay within. Another hand cupped her breasts, before lifting to stroke the sensitive skin under her arms. Kisses, pressed to her neck and shoulders, made her shiver. The sensation of an unseen lover's tongue tracing the contours of her ear, finally woke her up with a start.

It had been so vivid, she could almost swear it was real. Consciousness swept through her like an incoming tide and the sensations did not vanish as sleep receded. Her eyes snapped open.

In the lamplight, she could see Alice Fallon's face, no more than a few inches away from hers on the pillow. Jessica froze and then looked round in desperation, trying hard to get her bearings and some sense of what was going on, struggling to separate dream images from reality.

Alice stroked Jessica's hair back off her face, then leaning forward, eyes alight with love and passion, kissed her gently on the lips.

Jessica took a long gasping breath, torn between protest and passion. Her body was alight with need. The hand that worked its magic between her thighs was sliding deep inside her, a thumb lifting lazily to brush her clitoris.

'My God,' she whispered, 'what are you doing here?'

Alice grinned. 'I came up to see if you were all right. I thought it's what you wanted. When I came in you seemed to know it was me.' She ran her tongue along the crest of Jessica's shoulders and she moaned softly without thinking.

'I was asleep,' Jessica protested. 'I thought I was dreaming,' she stopped, feeling her colour rise. 'Where's Harry?'

Alice stroked her waist, sliding her hand back up towards her breasts.

'It's all right, he's downstairs with the others waiting for the cabaret to begin. He told everyone you've got a headache. Jack and I were worried about you,' she whispered.

Jessica glanced around the room in desperation. 'What if Harry comes up to find me?'

Alice snuggled closer, dropping her head so that she could draw a nipple deep into her mouth. Jessica groaned, torn between begging Alice to leave before they were discovered and desperately wanting her to stay. She wriggled away from Alice's compelling touch, trying hard to regain some sense of control.

'Alice, please stop. What are you really doing here?' she said.

Alice looked uncomfortable. 'I came to try and persuade you to think twice about accepting Stolworthy's offer of marriage.'

Jessica looked into her eyes. 'And seduce me?' she said quietly.

Alice looked away, reddening.

'That wasn't what I intended. You just looked so beautiful lying there. You're very hard to resist. When I called your name you reached out and pulled me closer.' She paused. 'I thought you must have known who it was.'

Jessica shook her head. 'I was dreaming,' she stopped and smiled. 'Maybe it is what I wanted. I really don't know any more.'

Alice smiled, stroking the puckered rose of her nipples with a single finger. 'It's all right. Don't fight it, can't you remember how good it feels?'

Jessica shivered. Her dreams and the touch of her unseen lover had already lit the fire inside her.

She stared at Alice. 'Yes,' she murmured. 'I remember.'

'Then why not just lie back and enjoy it? You know I won't ever hurt you.'

Her voice was gentle and unthreatening, every word emphasised by the soft circling of her fingers. She guided Jessica back onto the mattress, planting kiss after kiss on her aching flesh.

Instinctively, Jessica moaned, unable to resist the other woman's tender assault. Alice's gentleness was a stark contrast to her afternoon spent in the crystal room. Each fluttering kiss seemed not just to excite her but heal her too. Alice worked lower, spiralling down over her breasts and belly, lapping at Jessica's tender skin.

As Alice's fingers slipped into the warm junction between her thighs, Jessica let out a long throaty sob. With hesitation she opened herself, lifting her hips up to meet her lover's tongue. She slipped two fingers inside her fur-trimmed mound to open herself wider, relishing the little arrowhead of Alice's tongue as it found her clitoris.

Alice moaned appreciatively. 'My God,' she murmured, 'you taste like—'

Before Alice could finish her sentence, the door to the bedroom, which had been ajar, slowly opened.

To Jessica's horror, Harry Stolworthy was framed in the doorway. He looked first at Jessica and then Alice, as she scrambled to pull a sheet over them both. His expression was unreadable.

'So, this is what you get up to when my back is turned, Jessica?' he said in a low, even voice. He glared at Alice. 'They're looking for you downstairs,' he said. 'I wondered if I might find you up here.'

Alice began to protest but Harry lifted his hand to silence her.

'Well, Jessica? What have you got to say for yourself? Is this the kind of behaviour I can expect from you once we're married?'

Jessica reddened furiously. 'Harry—' she stopped. What was there she could say?

Harry closed the door and walked over to the bed. He looked down at them both and then snatched the sheet away. Springing forward he grabbed hold of Alice. With his hands locked tight in her hair, he dragged her towards him and kissed her fiercely, then pulled away, licking his lips.

His eyes flashed with a peculiar inner fire. 'So now we both know how my fiancée tastes tonight,' he said, relinquishing his hold on the blonde woman. He crossed the room and dropped into the chair beside the fire. His face was impassive now, his tone clipped and cold.

'Perhaps you'd like to show me, Jessica, what it is that Miss Fallon here can offer you that I can't? I'd be quite intrigued. Life with you gets better and better. You really are quite a remarkable find.'

He turned his attention to Alice. 'Why don't you touch her, Alice, slide those delicate little hands of yours up between her legs and make her cry out for more? Or does she prefer it when you use your tongue?'

Alice's face flushed crimson. 'How dare you!' she snapped. 'We all know about your tastes.'

Harry smiled. 'I'm sure you do and I intend to share everything with Jessica once we are married.' He looked back at Jessica, still smiling, though she noticed it didn't warm the light in his eyes.

'Let me tell you what I'd like you to do, my love.' His voice had lowered to a purr. 'I'd like to watch this little tableau through to its conclusion. Why don't you just lie back on the bed and open your legs for Miss Fallon. Pretend I'm not here.'

Alice scrambled off the bed, dragging one of the sheets with her.

'Stop it, Harry, I've had quite enough of this,' she snapped. 'I'm not going to take part in one of your little charades.' She turned round to look at Jessica. 'Come with me. Don't stay here with him.'

Jessica looked first at Harry and then Alice, torn between the two of them. For a moment it seemed impossible to think. If she followed Alice she would eventually be alone again, caught up in a love affair with her friend that was neither acceptable socially nor likely to last for more than the few days they were at Malestone. Harry could offer her marriage and a gateway into a world of sexual experience that she had never dreamed of - all masked by an air of respectability.

Harry seemed to be able to sense her uncertainty and smiled, holding out his hand.

Jessica looked at Alice. 'I have to stay,' she said quietly.

Alice stared at her in disbelief. 'You have to stay?' she repeated. 'Tell me one good reason why, for God's sake?'

Harry stood up and straightened his jacket.

'You have your answer, Alice. I suggest you leave now and get back downstairs to your little cabaret, unless of course you'd like to stay and finish what you started?'

Alice didn't move. 'Why, Jessica?' she whispered.

Jessica couldn't find the words to explain.

Alice turned and glared at Harry. 'You pig,' she hissed.

Harry smiled. 'What can you offer her? A furtive little affair? Something that can never be public? All those lies, all that pretence? I really don't think Jessica is that kind of woman.' He smiled triumphantly. 'I intend to make her my wife. What can you offer as an alternative?'

Jessica stared at them both. It almost seemed as if they had forgotten she was there. Alice grabbed her clothes up from the chair beside the bed and stormed out, her face a mask of fury. As the door closed, Harry turned to Jessica. He smiled, eyes moving down slowly over her naked body.

'So,' he said, quietly, 'an evening away from me and you feel the need to take someone else to bed. I shall have to remember that.'

'Harry, it wasn't like that—' Jessica began.

He shook his head. 'It really doesn't matter. Come here.' His voice dropped to a low commanding tone.

She shivered and began to gather the sheet up around her.

'No need for that, my dear,' Harry whispered. 'There's nothing you have to hide from me.'

She climbed nervously off the bed, wondering what he had in store for her. For some reason the authority in his voice excited her. As she crossed the room she was aware of the cold nipping at her skin, raising goose bumps. He indicated she should stand in front of him.

'I want you to touch yourself. Show me all those interesting places that Alice's tongue made wet and warm.'

Jessica reddened. 'I can't,' she murmured thickly, 'I really can't.'

Harry smiled wolfishly. 'Show me. After all, when we're married every part of you will belong to me,' he said, as if she hadn't spoken.

Jessica swallowed hard. He was right. She had chosen him rather than Alice and in doing so some part of her had agreed to do what he wanted.

She lifted one hand to her breast and began to circle her nipple, while the other snaked down over her belly to explore the dark triangle of hair between her legs. The lips opened under the slightest touch and she stroked along the engorged ridge of her clitoris. The heat was breathtaking. As she worked lower, down into the soft confines of her sex, the inner lips still glowed from Alice's kisses.

'There,' purred Harry, 'not so hard, was it?' His eyes were alight with approval.

Her touch rekindled the fire that her dreams and Alice had already lit. Dipping again and again into the depths of her quim she felt her muscles contracting around her fingertips. The sensation made her gasp and she began to circle her clitoris in earnest. Harry leaned back and watched her, eyes moving back and forth across her skin. Slowly, he began to smile.

Self-consciousness, fear and reluctance receded as the waves of pleasure began to build. She thrust her fingers deeper and deeper, relishing the wetness and heat she found there.

On and on, the spiral wound tighter and tighter, until she felt the first glorious surge of excitement flare like a beacon. Gasping, she rode the sensations out until she could bear no more.

Harry's hands lifted to his trousers and slowly he unbuttoned his fly. Mesmerised, her body still shaking from the release of passion, she watched as he pulled out his cock, stiff and as pale as ivory in the gloom.

'Come closer,' he whispered. As she moved towards him, he reached up and pulled her down onto her knees. She gasped at his roughness. Taking hold of her hand, he pressed her fingers, still slick from her juices, into his mouth. The sight and sensation of him lapping at each finger in turn was electrifying.

She found it impossible to resist the pull of his glittering grey eyes.

While his tongue worked along each finger, he stroked her hair, pulling her closer still. Just as she began to relax he pulled her face down into his groin. There was no doubting what he wanted from her.

She opened her mouth and ran her tongue across the end of his cock, closing her lips around the ridge of the head, slipping her tongue into its single sensitive eye.

Her hands instinctively moved to grip the length of his shaft, easing the foreskin back and forth. She could already taste the salty lubrication oozing from him and shivered as the flavour filled her mouth.

On the floor, crouched between his knees, Jessica felt as if she was a supplicant worshipping at an ancient altar. She realised, in the same instant, that his dominance excited her. Something about the way he claimed her as his own made her stomach contract.

She tried to work out whether it was him or the things he could show her that she craved so much. His fingers began to work through her hair, tightening and loosing as her mouth and hands closed around his cock.

'Put your hand between your legs,' he purred, as his excitement intensified.

She did as he asked, startled again by the thick silky moisture that trickled out onto her fingers.

The way her sex felt, the feeling of Harry in her mouth and the sound of his voice, loosened her grip on the rational thoughts she had been forming.

Her fingers found her clitoris, still glowing white hot. Its ancient hunger was renewed by every fleeting caress of her fingertips. She heard Harry's breath quicken and suddenly the only thing she could think about was bringing them both to the point of no return.

As his cock convulsed, flooding her mouth with warm seed, Jessica's sex contracted sharply, as if he had been buried deep inside her. As he pressed forward again, gasping and snorting, her body was drawn along with his into the molten furnace of orgasm.

Chapter 13

23 December

When Jack woke up he felt another monstrous headache stir and wake with him. He had not intended to get drunk - in fact, after his hangover the morning before he had sworn he would never get drunk again. But when Alice Fallon had arrived back downstairs, her expression tight and furious, his first instinct had been to reach for the brandy bottle. The rest of the evening, including the revue, was a complete blur.

Tentatively, he opened one eye. Beside him, curled in the crook of his arm - which was as dead as a dodo - Helen, the red-headed Prince Charming, was sound asleep. He groaned, carefully extricated his senseless limb and peered at the clock. It seemed, as he attempted to make his legs obey him, that Alice and Helen were taking the role of nurse maid in turns. He wondered what they would demand in return.

He strained to remember the events of the previous evening. He wasn't sure exactly why he hadn't noticed Harry Stolworthy leave the party. He had been stunned when Alice pinned him up against the wall to complain about his oversight.

Alice's account of the goings-on upstairs in Jessica's bedroom had been garbled, but graphic. Finally, when words failed her, she had snatched the brandy balloon out of his hands and drained the contents in a single gulp, before heading into the ballroom in the wake of Bunty, Miranda and the others.

Perhaps, he thought, as the blood pumped back into his arm, giving him pins and needles, Alice would wake up feeling as dreadful as he did. He groaned and rolled out of bed, feeling as if someone had installed a steam hammer where his brain had once been.

When Jessica got downstairs for breakfast, Malestone House seemed to be buzzing with activity. She realised as Harry came up behind her and slipped his arm through hers, that today was the day of the pantomime. In amongst every thing else, the performances seemed to have slipped her mind. Harry pulled her closer, fingers stroking her spine.

'I think that we ought to announce our engagement,' he said, pulling her into his arms. 'Why wait any longer? We could tell everyone today.' He glanced around the room. 'The sooner it's official the sooner we can leave.'

She stared at him. 'Harry, I have to stay, I've promise Alice.'

'You didn't help her yesterday and she seems to have managed all right. I'd like to get back to town. There are so many things we have to arrange.'

In daylight, away from the feverish activities in her bedroom, Jessica's doubts fluttered back like dark crows. She knew she didn't want to leave Malestone with Harry; a least, not yet.

'Why are you in so much of a hurry?' she asked in an undertone. 'I've already said I'll marry you, haven't I?' She tried hard to keep the hint of anxiety out of her voice. 'I chose to stay with you last night, not Alice. Isn't that enough for the moment?'

Harry sniffed. 'You mean you seriously considered there was a choice?'

Before Jessica could reply, Alice appeared from one of the corridors carrying a bundle of material. She looked first at Jessica and then at Harry. Whatever Alice thought or felt her expression revealed nothing.

'Morning,' she said briskly. 'You missed a damned good show last night. Bunty was on top form. I hope you're feeling better.'

Jessica nodded.

Alice handed her the cloth.

'Good. In that case perhaps we can get started straight away. We've got an awful lot to do.'

Jessica started to protest. 'What about breakfast?'

'We'll have to make do with a round of toast and a pot of tea. I've already asked the maid to bring us a tray in.'

Jessica, sensing that Alice was in no mood for discussion, slipped out of Harry's arms.

'If you'll excuse me,' she said to him, and before he could protest, followed Alice into the ballroom.

Inside, she saw that in her absence the stage had taken shape. Curtains had been hung on long poles to create a proscenium, the footlights were all in place and two rows of chairs were arranged just beyond what was obviously going to be the orchestra pit. Everywhere people were bustling back and forth carrying or arranging things. It seemed that several other members of the cast had also decided or been asked to miss breakfast. Alice headed towards them, walking quickly.

Jessica hurried to catch her up.

'Alice, about last night—'

Alice swung round. 'I haven't got anything to say. You made your choices, you're not a child. I'm just a little annoyed that you didn't come and help me with the show, presumably you and Harry were otherwise occupied?'

Jessica flinched.

Alice's expression softened. 'The thing is, Jess, I'm just worried that Harry's taking you for a ride. I think you're so obsessed with him that you can't see beyond what he does for you physically.' She stopped, taking a deep breath. 'I rang Charlie yesterday to see what I can find out about Harry. Please, if you value our friendship, wait until I hear from him before you commit yourself to something you'll regret.'

Hearing Alice's simple appeal, her words straight from the heart, made tears bubble up behind Jessica's eyes. She stepped forward and embraced her friend.

'How could you think I don't value our friendship? It isn't that I love you less, it's that - it's that—' she stopped abruptly. She had intended to say that she loved Harry more, but the words wouldn't form themselves in her mouth.

She stared at Alice, realising she couldn't say it, because it wasn't true. She wasn't going to marry Harry because she loved him - or ever imagined she would - but simply because he had asked her and she could think of no reasonable excuse for not accepting him.

Upstairs, Jack was getting changed. He'd been happy to let Felicia Gudgeon take over the role of hostess to his guests and didn't protest when she suggested everyone went down to the stables to look at Jack's new hunter before breakfast. It was a relief to be alone.

From downstairs, he could just make out the sounds of the stage hands transforming Malestone's ballroom into a theatre. Hanging on his wardrobe door was the frock coat and breeches Alice had had pressed and altered for the fancy dress ball on Christmas Eve. Everything was organised, the cabaret had been a great success and in some ways, the house party was going far better than he had anticipated. Certainly, all the guests seemed to be having a whale of a time - if only he could say the same thing about himself.

He looked into the mirror above the sink. His normally healthy complexion was pale, his eyes watering and bloodshot. He grimaced at his reflection.

It was time to talk to Jessica, however hard it might be. He glanced down at the contents of the washstand beside the sink. Amongst the more usual items was a bunch of keys. He had had the butler give him the keys to the corridor that led to the crystal room. Seeing them glinting amongst his things made him flinch. He picked them up and weighed them in his palm.

It was hard to reconcile everything he felt about finding Jessica with Harry Stolworthy. Even as he turned the keys over in his fingers, he was aware that part of his anger was fuelled by jealousy. For an instant he imagined slipping his cock deep inside her, feeling her body move in time with his, as he plunged deeper into the wetness and heat of her sex. He could almost feel her writhing under him and see the sweat rising between her breasts. He shuddered, so caught up in his own intense fantasy he could almost smell her pleasure. The thought made his mouth water and set his senses reeling.

He hefted the keys once more and then slipped them into his pocket. Whatever else happened, he would see that Stolworthy didn't get the chance to use the crystal room again.

He had no idea what else he had inadvertently told Stolworthy about Malestone. The crystal room wasn't the only room in the house that had two-way mirrors or viewing panels. He had tried desperately to remember when he had told Harry about the house's secrets, and came to the conclusion it had been years ago, in some drunken revel that he had long since forgotten.

Slowly, painfully aware of the throbbing in his skull, Jack finished dressing, and headed out onto the landing. Just as he was about to go down the stairs he saw two figures in the hall below him. It seemed that thinking about Harry had conjured him up. He was standing by the Christmas tree deep in conversation with one of the Haywood twins. Their voices were low but it would be impossible to misinterpret their body language. As Harry leaned closer to the beautiful blonde boy, every part of him seemed to be alight with desire.

The boy grinned and peered flirtatiously at Stolworthy, then giggled as Stolworthy lifted a hand to stroke at the twin's exquisite, androgynous face. Stolworthy was propositioning the boy and it seemed he did not mind in the slightest.

As Jack watched, the twin leaned closer and brushed Harry's cheek with his lips, before he turned and scurried back into the shadows. Furious, Jack hurried down the stairs and into the hall.

Stolworthy was hot on the boy's heels and oblivious to Jack, who was torn between calling Harry back and seeing what was to follow. Keeping to the shadows he hurried after them.

Malestone House had been extended several times over the years and beyond the main hall and public rooms, the corridors were like a maze. Keeping well behind them, Jack stayed hidden until Harry and the twin slipped into what had once been the gun room. Jack frowned - it was another place where the interior could be observed if the viewer knew the room's secrets.

He crept along the corridor until he reached the next turning, wondering who he would meet at the small grill that overlooked the old gun room. To his relief the corridor was empty. Set at eye level in the wall was what looked like a ventilation grill. With practised ease, Jack slid it aside and peered into the room, wondering what he would see within.

Inside, caught like a print in the grill's single eye, was a dark leather *chaise* on which Stolworthy was arranging cushions. Beside him, one of the twins was rubbing his hands and nervously running his fingers through his hair.

Stolworthy looked up at him. 'Your brother is coming too, isn't he?'

The boy nodded and glanced at his watch.

'He ought to be here any minute. I've already told him to go and get Jessica.' He smiled. 'You know, I really like her.'

Stolworthy laughed, as Jack heard footsteps approaching along the main corridor. He picked out Jessica's voice immediately.

'Are you supposed to be down here?' she said nervously. 'I thought Alice said the other curtains were in the...' Her voice faded as the door to the gun room opened.

Jack pressed his face hard against the grill and watched the girl and the second twin walk into the room.

'Harry?' Jessica said softly, looking from face to face. 'What are you doing here? I thought you were going in to breakfast. I'm on an errand for Alice.'

Harry grinned and lifted a finger to her lips to silence her.

'I was so sad when you had to go off and work. I thought I might divert you for a little while.' He grinned at the twins. 'It shouldn't take long. Alice will never miss you. Besides, Bobby here was so sad that he missed out on the fun yesterday.'

Jessica reddened. 'Harry, I really haven't got time for this now, I—'

Harry leaned forward and kissed her. 'Oh, but I think you have, my love.' His tone had subtly changed. Jessica stared at him.

Harry continued. 'These are my friends. Rather like Alice Fallon is your friend.'

Jessica stiffened. 'Harry—' she began to protest. He circled her like a cat playing with a mouse.

'Don't be shy,' Harry purred softly, stroking her breasts with his fingertips.

Jessica felt her nipples harden through her clothes. The twins looked at her with expectation, but all she could see clearly were Harry's eyes glittering darkly. He nodded towards the couch.

'I thought we could share the pleasure today, my love.' His hand slipped lower, sliding up between her legs so that his palm and fingers worked against her sex. She reddened dramatically.

'Why are you doing this, Harry?' she murmured as he stroked at the sensitive cleft between her legs. His touch lit a series of tiny beacons in her mind.

Harry was closer now. 'Because I know part of you loves it. All those years without being loved, they've left you so hungry.'

He grinned, bending so that his lips closed around one nipple. He breathed out hard, warming her skin and making her tremble.

'But I can help you with that.' He stood up and circled her chest, fingers working at the fastenings of her dress. 'I can help you discover so many wonderful things. But maybe I've already said that.'

The buttons on her dress gave way and he slipped the material down over her shoulders. She felt powerless to resist him. He was right; some part of her loved the sense of obedience - of surrender - and relished the things he had helped her to discover. What stunned her was that she had never been aware it was there until Harry had seduced her.

Now, as his fingers worked under the shoestring straps of her camisole, she wondered if she had been waiting for someone like Harry, someone who recognised her need. The thought shocked her almost as much as the sensation of Harry's eager fingers nipping at her breasts.

He began to roll her erect nipples between them. She groaned and lay back against him, surrendering to the welter of feelings.

She barely noticed him sliding her dress down over her hips. The camisole top followed, falling like a whisper over her glowing flesh. One hand worked down over her belly, finding and then tracing the contours of her sex. His fingers seemed to touch everywhere except the one spot that bayed for his caresses. She writhed against him, pushing her hips forward so that he would touch her clitoris. Again and again he avoided the little peak until she could hardly bear it. As she wriggled, her dress moved lower and lower until all she had to do was step out of it.

Harry purred his approval and then with a single movement caught hold of her knickers and pulled them down. She had almost forgotten the twins were there, until another pair of hands joined Harry's. She felt warm breath on her belly and, gasping, looked down to see one of the twins on his knees at her feet. His fingers slid her panties lower, jerking them down over her ankles. As he did so, he planted a single wet kiss on her quim. The touch was as intense as a firebrand. His tongue sought out the throbbing bud Harry had neglected, and as his tongue worked across it, she let out a tiny sob of delight.

With a single movement, Harry guided her back onto the *chaise*, and she lay back amongst the cushions, revelling in the twin's caresses.

Harry bent over her, opening her legs wider, so she was straddled across the cold dark leather. As if he were the conductor of her seduction, he lifted her hips and slid a cushion under her so that every moist fold, every inch of her nakedness was exposed for the other man's explorations.

Jessica's fears and doubts receded in the face of the pleasure. She could hardly believe how good the touch of the boy's tongue felt. Closing her eyes, she relinquished all control. His touch was as delicate and knowing as Alice Fallon's. She lifted herself up onto his mouth, chasing his lips with her body.

Close by, she heard Harry murmur his approval. Just as she thought there could be nothing else but the long slow spiral out towards satisfaction, she felt the brush of a leg on her cheek. She glanced up into a face identical to the one that was pressed eagerly between her thighs. The other twin was naked, his cock jutting towards her, as desperate and eager as her own body was for release. He straddled her and without hesitation, she guided his shaft into her waiting mouth.

The taste of salt and masculine musk flooded her mind and she began to stroke him, relishing his weight and heat. He repaid her with a long throaty groan, as she began to work him with lips and fingers. Her sex ached, longing to be filled. Between her legs, as if the other twin could read her, a single finger pressed deep inside her.

Her sex convulsed, sending an arc of light up through her belly. She lifted up to receive his offering and almost cried out as he shifted position and slid his cock deep inside her. The boy's thumb replaced his tongue, keeping up a steady circling pressure on her clitoris. There was nothing left in her mind but pleasure and the sure, compelling ride out towards oblivion.

Behind the grating, Jack felt a glittering shard of fury, but he couldn't tear his eyes away from the scenario being played out in the gun room. The temptation was to burst in and unseat the Haywood twins. He shivered, fighting the excitement that threatened to engulf him. He knew he didn't so much want to rescue Jessica as share the pleasure the three lovers were experiencing.

He wanted to plunge his cock into Jessica's obviously eager body and bring her to an earth-shattering climax or feel her lips drawing him into her mouth, while her fingers cradled and stroked his aching balls. He could already see her excitement building and imagined her sex tightening around his shaft like a warm glove.

He was so entranced by the idea, that he was barely aware of Harry Stolworthy until the man moved. Jack stared at him and saw the look on the other man's face. Stolworthy was eyeing up the scenario with a kind of professional detachment. The expression was so at odds with the events unfolding on the *chaise* that Jack couldn't help but stare at him.

As Jessica began to writhe, her body flushed and totally at one with the twins, Stolworthy grinned and turned away. The expression on Harry's face made Jack's excitement drain away. The one thought that glowed in his mind was, what was Stolworthy up to?

On the *chaise*, the three lovers strained and thrust, grabbing on tight to their last few moments of excitement. When the final aftershocks shuddered through them, they collapsed down onto each other, struggling to catch their breath.

Jack looked away and slid down onto the floor in the corridor, forcing his mind to clear. After a few minutes he heard the gun room door open and close. He peered round the corner and saw Jessica hurrying back towards the main house. Seconds later the twins followed, leaving only Stolworthy, alone.

Jack got to his feet and tidied his clothes, composing himself. As the gun room door opened and closed for a third time he waited a few seconds and then stepped out into the corridor and followed Harry, who was walking briskly back towards the hall.

'Stolworthy,' he snapped to Harry's disappearing back.

Harry, obviously unaware that he had been observed, turned round, his face the picture of innocence.

'Good morning, Jack,' he said, with measured good humour. 'I was just exploring a little, I hope you don't mind.'

Jack felt an icy knot of anger growing in his belly.

'What the hell are you playing at?' he growled.

Harry looked bemused. 'I beg your pardon?' he said evenly. 'I'm not sure that I follow you.'

Behind him, the door to the drawing room opened and several of the players, including Bunty Redknap, appeared. They were deep in conversation and apparently oblivious to the confrontation between Jack and Harry.

Jack indicated the stairs. 'I think we ought to go to my office.'

Harry lifted an eyebrow. 'Are you propositioning me?' he said with a wry smile. 'My, but life here at Malestone is exciting, isn't it? What exactly had you got in mind?'

Jack felt the fury bubble up. 'You little bastard,' he hissed. 'I want you to tell me exactly what it is you're up to.'

Harry's eyes did not leave his. 'What, may I ask, has it got to do with you?'

Jack snorted. Stolworthy was right - in reality the answer was nothing. Wasn't everyone else at Malestone hell bent on enjoying every sexual pleasure that was on offer? And if he asked Stolworthy to leave, wasn't there a very good chance that Jessica would go with him? He struggled to keep his hands firmly by his sides. The temptation to punch Harry Stolworthy was almost unbearable.

'The little scenario you just played out in the gun room?' he hissed. 'Jessica Harper is a friend of mine.'

Harry laughed. 'Really? Aren't you overplaying your hand a little, Jack? From what I can gather, she was invited by Alice as a glorified stage hand. And the gun room? I really had no idea you were a voyeur, Jack. You should have come in and joined the fun. At the very least you could have had a comfortable chair from which to enjoy the performance.' He grinned unpleasantly. 'Quite a find, our Miss Harper. Has she told you we're going to be married?'

'Over my dead body,' Jack snapped.

Harry pulled a face. 'A touch overdramatic, Jack. After all, if you saw this morning's little performance you know damned well I didn't have to force her.' He grinned again. 'Quite the reverse, she loves it. It's difficult to credit, really, someone like Jessica having so much fire in her belly.' He paused, as if waiting for Jack to reply. 'Well, may I go now?'

Jack stared at him impotently. Harry was right. Jessica wasn't a victim. She knew her own mind. Then it struck Jack what the problem was. He wasn't concerned about Jessica's motives but Stolworthy's.

He glared furiously at the other man.

'Why are you doing this? If you wanted a whore the house is knee deep in them. You could have had any one of the guests, male or female. What the hell are you up to?'

Stolworthy tugged at his cuffs. 'As I've said, Jack, this has nothing whatsoever to do with you.'

Jack sensed he was close to the truth and couldn't keep his anger in check any more. Leaping forward, he grabbed Stolworthy by the lapels and thrust him hard up against the wall.

'Tell me why you're doing this,' he hissed between gritted teeth, 'or, as God is my witness, I'll knock your bloody head off.'

Stolworthy, his face ashen, was about to speak, when the double doors to the hall swung open and Felicia Gudgeon and a small group of Jack's house guests hurried in out of the cold. Felicia cast a knowing eye over Jack, who still had Harry bundled up against the wall.

'Play nicely, children,' she said wryly, slipping off her coat. 'I leave you alone for five minutes and you're at each other's throats.'

Jack relinquished his hold on Harry's jacket. Harry immediately stepped away from him and began to rearrange his clothes.

Jack, unable to think of anything to say, turned on his heel and headed back upstairs to his office, mind blazing with anger. Still shaking, he poured himself a stiff brandy and stood by the window looking out into the park. Outside the first flakes of snow began to fall.

The rest of the day was devoted to preparing for the pantomime. Jessica had very little time to think about what had happened in the gun room, or at least, she tried hard to keep the thoughts under control. As she moved her body reminded her time and again of the twins' attentions.

Some of the male members of the cast brought in the piano and the rest of the instruments, while everyone else went through their lines one last time. By late afternoon the ballroom seemed to be teeming with people and row after row of chairs were arranged over the polished wooden floor.

Jessica and Alice had no time to talk. Jessica helped slide the backdrop for the opening scene of Cinderella into position and then looked out over the makeshift auditorium. 'There seems to be an awful lot of seats,' she said in an undertone, as Bunty Redknap arranged bundles of sheet music on the music stands.

He looked up and grinned. 'Hasn't Alice told you? Jack invited his tenants and their families up for the performance, so we'll have to make sure it's all above board, darling.' He winked conspiratorially. 'No funny business, if you know what I mean?' He paused and licked his lips. 'But there will be lots of time for that later. I'm looking forward to tomorrow night's fancy dress party, myself.'

He pouted and struck a pose. 'Just you wait and see what I've come up with. It's absolutely stunning, even if I do say so myself. And those naughty twins, I really can't wait to see what the boys have chosen.' He grinned.

Jessica stared at him. Between her legs she could still feel the remains of the twins' passion, and she shivered. She'd totally forgotten about the party and certainly hadn't given any thought about what she might go as.

Behind her, Alice was going through the running order on her notebook.

Jessica turned. 'Would it be all right for me to borrow a costume for tomorrow night?'

Alice, obviously preoccupied, barely looked up.

'Help yourself,' she said. 'But for goodness' sake don't take anything off the rails tonight. It's complete chaos already. Have you seen Cinders' broom by any chance?'

Supper for the theatre troupe was served early, as a running buffet, in the breakfast room. Jessica, cradling her plate, wandered amongst the players, now all transformed into their characters in the pantomime. There was an expectant, excited atmosphere in the room. Some of the actors talked in subdued voices, while others read through their lines.

Jessica felt isolated as she moved between them. She wasn't part of their world any more than she was part of Jack's. She couldn't really slip out from this dining room and into the one where his house guests, including Harry, were about to dine - she didn't fit in either place. The twins, over by the buffet table, were deep in conversation, though she found it hard to contemplate talking to them after the events of the morning. She wondered if they had given her a second thought since slipping out of her compliant body.

She was beginning to feel maudlin. As she watched the rest of the troupe finish their meal, Alice came over and slipped the prompt script into her hands.

'Another half an hour, then we'd better get everyone up on stage. You shouldn't have much to do. They like to adlib anyway.' She stared angrily across the room. 'Won't be a minute, I must just go and take that bottle of port away from Bunty. Lord only knows what'll happen if he gets drunk.'

Chapter 14

The Performance

Jessica had never been backstage during a live theatre performance before - albeit that Alice's show was small, it was exciting to be behind the curtain waiting for the audience to take their seats.

In the wings, the twins, dressed as medieval pages, were ready for the show's opening number, which would conclude with the curtains opening up on to Cinderella's kitchen. Jessica found it hard to watch them without seeing Harry's face as they had made love to her and imagining their hands and bodies working on hers. Catching her look, one of the boys winked at her and tipped his hat. She blushed and quietly slipped out of the prompter's chair and into the little anteroom adjoining the ballroom, where the rest of the cast were putting the finishing touches to their make-up.

Alice, busy dressing Miranda's hair, grinned up at her and then pointed to her watch.

'Five more minutes. Can you just see if anyone else needs any help?'

Jessica nodded, relieved to be away from the twins' undivided attention, set about doing up buttons and generally mothering the cast who were keyed up and ready to go.

Alice took a final look at her watch and then beckoned to Jessica. 'We'll go up into the wings. Bunty should be starting any second now.'

Right on cue they heard the opening bars of the overture and seconds later the curtains began to open. Alice waved the twins on to begin their narrative song.

Jessica peered out beyond the footlights into the audience. Harry was sitting in one of the aisle seats, his attention fixed on the stage as the boys danced and sung their way through their act.

In repose he looked extremely handsome. People would consider him a good catch, with his well cut suit and perfect manners. Excited by the atmosphere around her, she tried hard to quash the doubts that continued to surface inside her head. She certainly couldn't accuse him of not being attentive. He had helped her to discover a wild and astonishing depth of passion.

She glanced back over the audience and was stunned to see Jack Healy, sitting on the far end of the first row of seats, looking at her. She took a step back, trying to press herself into the shadows of the wings but even then his gaze stayed on her. His expression was neutral, though his eyes glittered in the darkness. For some reason when she looked at him, her stomach contracted sharply and she felt her pulse quicken. If Harry Stolworthy hadn't arrived at Malestone, things might have been very different. She looked away and turned her attention back to the sheet of paper with the running order on it. As the boys' song came to an end, with the tumultuous burst of applause, the curtains opened with a lurch to reveal Miranda sweeping the floor with a besom.

'Marvellous, marvellous, everyone,' Bunty Redknap crowed triumphantly as he passed another glass of champagne out across the crowded anteroom.

The pantomime had received a standing ovation. Outside in the hall, the audience, guided by the staff at Malestone, were making their way back out into the cold winter night, while backstage, the tiny room was heaving with the entire cast and Jack's house guests.

Jessica found a relatively quiet spot over by the fireplace and sipped her champagne, feeling elated and excited that everything had gone so well. The players, still in costume and make-up, were congratulating each other, laughing and comparing notes, reliving every second of what had proved to be a superbly successful evening.

The room was very hot with everyone packed shoulder to shoulder. Jessica was about to make her way through the crowd to find Alice when Jack pushed his way through the people to stand beside her.

She smiled and lifted her glass in salute. 'It was a great night. I think everyone had a wonderful time. You ought to congratulate yourself on such a wonderful idea.'

Jack nodded. There was something about the way he looked at her that was both unnerving and exciting. She swallowed hard, struggling to avoid his intense gaze.

'It was good, wasn't it?' He smiled and moved a little closer. 'I have been trying to find a way to talk to you for days,' he said softly.

Jessica shivered. 'If you're going to talk to me about Harry—' she began.

He shook his head. 'No, I don't want to talk about him. I want to talk about you.' He glanced around the sea of faces and bodies. 'Can we go somewhere else?'

'Harry will be here in a minute,' she said in a low voice.

Jack lifted an eyebrow. 'Are you sure? I saw him with one of the twins a few minutes ago. They seemed to be very keen that I shouldn't hear what they were planning.'

Jessica tried hard to ensure her face revealed nothing. It was obvious that Harry was intrigued by the two boys. She smiled. 'Well, in that case I'd be delighted.'

Jack offered her his arm. 'There's another way out of here,' he said in an undertone. 'Let me show you.'

Lifting aside one of the heavy drapes that framed the windows, Jack led her through a hidden door into a shadowy passageway. In spite of herself, Jessica felt a little flurry of fear and tried to disguise it with a laugh.

'What's this?' she said with forced good humour. 'A secret passage?'

Jack looked back at her, eyes ablaze. 'Yes, Malestone is full of secrets. I thought perhaps you already knew that.'

Jessica stiffened. 'I don't know what you mean,' she began.

The corridor seemed to be getting increasingly narrow and darker with every step. There was barely room for them to walk side by side and Jessica's feeling of anxiety was increasing with every yard. She sensed that Jack was trying to tell her something, but she had no idea what. As her eyes adjusted to the gloom she could see that there were other doors set into the unplastered walls. Finally the corridor forked left and right, both forks leading up to flights of stairs.

'Where are we going?' she murmured, suddenly feeling terribly alone and vulnerable.

Jack spun round. 'I'm surprised you don't already know. This way' - he lifted a hand to indicate the staircase to the left - 'leads to a room my father had built for his mistress. Perhaps you've heard of it, the crystal room?'

Jessica stared at him. 'A secret way in?' she whispered, feeling her colour rise.

Jack grinned, his teeth looking unnaturally white in the gloom. 'Not exactly, this leads to a little room behind it. My father and his friends liked to watch.' He stopped. 'Do you understand what I'm saying?'

Jessica shook her head nervously.

Jack sighed. 'There's a two-way mirror in the room. You must remind me to show you sometime before you leave. It overlooks the bed. It's perfect for a little voyeurism.'

Jessica struggled to maintain her composure, thoughts racing through her mind. Had Harry known about the two-way mirror? 'And this one?' she whispered, pointing to the stairs on their right.

Jack smiled. 'My father's bedroom. Would you like to look at it? He was a collector of curios and antiquities. He had the passages built when he had the house extended, so he could move around without anyone knowing exactly where he was.'

'Are there many secret passages?'

Jack shook his head. 'No, not really, but there are lots of places where he could oversee the goings-on in the rest of the house. He liked to see what was happening under his roof.' Jack paused and then offered her his hand. 'Why don't you come with me and see what we can find tonight? It might be very educational.'

Jessica shook her head. 'I don't think so,' she began.

To her surprise, Jack spun round and grabbed hold of her shoulders. 'Why not? What is it you're afraid of? Are you worried that you might find Harry with one of the twins or one of the other guests? It seems to me that his tastes are fairly catholic.'

Jessica froze. Jack's face was no more than a few inches away from hers. She could hear her pulse thumping in her ears and could sense his fury. She tried to wriggle free of him but it just made him hold her tighter.

'Please let me go,' she whispered unsteadily.

Jack pushed her back against the rough wall, his lips seeking hers. At first she was so stunned she felt unable to resist and then her fear was replaced by a roaring, bubbling torrent of desire, so astonishing and unexpected that the breath caught in her throat.

She felt her body respond and held him tight, gasping as his arms encircled her, her lips working against his. Jack groaned, his tongue lapping at her lips, seeking entry. Her nipples hardened, brushing against the front of his dress shirt and for an instant she felt every part of her body reach out to him, begging for satisfaction.

He relaxed the grip on her shoulders and let his hands drop to her breasts. She could already feel his cock pressing against her, hard and eager for her caresses. As his fingers stroked at the pert hard buds she was suddenly aware of where she was and what she was doing. Gasping for breath, she broke away from him, eyes alight with confusion and desire.

'No,' she cried. 'No, I can't, Jack.'

He took a step towards her. She felt his need draw her like a magnet, but what was more disturbing was the glowing hunger that she felt for him. She longed to take him in her arms and share everything she had. She wanted to feel his tongue working deep in her sex, and his cock and his fingers. She imagined him taking her then and there and them both being burned up by the heat of the passion.

Afraid, not of what Jack wanted from her, but what she felt, Jessica backed along the wall. She had never felt this before - not for Robert, not for Harry; this desire was so close to insanity that she couldn't bear to think where it might lead.

As she moved, eyes firmly on Jack, she felt the wall's surface give way to a wooden door and struggled to find the handle. Behind her, Jack was advancing towards her. She felt the cold metal handle in her fingers, twisted it and was relieved to feel the door open. Without hesitation she stepped through.

She wasn't quick enough to stop Jack following her and found herself in a small alcove behind what seemed like a heavy tapestry. Jack was at her shoulder, his breath hot on her skin.

She was about to pull the heavy cloth aside and escape, when she heard voices on the far side and recognised one as Harry's. The coincidence was almost more than she could cope with. How could she step out from her hiding place with Jack behind her?

In the few seconds that she hesitated, she felt Jack's hands snaking up around her torso and cup her aching breasts. His lips closed on her shoulders, biting and kissing, lifting a floodtide of desire in her belly. Unable to speak, powerless to resist, she knew she had no choice but to comply with what he wanted, and more compelling still, there was nothing she wanted more. She turned to face him, knowing that her passion and need were equal to his. He stared down at her and then gathered up her skirt. He was rough and unstoppable.

His hands parted her thighs, ripping at her knickers. She swallowed down a whimper of fear and desire as the fabric gave way, exposing her to a touch that was raw and frantic.

She leaned back against the rough wall, opening her legs, giving him complete access to every part of her. His fingers plunged into her wetness. Reaching forward, she caught hold of his trousers, sliding her hand down to cup and stroke the impressive bulge in the front of his trousers. He bit his lips, struggling to stifle the noises of pleasure and then grinned at her as her fingers sought to free him. As his fly buttons gave way under her explorations, his cock sprung into her hand like a loaded pistol. He lifted his hand to the back of her neck, and knotting his fingers in her hair, kissed her with a savagery that took her breath away. She returned it with equal vigour, relishing the sensation of his throbbing cock cradled in her palm.

Roughly he grabbed hold of one of her legs, dragging it around his waist and then without hesitation she guided his shaft deep inside her. Her body opened up in his path and she shivered. Every thought, every sensation centred on her sex, where he breached her. She hissed softly as he began to move, each thrust matched by her own. She could hardly believe anything could be so all-consuming. She thrust again, driving him deeper still. He pressed his lips to her throat, lapping at the sensitive flesh, while his fingers nipped into her thighs and buttocks, holding her so close to him that it seemed as if they had become a single creature, welded together by a completely overwhelming desire.

Jessica struggled to keep quiet, her mouth pressed up tight against Jack's broad shoulders as he drove on and on. As a counterpoint to their passion, she could hear Harry's voice in the room beyond the tapestry. He was not alone, but talking with one or two other men. Her mind was so full of Jack's caresses that she found it impossible to concentrate on what Harry was saying. Even so, his words seemed to filter through into her mind, like the backbeat to a compelling tune.

He was talking business, asking the men for money as an investment. Jack, as if he sensed that her attention was slipping, pushed his hand back between her thighs. His fingers brushed up against her clitoris - it was all she could do to stop herself from screaming out. His touch seemed to ignite a roaring flame. She grabbed at his back and kissed him hard, letting herself be sucked down into a swirling sea of sensations.

Her kisses made him gasp and then he began to move his finger more rhythmically, until all she was aware of was his body against hers, his lips, his fingers and the devastating thrust of his cock as it plunged deep inside her. She felt as if she would die and imagined that they were alone in some secret place in the universe, flying out amongst the stars to be burnt up by the heat of the sun.

As she felt the first roaring, white-hot waves of orgasm sweep through her, she pressed her face back against the shoulders of his jacket, biting into the fabric to smother the cry of ecstasy that bubbled up in her throat.

She could hear and feel Jack's breath, coming in short explosive bursts, and inside her throbbing quim she felt his cock convulse and flood her with his seed. Coming back to reality was almost like regaining consciousness.

She stared up at Jack Heally, hardly able to believe what she had done and at the same time immeasurably pleased that she had done it. He grabbed hold of her hand and dragged her back into the darkness of the passageway, leaving the sodden remains of her panties in the alcove.

The last thing she heard as she closed the door to the secret passage was Harry Stolworthy saying in a confident voice, 'Of course, Jessica and I will be married by then, and that will make an awful lot of difference to my life.'

In the darkness, the weight of what she had done flooded through her.

'Jack?' she whispered in the darkness. His reply was to pull her into his arms and kiss her again. She wriggled free. 'I can't do this,' she gasped almost hysterically. 'Please, let me go. I have to go back and find Harry.'

'Why? Don't you understand how I feel about you? You can't leave me now.'

Jessica felt a chill of anxiety. 'I'm going to marry him,' she said with a degree of confidence that belied all her fears.

'Why?' whispered Jack incredulously. 'I don't understand.'

She stared at Jack, completely unable to find an answer that made any kind of sense at all.

'I have got to go,' she said again and slipping her hand out of his, hurried back along the gloomy corridor towards the door that led into the ballroom.

Part of her fear was that she thought - even given the passion Jack had lit in her - that he wanted her purely as another trophy, another head on the gun room wall, whereas Harry, for all his faults, wanted to marry her. She would be his and his alone. It sounded so irrational that she couldn't bring herself to say it.

Without looking back, Jessica opened the door at the far end of the corridor and stepped out from behind the curtain into the busy, crowded little room that backed onto the ballroom. It didn't seem that anyone had noticed she had been missing. Taking another drink from the tray, she set off to find Harry.

Jack stood alone in the passage and watched Jessica vanish into the darkness. He ought to go back into the main house and play host to his guests. The idea did not fill him with much enthusiasm. What he should have done was tell Jessica about Harry arranging for her seduction to be viewed in the crystal room, but he suspected that she might forgive Harry even that. Women were a complete mystery.

He sighed, just as a door on his right swung open and flooded the dusty corridor with light. Felicia Gudgeon struck her head round and peered into the corridor.

'So there you are, Jack,' she said. 'I wondered where you'd got to. I was running out of places to look. What are you doing skulking round there in the dark? Surely it's far too early for anyone to be up to no good, or were you hoping to catch the eager few?' She grinned. 'Found anything exciting on your travels?'

Jack shook his head and slipped his arm through hers.

'No,' he said flatly. 'Come on, I could really use a drink.'

Felicia curled happily into the crook of his arm. 'I've missed you. What are you going to wear tomorrow for the fancy dress party? George seems to think he and I ought to come as Napoleon and Josephine. What do you think?'

'With an ample expanse of bosom exposed?'

Felicia grinned. 'Well, of course, darling. Or Alice has got these other costumes, a Roman emperor and empress. If we wore those I'd get to show an awful lot of leg as well. Which do you think would suit me best?' She looked up from under her eyelashes, aping coyness.

Jack smiled at her, grateful that some women remained deliciously predictable, whatever the circumstances.

Jessica made her way out into the hall, where the overspill of revellers from the backstage room were happily chatting in small groups around the Christmas tree and the log fire. It all looked remarkably normal and civilised except that here and there, some of the theatre group were still dressed in their costumes and had their garish make-up on.

Bunty Redknap, cradling a bottle of champagne, was supervising the return of the piano to the spot by the cocktail cabinet. Alice was nowhere in sight. Jessica wondered where Harry had got to and tried to work out which room the tapestry curtain might have hung in. Just as she was about to set out to explore, Harry appeared from under the stairs, spotted her and hurried over. He did not look overly pleased.

'So, there you are,' he said in a slightly exasperated tone. 'I've been looking everywhere.' His expression softened. 'I've been worried about you. I see you've got a drink.' He leaned closer and pressed a kiss against her cheek. 'You feel very hot, you're not sickening for something, are you?'

Jessica blushed. 'No, I'm fine, really.'

Harry grinned. 'Good, I've been thinking about our engagement announcement. I think we ought to tell everyone tomorrow night at the fancy dress ball.' He smiled. 'I've been thinking about our costumes.'

Jessica nodded, distractedly. Across the room, Jack was making his way to the cocktail cabinet accompanied by Felicia Gudgeon. As if he sensed her watching him, he looked up. When their eyes met, Jessica blushed crimson. Between her legs she could still feel the moist glow of his caresses. Her colour deepened, while beside her, Harry babbled on about his ideas.

'Well,' he said, suddenly. 'What do you think?'

Jessica stared up at him, realising she hadn't heard a word he had said.

Harry sighed. 'Leave it to me. I'll arrange everything.' He looked at her more closely. 'Are you sure you're all right?'

Jessica bit her lips. 'Actually I do feel a little strange,' she said.

He took hold of her hand. 'Why don't we go upstairs? It'll be cooler up there and I can show you what I've chosen for tomorrow night.'

She didn't protest as Harry led her away from the main group, aware as they left that Jack's eyes were on her every step of the way. Harry was right. It was much cooler upstairs, and away from Jack she began to feel more at ease.

'Here we are,' said Harry, opening the door to his room.

It struck her that she hadn't been in it since they had met. It was far grander than her own little bedroom up under the eaves. As she stepped inside, he rounded on her, eyes alight.

'I'm glad we're finally on our own,' he said in an undertone. As he spoke he slid his hands up over her thighs and gathered up her skirt. His finger brushed the outside of her quim and as he found the soft naked hair, he froze, the expression on his face hardening.

'You haven't got any underwear on,' he said accusingly. His finger slid deeper into the wet hot pit that lay between her legs.

Her expression must have betrayed her. His eyes darkened. 'Was it Alice?' he whispered thickly. 'I haven't seen her since the performance and I couldn't find you either. Have you two been having a little fun behind my back?' His finger pressed deeper inside her. She flinched. 'Did her pretty little tongue slide up here and make you so very wet or was it someone else?'

Jessica, unable to think of anything to say, felt herself tremble. Harry's hand lifted to the neckline of her silky cocktail dress.

'Well?' he snapped. His fingers closed on the thin fabric and he wrenched at it furiously, making her shriek as the stitching gave way. The material tore like tissue, exposing her breasts and belly. She knew Harry would be able to see the red marks of Jack's excited kisses.

He smiled without humour and wrenched the fabric again. It fell to the floor like a silken flag. 'What am I going to do with you?' he said, his eyes working back and forth across her exposed body.

'Harry—' she began.

He glared at her. 'I really don't think I want you to say anything,' he said thickly, his gaze moving up to her face. 'Come over here.'

Stepping out of the ruins of her dress she obediently stepped closer. He pulled her tight against him.

'Look over there,' he said. She followed his eyes. Hanging over the chair was a pile of pastel gauze. 'I thought tomorrow we could go to the party as master and harem girl. What do you think?'

Jessica nodded.

'One thing a master demands from his slaves is complete obedience,' he murmured. 'I don't think you've really grasped that concept, have you, my love?'

Jessica felt her pulse skip a beat.

Harry continued. 'I really think it's something you need to learn if we are to understand each other better. I am the one who decides who you make love to. Is that clear? The decision is mine, not yours.' He grabbed her wrists and snatched up a tie from the end of the bed. Wrapping it round them, he knotted it tightly.

'There,' he said quietly, 'I think that's better. Now what else?'

He smiled, took a handkerchief from his pocket and secured it around her eyes. Plunged into darkness Jessica felt completely helpless.

Rough hands guided her towards the bed and she almost felt relieved when he rolled her over onto her belly, face down on the mattress. He grabbed her wrists and lifted them above her head, securing them to the bedhead. She strained to try and pick out some sound, some clue to what he had in store for her. He caught hold of her hips and pulled her up onto her knees.

She could hear him breathing heavily and fought the temptation to speak - after all what had she got to say? Between her legs she could feel the remnants of Jack's passion, trickling out onto her thighs.

She heard Harry laugh wryly. 'My, what a pretty picture you make,' he purred. 'You ought to see yourself.' He ran his hands over her thighs, pausing to run a finger over the dripping lips of her open quim.

'A master needs a little something to help keep his harem in order,' he whispered. 'I borrowed this from Alice, though I believe it belongs to Jack. Perhaps we ought to ask him.'

As he spoke, Jessica heard a terrifying hiss and the next instant a streak of searing pain exploded across her buttocks. She screamed out in pain and surprise as the sensation echoed through every nerve-ending like molten lead. She had no doubt that Harry was using the riding crop Alice had borrowed for the coachman. But all thoughts were burned away as the pain exploded again deep inside her mind.

Her body screamed out in protest, and she began to sob. Harry bent closer to her, so close she could feel his breath on her hot, red face.

'You will learn, my love,' he said in an unemotional voice. 'And you will never, ever forget.'

The crop cracked again. Jessica flinched, feeling tears of pain and humiliation course down her face.

'Just three more,' said Harry. 'I think that will be enough. Don't you agree?'

Jessica was too shaken to speak. Harry repeated his question and then brought the whip down again.

'Answer me,' he said in a firmer tone. 'Or would you prefer it if I carried on a little longer? Would you like me to stop after six?'

Jessica drew in a long ragged breath.

'Please, Harry,' she said in a voice ragged with emotion. 'Please stop.'

'Of course, my dear,' he said triumphantly. 'Just two more and it will all be over and done with.'

Jessica braced herself for the next blow, and the next, then held her breath waiting to see if Harry would keep to his word. The next thing she felt was Harry pressing kisses to her backside, lapping at the skin that still felt as if it were glowing red hot. His fingers traced what she assumed must be the weals the crop had left. He worked lower, dipping a finger inside her and then tracing the sensitive bridge of skin between her sex and the dark tighter entrance behind.

'You're so tight,' he purred, a finger working at the tight puckering. 'You have no idea how much I need you,' he whispered. 'You are very important to me. All I ask is that you do as I say and then everything will be all right.'

Jessica wasn't certain whether his words were meant to reassure her or give her comfort, but they did neither.

She felt her body beginning to relax under his caresses. The bizarre combination of pain and pleasure had lowered her resistance to his explorations.

A finger slipped inside her quim, another lifted to brush her clitoris. Without thinking she flexed the muscles in her stomach, lifting her hips to let him have greater freedom. As she did, Harry slipped a single finger into the puckered closure of her backside.

The sensation made her shiver. She remembered the twin's slim cock following the same route and the sense of constriction and delight it had given her. While her mind was repulsed her body had relished the new sensation.

Behind her, she could feel Harry moving and swallowed hard. It was obvious what Harry's intentions were. She tried desperately not to tense up as she felt the head of his cock nosing at the tight little bud. His shaft was far bigger than that of the twin's.

He massaged her back, his other hand still working at her sex, fingers stroking her pleasure bud.

'Relax,' he murmured, as he tried to enter her. 'Pant, don't fight me, this will feel so good for both of us.'

Jessica tried hard to work with him, willing her body to comply. She needn't have worried, her body opened up to him like a flower blossoming - but her mind stayed closed tight shut. Was this what Harry really wanted from her? Was he only interested in the pleasures that the twins could offer him? She struggled to control her thoughts, praying the pleasure that was growing under Harry's fingertips would build into an inferno and her fears would be swept away in the blaze.

Behind her, Harry let out a soft grunt of satisfaction as he moved deeper into the tight tunnel. She took a deep breath, trying to concentrate every thought on the heat that glowed between her legs. As if reading her mind, Harry renewed his attentions, his caresses becoming faster and faster.

As the first waves began to gather in her mind, she imagined Jack Heally's dark features as he had clung to her in the alcove. The memory of the satisfaction he had given her made her gasp.

Harry dragged her further onto him. Overwhelmed by the heady mixture of fear and pleasure, Jessica began to move with him, praying that if she cooperated it would soon be over.

Chapter 15

Christmas Eve

Jessica woke with a start and sat bolt upright in bed. The room was dark. She reached up to touch her face. As she struggled to get her bearings, memories of where she was and why she was there came flooding back. It seemed that sometime during the night Harry had taken off her blindfold and untied her wrists, although her shoulders and buttocks still ached from having been secured to the bed and horsewhipped. She stared into the darkness until her eyes could pick out details in the shadowy room.

Beside her, Harry lay on his side. In the gloom, his skin looked like ivory. She wondered whether she ought to go back to her own room - until she remembered that Harry had ripped her evening dress to shreds. As the thought formed in her mind, Harry rolled over and, reaching out towards her, caught hold of her wrist.

'Lie down,' he murmured sleepily, tightening his grip. She had very little choice and slid down beside him. He snuffled contentedly and guided her hand into his groin. His cock was as hard as iron and pulsed in her fingers.

Jack was woken by Felicia Gudgeon poking him in the ribs.

'Wake up,' she hissed. 'You're dreaming again.'

Jack blinked frantically and tried to work out where the hell he was. Felicia hadn't been with him in his dreams, surely it was Jessica who should be curled up alongside him. He peered at the woman's face, struggling to make out her features and then winced as she turned over and lit the lamp. At least he was in his own bedroom.

He stared at his diminutive blonde companion, the smallness of whose frame was accentuated by the contrast with his dark muscular body.

'What are you doing here?' he said thickly, rubbing his eyes.

Felicia pouted. 'Oh, that's charming, I must say. All night long you've had your hands all over me.' She grinned, stretching out against him so that her breasts brushed his chest. 'Now do you remember?'

Jack nodded. After the pantomime, he and George Gudgeon had retired to the confines of his office to crack a bottle of vintage brandy George had brought him as a gift.

As if Felicia was privy to his thoughts, Jack said, 'Where is George?'

Felicia rolled her eyes heavenwards. 'Sound asleep, I should think. I told him I was going to sleep in another room so that his incessant snoring wouldn't keep me awake. His problem is that he thinks he's still thirty and can drink all night along with the rest of the boys. I had your butler put him to bed.'

Jack licked his teeth. He remembered that George was very, very drunk, and more importantly, he remembered quite clearly that he hadn't been. He'd managed to resist the temptation to hit the bottle, even after Stolworthy had vanished upstairs with Jessica. Jessica - he felt a little ripple of something bittersweet; even her name had an effect on him.

Felicia looked up at him with world-weary eyes.

'You know you talk about her in your sleep, don't you?'

Jack stared at her, wondering if perhaps she could read his mind.

'Who?' he said defensively.

She laughed. 'Don't by so coy, Jack. Jessica Harper, who else? It's not very flattering when someone's got their fingers in your pussy to be called by another woman's name, you know.' She grinned. 'Not that I minded too much, after all, I got what she should have had.' She settled back amongst the tangle of sheets and pillows, lifting a finger to circle her ripe pink nipples. 'And I'm here now. Perhaps you'd like to show me again what you have got planned for her?'

Jack grimaced and then rolled closer to plant a kiss on one tight little nipple.

'If you insist,' he said, well aware of the throbbing angry erection he'd woken up with.

Felicia stretched like a well loved cat.

'What I don't understand, darling, is why, if you're so obsessed with this girl, you haven't leapt on your white charger and rescued her from the clutches of the dreadful Harry Stolworthy? It seems such a simple solution, or am I missing something? Why don't you just whisk her away from him?'

As she spoke, her hand slipped down the bed and settled on his shaft. She knew exactly what he needed and tightening her grip, began to move her fingers up and down with firm strokes, filling his mind with an ancient sense of contentment. If he wanted to continue the conversation he would have to make his point fairly swiftly, before need overcame reason.

He caught hold of her wrist, slowing the rhythm. 'There's no point in rescuing someone who doesn't want rescuing.'

Felicia snorted. 'How ridiculous you men are. It's perfectly all right to rescue someone who doesn't know they need rescuing - that's different. Besides, I'm sure Jessica would be very flattered, I know I would be.' She looked up at him. 'What interests me is what you intend to do with Jessica once you have extricated her from Harry's clutches. Set her free? Send her back to her little teaching job?'

Jack reddened. 'Something like that.'

Felicia tightened her grip on his cock and slipped her other hand lower to cradle his balls.

'In that case,' she said, wriggling down the bed, 'you're a bigger fool than I thought you were. Now just shut up and fuck me. You've been driving me crazy all night long. I was very tempted to take matters into my own hands and still will unless you stop mooning around like a lovesick calf.'

Jack smiled, sliding down beside her. 'What would you like?' he whispered.

Felicia giggled and lifted a leg up over his hips. 'How does everything sound?'

'Greedy,' said Jack, drawing a single finger over the wet, hot lips of her quim.

Felicia's eyes darkened mischievously. 'Oh, that's me,' she said, and pulled him closer.

Jessica had assumed, with the pantomime over, that the atmosphere in Malestone would be less tense and excited - in fact the reverse was true. When she and Harry arrived downstairs for breakfast, everyone was talking about what they intended to wear for the fancy dress party. Jessica was relieved to see that Jack's chair at the head of the table was empty.

Alice looked up as they took their places at the table. 'Good morning,' she said to Jessica, pointedly ignoring Harry. 'If you don't mind, I really could do with your help this morning to organise all these damned costumes. Everyone wants to raid the theatrical wardrobe.'

Jessica was about to agree when Harry butted, in.

'How long will it take? Jessica and I had planned to go into town today.'

This was news to Jessica, who looked first at one and then the other. She sensed that Harry was staking a claim on her time - declaring his ownership of her. Alice Fallon's expression hardened.

'I'm not sure,' she said slowly. 'I imagine we'll be done by lunchtime.'

Harry nodded. 'That will be fine. Jessica and I planned to have lunch in King's Lynn and do some last minute shopping. So, shall we say she'll be finished by twelve?'

Alice nodded. The uneasy silence between the three of them was shattered by the arrival of the Haywood twins and Bunty Redknap, who were all wearing long woollen scarves and outdoor boots. The twins had glowing, wind blown faces and were grinning madly.

Jessica couldn't help but notice the way Harry turned instantly to follow the sound of their voices. The twins looked almost boyish with their pink cheeks and wind-tussled hair.

'We've been out for a walk to work up an appetite,' one of the twins announced happily. 'Gosh, it's so cold out there.'

'Almost cold enough for snow,' added the second twin. 'The sky's very overcast, maybe we'll have a white Christmas. Oh, and we saw some deer in the park.'

Beside them, Bunty, evidently not so enamoured of the great outdoors, grimaced.

'Too bloody cold for me. I'm planning a long lazy day curled up in front of a fire somewhere.'

Their comments fuelled a series of conversations about plans for the day. Costumes were the first priority, followed by various ideas about walking, riding, playing cards and billiards.

Jessica sat back, aware that Harry was watching her intently. Alice turned her attention to Bunty, who was still breathless from his walk.

'I didn't know you had planned to go into town?' said Jessica quietly to Harry.

He smiled. 'I thought I'd surprise you.' He moved closer, brushing her ear with his lips. 'I wanted to get you a present,' he purred. 'After all, tomorrow is Christmas Day.'

Jessica nodded, wondering what he had in mind. He slid his hand down over her thigh. 'Have you got any underwear on?'

Jessica blushed. 'Yes, of course,' she whispered uncomfortably.

Harry grinned salaciously. 'What a great shame,' he murmured. 'I quite like the idea that you haven't got any on. Perhaps you could take them off when we go out to lunch?'

His fingers brushed the mound of her sex.

'Just a thought,' he said.

The morning passed quickly. By half-past eleven nearly every rail, previously laden down with costumes and props, was empty. Alice groaned and looked at the notebook she had filled in to help her keep track of who had taken what.

As the final house guest left with a costume, Jessica glanced up at the clock above the fireplace.

'He said twelve,' Alice said with a sharp edge to her voice.

Jessica nodded. 'I know.' She paused. 'Please don't let this thing with Harry spoil what we have.'

Alice grimaced. 'You're asking rather a lot.'

Anxious to change the subject, Jessica ran a finger along the remaining clothes. 'What are you going to wear tonight?'

'I've squirreled Cinderella's ball gown away for myself. What about you?'

Jessica pulled a face. Her answer would bring them back to Harry. She shook her head. 'I'm not sure.'

Alice sighed. 'You should have said something. We could have sorted something nice out for you before the rest of the mob got their hands on the clothes.' She stared at the rather bedraggled selection that was left. 'I think there's most of the pirate suit there or—' she looked up at Jessica, who found herself glancing back at the clock.

'Aren't you at least going to look?'

Jessica reddened. 'I think Harry has already sorted something out for me.'

'Oh, I should have guessed. Several of the costumes went walkies before last night's pantomime. What did he get you?'

Jessica found it impossible to answer. She had barely looked at the pile of gauze on the chair in Harry's room, but she did remember what he'd said - harem girl and master. She couldn't bring herself to tell Alice, feeling that it would confirm her friend's suspicions about Harry.

She was saved from replying by the arrival of Jack, who stood in the doorway with his costume over his arm. As their eyes met, Jessica felt a *frisson* of excitement that startled her. Her whole body seemed to tremble as he walked towards her.

'Hello, I didn't realise you were in here,' he said in a low even voice, eyes never leaving hers. 'I'm sorry I missed you at breakfast.' He took a step closer so that they were barely an arm's length apart.

Jessica held her breath, wondering what he was going to do or say. Her pulse quickened, hammering out a frantic rhythm in her ears.

'Morning, Jack,' said Alice. Jack jumped and then spun round, as if he was surprised to see her there.

Alice Fallon shook her head. 'This is quite beyond belief,' she sighed, as if neither of them could hear her. She nodded at the jacket over his arm and said briskly, 'What seems to be the trouble with your costume?'

Jack appeared to struggle to remember why he was there. 'Buttons,' he said after a few seconds. 'I tried the jacket on and found there were a couple missing.' He looked again at Jessica and, to her complete surprise, blushed.

Alice, meanwhile, had taken the coat away from him. Jack turned and caught hold of Jessica's hands.

'You and I need to talk,' he whispered.

Jessica felt a flush of heat. 'We tried that yesterday and look where it got us,' she said, aware Alice was listening to every word.

Jack groaned. 'You are driving me mad,' he hissed. 'I can't stop thinking about you. I even dream about you, for God's sake. I can't let you—' He froze as Harry Stolworthy stepped into the drawing room.

Harry looked first at Jessica and then Jack, his face impassive.

'Good morning,' he said evenly. He nodded towards Jessica. 'I presume you've finished work, my dear. I think you ought to go and get your coat. Our cab will be here any minute.'

Jessica had never felt so uncomfortable in her life. Disentangling her hands from Jack's, she hurried past Harry and out into the hall, her face scarlet with embarrassment. When she looked round, Harry was still framed in the doorway, Jack still standing by the rail of costumes, as if they had both been frozen to the spot. She ran upstairs to get her coat, her mind reeling with confusion.

Jack had only to look at her and she felt a flare of need and tenderness and passion that was all consuming. She could still feel the light touch of his fingers on hers and see the look of desire in his eyes.

As she closed the door of her bedroom, tears unexpectedly welled up behind her eyes. She struggled to swallow them down and put on her coat.

The little railway station, where Jessica had arrived a few days earlier, was quite busy when she and Harry Stolworthy arrived to catch their train. The platform was bustling with travellers making their way home for the Christmas holidays. Above them, the sky was overcast and ominous, promising the snow that the Haywood twins had predicted.

Jessica and Harry had travelled in uncomfortable silence from Malestone House. Once Harry had bought their tickets, he rounded on her, eyes cold as the winter wind that roared along the platform. He slipped his arm through hers and guided her towards the waiting train. For a moment, she caught sight of their reflections in the dusty windows and realised that they made a handsome couple. Harry, tall with his angular face and mop of blond hair; she, smaller with tiny features and a dark bob, wrapped up against the cold in her new winter coat. Their appearance was at odds with the relationship that bound them together.

'Have you got a crush on Jack Heally?' he said, opening the door to an empty first class carriage. Jessica's stomach was tied up into a tight unhappy knot. The image of the perfect couple vanished from mind as he helped her inside.

'It's not like that,' she said in a small voice. 'I tried to tell you I needed time to think about marrying you. You seem to be in such a rush. I think—'

Harry's expression dried the rest of the words in her throat.

'Just yes or no will be sufficient,' he said, tugging off his gloves. 'I saw the look in Jack's eyes.' He glanced up at her, a hint of a smile on his lips. 'But don't worry, I'm not angry, in fact quite the reverse. I find it extremely flattering that other men are attracted to my fiancée.' He indicated that she should sit and then took the seat opposite her. 'Of course, I would prefer it if they looked but didn't touch.' He leaned forward and slid a hand up under her coat. His fingers grazed the inside of her thighs. 'Unless, of course, I tell them to,' he purred.

Jessica shivered.

'And I'm rather disappointed that you didn't take my suggestion to heart,' he said, sitting back into his seat.

'What suggestion?' Jessica said. She glanced out of the window. The station master was prowling along the platform, with a whistle in his mouth and a flag in his other hand. A few more seconds and the train would be leaving.

Harry aped disappointment. 'Oh come, come now, Jessica. You really ought to remember. I told you at breakfast that I would much prefer it if you didn't wear any underwear.'

Jessica stared at him. 'I beg your pardon?'

Harry smiled. 'So, if you just stand up now, we can rectify the situation. Can't we?'

'Are you serious?'

Harry nodded. 'Oh, absolutely. Stand up.'

His eyes were glittering and she felt an erotic charge arc between them. Despite her attraction to Jack she couldn't deny the desire she felt for Harry. It disturbed her that she could feel this way about a man who was so obviously amoral. His dominance added an extra dimension that she was almost afraid to admit excited her.

'Well?' he said softly, 'what are you waiting for?'

Slowly, almost as if she was on the edge of a dream, she stood up. The train sighed and began to move. Her hands gathered up the hem of her coat and she slid her cold fingers up over her legs, eyes firmly fixed on Harry. His face was alight with expectation.

'Let me see,' he murmured. She hoisted the skirt higher, so that her legs and thighs were exposed. He grinned. 'Very good, now take them off.'

She swallowed hard and slipped her knickers down, aware of his eyes on her as real and tangible as his fingers. As the thin fabric slithered down to her knees, he smiled and stooped down to help her slip them over her feet. She let go of her coat, feeling her face reddening as Harry rolled her panties into a ball and stuffed them in his pocket.

It was just in time - a split second later the ticket collector appeared in the corridor and slid the carriage door open. Jessica, still standing up, hastily took her seat. Behind the ticket collector was a distinguished looking man with greying hair, carrying a large suitcase.

The ticket collector smiled and touched his cap.

'Excuse me sir, madam. Would you mind if this gentleman joined you? The other first class carriages are full.'

Harry got to his feet. 'Not at all. We'd be delighted, wouldn't we, darling?'

Jessica, still blushing furiously, nodded.

The man stowed his bag in the overhead luggage rack and then turned to press a few coins into the ticket collector's hands.

'How long will it take us to get to King's Lynn?' he said pleasantly, as the uniformed man slipped the coins into his waistcoat pocket.

The ticket collector pulled a face. 'Usually it takes about half an hour, but we may be a bit longer today. There's been a bit of a problem on the line out at Basingham. Shouldn't take more than an hour, though.' He nodded along the corridor. 'We've got a buffet car if you'd like a pot of tea or something. Would you like me to call the steward for you, sir?'

Before the man could reply, Harry said, 'No need, my fiancée has already said she's going to go and have a cuppa. I'm sure she wouldn't mind ordering for you at the same time, would you, my dear?'

Jessica stared at him. It was all complete lies, she had said nothing of the sort. Harry smiled.

'Would you, my dear?' he repeated more firmly.

Jessica shook her head. 'No, not at all.'

The elderly man smiled. 'How very kind. Actually, I'm fine, thank you. I'm just delighted to get a seat.'

Harry waved Jessica to her feet. 'Why don't you let the ticket collector direct you to the buffet?' he said. Dumbly she stood up, completely mystified by his behaviour. Picking up her bag, she caught his eye, trying to guess at an explanation.

'But do hurry back,' he said lightly. 'You know how I miss you.'

Jessica had no trouble getting a seat in the buffet car and ordered a pot of tea. Watching the bleak Norfolk landscape roll by the windows, she wondered what she ought to do. Harry had shown her things that she could barely have imagined, and Jack... Feeling the tears threaten, she stared down into her teacup. Jack Heally had offered something else. If she wasn't very careful she could easily fall in love with a man like Jack. The trouble was men like Jack didn't fall in love with girls like her.

She found her thoughts dwelling on the way he had made her feel, his skin, his fingertips against hers, the pressure of his cock deep inside her. To her surprise, the fantasy took hold; she felt her excitement growing and struggled to drag her attention back to the view from the window. After a few more minutes she drained her teacup. She ought to be getting back to Harry.

When she arrived it was quite obvious that something was going on. Harry was grinning and their travelling companion looked up expectantly when she stepped into their carriage. She had barely had a chance to close the door before Harry leapt to his feet and pulled the blinds down.

Jessica stared at him in astonishment. 'What's going on?' she hissed.

Harry nodded towards the man. 'Lift up your skirt, my dear,' he said. 'I've told our friend here that you aren't wearing any underwear.'

Jessica blushed. The man's eyes travelled over her body as if he could almost already see what lay beneath. She shivered.

'Are you serious?' she said in a tiny voice.

Harry nodded. 'Oh yes, my dear. You ought to be flattered. I told you that I really don't mind other men finding you attractive, as long as I can choose who gets to benefit. Now, lift your skirt, there's a good girl, let him see just how beautiful you are. Who will ever know?' As he spoke he moved closer and pressed his lips to her neck. His kiss was like molten gold.

Jessica was shocked and, at the same time, excited by his suggestion. The idea of exposing herself to a total stranger was astonishing but she didn't resist as Harry's hands slid down over her coat and began to hoist the hem higher.

In his seat, the elderly man licked his lips as if he was being presented with a banquet. Higher and higher Harry lifted her coat. She could feel the air in the carriage against her naked flesh like the breath of an eager lover.

Finally, the material brushed against the top of her thighs and the man let out an appreciative moan. Slowly, he extended a hand, as if he could hardly believe his eyes, and stroked tentatively at the dark folds of her sex.

Jessica shivered. His fingers were cold and dry, as if he were exploring an artefact from an alien culture. As his fingers parted the lips and found the warmth within he closed his eyes for a second and sighed.

'Would you like to see more?' Harry said.

The man nodded. 'Oh yes,' he murmured.

Harry grabbed Jessica's coat up in one hand and began to struggle with her buttons. His touch was rough and perfunctory.

'Help me,' he hissed in her ear.

She stiffened and then took hold of her coat, while the old man continued to stroke her.

Harry undid her coat from top to bottom and then set about her blouse. All the time the old man's eyes followed Harry's hands. Triumphantly, Harry opened her blouse to reveal her camisole top. She already knew her nipples had hardened and glancing down saw them jutting forward through the thin fabric. Harry slipped his finger under the waistband of her skirt and pulled the camisole out, rolling it up so that the old man could see what lay beneath.

'Oh, my goodness,' the man hissed, 'how very beautiful. Would you mind if I touched them?'

Harry grinned. 'Help yourself. I'll add it to your bill.' Jessica closed her eyes as their companion stood up and began to stroke her pert nipples. She felt the brush of his hair and then shivered as he drew a single nipple deep into his mouth. His tongue began to lap at her while below his fingers finally slid deep inside her quim. She heard him grunt with satisfaction and then slowly he sank to his knees. She felt his breath on her belly and then gasped as his tongue joined his fingers.

His lips felt as cool and dry as his fingertips. His tongue darted back and forth in and out of the wet confines of her body. She could barely believe what was happening. When he found her clitoris she let out a long, slow, shuddering moan and leaned back against Harry. She could sense Harry's growing excitement. She felt his knee between hers, pushing her legs open, so that the old man could have greater access.

'Would you like to fuck her?' Harry whispered. 'You can feel how wet and tight she is. Wouldn't that be something to tell the other chaps at your club?'

The old man rested back on his heels. His lips were wet from Jessica's juices and his expression beatific. He shook his head.

'No, thank you, terribly kind of you to offer, but I prefer this. My wife never lets me do it, you see, and I do so love the way warm pussy tastes.'

Jessica blushed. He had refused Harry's offer with the same good grace with which he probably declined a second cup of tea or a slice of cake. His tongue began to work lovingly again at the folds of her quim, his cool fingers following close behind.

In spite of herself, Jessica began to feel her excitement growing. The man's touch was so delicate and knowing. Her pleasure began to build, rippling out in a spiral, as his tongue worked on and on. She struggled to catch her breath.

Behind her, Harry cupped her breasts and began to tug and twist her nipples. It was too much - Jessica felt the dam of passion burst, and ground her sex onto the old man's tongue, thrusting her hips out to accept his searching fingers.

Flares began to explode inside her head and she shrieked out as madness and pleasure overtook her. Gasping, she tore herself away, dragging her skirt and coat down over her throbbing sex. Turning away, she bent over the seat, supporting herself on her arms as she tried to catch her breath.

The old man, still kneeling on the floor, pulled out a handkerchief to wipe his face, and then just shuffled back into his seat. He looked up at Harry expectantly.

'Would you mind getting my suitcase down off the rack?' he said conversationally. 'I think I shall go to the buffet car and have a pot of tea after all. It must be at least another quarter of an hour before we get to King's Lynn.'

Harry nodded and did as he was asked. Jessica sat down, unable to meet the old man's eyes.

Their companion got to his feet and, opening his coat, pulled out his wallet.

'Here we are; five pounds, wasn't it?'

Harry smiled and extended a hand. 'Merry Christmas,' he purred.

'Oh,' continued the old man, 'and here's my card. Perhaps next time you're in Norwich, you might like to look me up? I know a rather charming whore who lives down by the railway station. She's an attractive little thing, nice and clean. Perhaps you'd like to bring along your young lady and we could introduce them. I'd rather like to see the two of them together.'

Harry tucked the bank note and the old man's card away in his pocket.

'Absolutely. We'd be delighted to accept your offer, wouldn't we, my dear?'

Jessica couldn't bring herself to answer. The sense of excitement and release was rapidly being replaced by disgust. She turned her attention to the blinds, imagining the view outside. She didn't look up until she heard the old man say his farewells and open the carriage door. As soon as she was certain he had gone, she spun round to stare at Harry.

'You sold me off to him like a cheap whore,' she snapped furiously.

Harry grinned. 'Not so cheap, my dear. Are you going to tell me you didn't enjoy it? You had the chance to say no, but you didn't, which rather suggests you quite liked the idea.' He moved closer and kissed her on the end of the nose. 'And you were quite magnificent.'

Jessica felt her colour rising - it had excited her. What worried her was where all this might lead. She bit her lip and looked away.

Before she could voice her fears, someone knocked at the carriage door. For one awful minute Jessica wondered if the old man had changed his mind and come back for more.

Harry was already on his feet and opened the door a fraction. The ticket collector glanced inside. 'Sorry to disturb you, sir, but I saw the blinds closed. I wondered if everything was all right in here?'

Harry smiled and glanced at Jessica. 'Everything is just fine, thank you. My fiancée felt a little faint.'

The uniformed man looked at her with concern. 'Would you like me to get you a glass of water, miss?'

Jessica shook her head. 'No, I'm fine now, really.'

As Harry guided the man back out into the corridor, Jessica wondered if that was true.

Chapter 16

Jessica's Christmas Present

Jessica and Harry had a late lunch in a little restaurant off King's Street. Jessica, her mind still full of the encounter on the train, could barely bring herself to speak as they ate. Fortunately, the restaurant was quite busy and Harry seemed keen to make light conversation.

Laughing and making jokes as he demolished a plate of roast beef, it seemed inconceivable that he could be the same man who had sold her favours to a stranger. When they'd eaten, Harry set about searching out Christmas presents and Jessica followed.

Harry's good humour continued as they explored the shops. It was odd - he was perfect company, leading her cheerfully between the throngs of people. This part of his nature was so different and so gentle, that she began to relax and genuinely enjoy being with him - if only he could be like this more often.

By late afternoon they were laden down with parcels. Every shop seemed to be crowded with people making last minute purchases though outside the heat and bustle of the shops, the winter wind was razor sharp and bitterly cold.

Harry led her into another busy street.

'One more shop, and then,' he said, pulling out his pocket watch, 'we really ought to make our way back to the station.' He slipped his arm through hers and pulled her close. 'It's been a lovely day, hasn't it?'

She smiled; except for the incident on the train she would have to agree with him.

'In here,' said Harry, pointing out a jeweller's shop. 'I've left your present until last.'

Jessica looked up into his eyes. The breeze had brought the colour to his cheeks and ruffled his blonde hair. He looked stunningly handsome, all wrapped up in his long winter coat. Arm in arm, they looked like any other respectable young couple. Harry stepped to one side and opened the door for her.

Inside the shop, an amiable, plump man stepped out from behind the counter.

'Good afternoon and the season's greetings to you both. Rather nippy out today.' He smiled at Harry. 'How may I help you, sir?'

Harry smiled in return. 'Good afternoon. I was rather hoping that we might take a look at some engagement rings.'

Jessica smiled. 'Harry, I don't think...'

He took her hand and pressed it to his lips, silencing her. His eyes met hers in silent appeal, while the man began to pullout trays of rings from under the counter.

'May I be among the first to offer you both my congratulations? What had you got in mind? A solitaire? Or perhaps a cluster? We have a very wide selection. Perhaps something in the window caught your eye?'

Jessica glanced down at the padded trays of rings with a bubbling sense of panic.

'What about this?' said Harry, pointing out an ostentatious bauble with a sapphire the size of a quail's egg. She saw the jeweller's eyes light up with avarice. It seemed that Harry had gone up a level in the man's estimation.

'A very nice ring, sir. The stones are quite exceptional. Would your fiancée care to try it for size?'

Jessica sighed, slipped off her gloves, and allowed the man to fit the ring on. It dwarfed her tiny fingers.

'Perhaps a little large for your hand, miss,' the jeweller said regretfully.

Harry pointed out another and another until the whole of the top of the counter was covered in ring pads. Jessica's mind was reeling. The price tags on some of the rings were more than she earned in a year. Harry did not seem in the least bit concerned.

Finally, Harry and the jeweller settled on a broad gold band with three large diamonds. Harry slipped it on to her ring finger and then held her hand up to admire the effect. Both he and the jeweller smiled.

'What do you think, darling? Rather splendid, isn't it?'

Jessica stared down at the ring and felt dizzy.

'It's awfully nice,' she began. 'But it's terribly expensive.'

Harry laughed. 'Oh, my dear, you really don't have to worry about things like that. I think it's perfect, though it is a little too large at the moment.' He looked up at the jeweller expectantly. 'I assume it can be made smaller.'

The man nodded and then added apologetically, 'Of course, sir, but I'm afraid it won't be until after Christmas. My workshop is rather behind at the moment, people off with colds and flu, you know how it is—'

Harry held up his hand. 'Please, don't worry in the slightest. My fiancée keeps chastising me for being in such a rush.' He held Jessica's fingers to his lips and kissed them gently. 'And I do understand, really I do.' His eyes met hers and he smiled. 'We'll call back some time next week and collect it.' As he spoke he slipped his hand into his pocket. 'Here's my card. Do you require a deposit?'

The jeweller looked down at the heavy, embossed card and then briefly at the two of them, then smiled and shook his head.

'No, no, not at all. I wouldn't dream of it, sir. I'll make sure the ring is ready for you by the middle of next week at the very latest.'

Jessica had an odd feeling and was about to speak, when Harry slipped his arm back through hers and said cheerfully, 'Thank you so much for your time. And a very merry Christmas to you and your staff. We really do have to be off, I'm afraid. We have a train to catch. Until next week.'

Outside, in the street, as they started to make their way to the station, Jessica turned to Harry.

'You gave him the wrong card,' she said.

He stared at her, a hint of mischief in his eyes. 'Pardon?'

Jessica took a deep breath. 'The card you just gave the jeweller, I'm sure it was the one the man gave you on the train.'

Harry looked puzzled, but didn't protest. 'Really? Are you certain?'

Jessica nodded. She knew it hadn't been Harry's name on the card.

He smiled and pulled her closer.

'It doesn't really matter, does it? It was a simple mistake. The chap knows who we are, I'm sure he'll recognise us again and we haven't really got the time to go back and sort it out now. We'll miss our train if we go back. The next one doesn't leave until nearly seven, and I don't know about you but I'm frozen through to the core.'

Jessica fell into step, slightly perturbed by Harry's explanation.

When Jack Heally went into the ballroom at Malestone, all traces of the stage had been cleared away, and the elegant room was a hive of activity. Alice Fallon was on a step ladder hanging Chinese lanterns from lengths of ribbon. Over by the windows, Felicia Gudgeon and Miranda were putting the finishing touches to the swags of holly that now lined the panelled walls, while other house guests and theatricals were busy moving chairs and tables.

Alice grinned down at him.

'Remind me, next time you invite me to spend Christmas, that it involves an awful lot of work and very little play.'

Jack pulled a wry face.

He extended his hand to help her as she climbed down the ladder and picked up another Chinese lantern from a box on a small table beside her.

'Costume all right now?' she said.

Jack nodded and then looked around the room again. 'I just came to see if Jessica was back from King's Lynn yet.'

Alice sighed and handed him the box of lanterns.

'Here, hold these, will you? No, she's not back. I expect they're catching the teatime train.' Alice paused, picking out another scarlet concertina of paper. 'I've been thinking, Jack. Perhaps this is a lost cause, after all, darling. I haven't heard a word from Charlie in London, and if there was any dirt to dish on Harry Stolworthy, trust me, that boy would have found it. He's got a real nose for gossip. And as we've both said, Jessica is an adult. Much as I'm loathe to admit it, it might be better for everyone if we backed off and left them to it. It really isn't any of our business.'

Jack felt the return of the unpleasant gripping sensation in his gut.

'No,' he said coolly, holding her gaze. 'And I know you don't really believe that either.'

Jack had seen the look of longing in Jessica's eyes when he had touched her earlier, in the drawing room. He had felt the desire arc between them. His mind was full of the memories of her hot eager body and the way she had moved against him when they had been in the alcove together. He couldn't believe that he meant nothing to her - or that she would be better off married to the bastard Stolworthy.

Alice leaned closer and rubbed herself against him like a sleek cat, seeking affection.

'Actually, I've nearly finished in here. It's absolutely ages until the party begins.' She smiled, her voice dropping to a teasing purr. 'There's nothing worse than waiting alone.'

Felicia, who had been watching them, shimmied over, grinning from ear to ear.

'Alice is right, you know.' She plucked the box of lanterns out of Jack's hands. 'They do say all work and no play makes Jack a dull boy. I think we've all had quite enough work for one day.' She pouted and, leaning forward, brushed her lips across his. 'Besides, who needs all the pain of unrequited love when you've got friends like us?'

Her hand, like a little white bird, fluttered down to cup his crotch. He instantly felt his cock stir into life, his mind already excited by the memories of making love to Jessica.

Felicia smiled and licked her lips.

'My, my, Jack Heally. We are keen, aren't we?'

Alice, meanwhile, slid a hand between the buttons of his shirt and playfully tweaked the hairs on his chest.

'Don't be so greedy,' she said to Felicia, her tone still light-hearted. 'I did proposition him first. Besides, you have him at your beck and call all year.'

Jack shook his head and grinned good-naturedly. His thoughts of Jessica were temporarily put to one side as Felicia's fingers tightened around his cock.

'No need to fight over me, ladies,' he said. 'There's plenty for everyone.'

Felicia giggled. 'That's what I was hoping you'd say. Where shall we go?'

Jack shrugged.

Alice glanced over her shoulder, towards the door of the little room the actors had used the previous night to get ready.

'Why don't we use the changing room? I've just put all the curtains in there.' She gave them both a sly look. 'At least we'll have something comfortable to lie on.'

Jack nodded, wondering at how some relationships, uncluttered by anything more complicated than mutual desire and simple friendship, could be so easy, while love, if that was what he felt for Jessica, was so torturous. The thought formed and made him freeze. Was he in love with Jessica Harper? Was that what this dark, unsettling pain was that formed every time he thought about her?

The idea was whisked away by Felicia, who began to undo the buttons of her white silk blouse. For an instant, he caught a glimpse of her pert breasts beneath and shivered. Oblivious to the other people in the ballroom, she slipped the collar down to reveal her delicate shoulders. She lowered her eyelids and peered up at him from under her long lashes.

'Well,' she purred, 'what are you waiting for? An engraved invitation?'

With a beautiful woman on each arm, he made his way to the back of the hall, and didn't resist as they led him into the little anteroom. They giggled conspiratorially as the door closed. Alice, standing in the centre of the room, pulled her cream woollen dress up over her head. Beneath she was wearing a pair of white silk camiknickers, cream stockings held up with garters and a pair of high, t-bar shoes.

Felicia eyed her appreciatively. 'How very forward you are,' she whispered and then set about pulling off her own blouse and skirt. Jack watched them with a mixture of growing desire and amusement. Like card sharps raising the stakes, they were trying to outdo each other. He wondered for a minute if he might prove to be surplus to requirements as the women eyed each other expectantly. Almost as if they heard the thought forming, they both turned towards him, eyes flashing with desire.

'Well,' murmured Alice, 'what have you got in mind?'

Jack smiled. 'It seems to me that you're doing all right working on your own initiative.'

Felicia grimaced and then rounded on Alice, taking her into her arms and kissing her fiercely. Jack felt his pulse quicken. He had always been excited by the fantasy and the reality of two women making love. He adored the way their delicate curves looked as they embraced each other. Alice moaned and kissed Felicia with equal fervour. Alice's fingers worked their way over Felicia's torso, stroking the stiff peaks of the other woman's breasts.

Jack knew each of the women's bodies well, but had never imagined they would ever make love together. Felicia moaned and closing her eyes, began to trace the line of Alice's spine, fingers lingering over each tiny bony prominence, her lips working hungrily at Alice's mouth.

Jack didn't know whether to join them, or just stand back and enjoy the spectacle. Felicia's hands snaked lower to find the fastenings of the camiknickers between Alice's legs.

Alice, getting more excited with every passing second, came to her assistance and between them they slipped the whisper of sheer fabric up over her head. Felicia, eyes dark, pupils dilated, ran her hands lovingly over Alice's naked body, sighing with delight.

Jack's mouth began to water as he imagined the way Alice's body felt. Felicia guided her back onto one of the bundles of curtains and then stood back to admire her prize.

'God, you look stunning,' she whispered. Alice, smiling lazily, held out her arms to Felicia.

'You too,' she murmured as they sank down onto the pile of dusty cloth. Jack watched Alice's fingers tracing a path down to Felicia's sex, which was still covered by a scrap of black silk, and decided the time had come to join the ladies, before they got too engrossed.

He ran his hands over Felicia's hips. Catching hold of her knickers he pulled them down, revealing her plump backside. She giggled and wriggled back against him, offering herself up for his pleasure. He slipped a hand between her thighs and met Alice's eager finger seeking out Felicia's clitoris. He smiled and left her to it, his own fingers exploring the sopping depth of her quim.

Beneath him, he heard Felicia moan in appreciation and then very slowly she began to ease back towards him. Alice's hand slipped away so he was left fingering Felicia. Felicia wriggled down amongst the curtains until her face was level with Alice's wet open pussy and without hesitation she buried her tongue deep inside it.

Alice let out a little shriek of delight and thrust her hips upwards. Jack could feel the heat of Felicia's body and sense her growing excitement as she got wetter and wetter. With one hand he undid his flies and guided his aching cock between the cheeks of her backside, nuzzling at the slick outer lips, begging entry.

Felicia glanced over her shoulder for a second. Her lips, glistening with Alice's fragrant juices, were drawn back in a contented smile.

'Oh yes, please,' she moaned, on the edge of a long throaty gasp.

Jack grinned at her and gently slid his cock home. Her body opened eagerly for him, and then, as he pushed deeper, closed like a tight fist around his shaft. The sensation made him gasp. The heat and the wetness never ceased to excite him and he began to move, matching his strokes to Felicia's compelling tongue as it worked its magic on Alice. As the threesome hit their rhythm, he grabbed hold of Felicia's hips, letting the tempo take him.

Sliding one hand lower, he sought out Felicia's pleasure bud and then smiled as he found that her fingers had already discovered it. She pushed back against him and moved her fingers so they stroked along his slick shaft.

Below them, Alice, her eyes tightly closed, was straining upwards onto Felicia's tongue. Her breasts were flushed and she had thrown back her head. As Felicia's lips brought her closer and closer to the point of release, she writhed from side to side. The look of sheer ecstasy on her face was enough to drive Jack wild.

He snorted and jerked Felicia hard back onto him. Felicia, sensing the end was in sight, let out a mewl of delight and he felt her fingers quicken on her clitoris, the heady vibrations echoing through his shaft.

The moment of release seemed to reverberate between them all, bouncing off one and then another, every convulsive shudder, every gasping thrust, repeated and renewed by the three lovers. Finally, as the last aftershocks faded, Jack rolled out of Felicia and slumped, sweating, between the two women on the curtains.

Felicia was the first to recover and curled up beside him. Her pert breasts brushing his chest set off an almost painful series of contractions in his exhausted cock. Alice moaned and curled into the crook of his arm, eyelids heavy. She sniffed and then peered at him.

'I don't suppose you thought to lock the door, did you?' she said, pulling one of the curtains over her warm body.

Jack shook his head.

Alice groaned. 'Shame, I was rather hoping we could just curl up and go to sleep for a little while.'

Jack stroked a stray tendril of hair away from her face and pressed his lips to her forehead. 'If you stay where you are, I'll lock it.'

Sliding out from between them, he crossed the room and turned the key in the lock. Glancing back, he found it hard to suppress a smile - the two beautiful young women were curled up, facing each other. Their pale skin was a stark contrast to the blood-red brocade of the stage curtains. Snuggled together, eyes closed, they looked like some wonderful, erotic version of babes in the wood. He hurried back across the room and slipped into the warm space they had left for him.

Jessica was pleased when the taxi-cab finally pulled into the long drive that led up to Malestone House. It had been a long day. The train journey back had been uneventful, though Jessica wondered if this had more to do with the fact that the train was packed with families, rather than any philanthropic decision of Harry's not to sell her services again.

As the car turned the final corner, Jessica saw the lights of Malestone picked out against the backdrop of trees and realised she would be pleased to see Alice, Bunty Redknap, even the twins - and Jack Heally. She glanced across at Harry who seemed preoccupied by the view.

Sensing she was watching him, he turned and smiled warmly.

'Rather a good day, all in all, wouldn't you say?' He took out his wallet and pulled out a five-pound note. 'Perhaps you'd like to pay the driver, my dear?' he said with a wink.

Jessica stared at him in astonishment, her anxieties returning as they got closer to the house. There was no doubt in her mind that the note he pressed into her hand was the one given to Harry by the man in the train. He leant closer and kissed her ear.

'Don't look so worried, everything is going to be fine. Just a day or two more and then we can go up to London for the rest of the holiday. There are several people there I'd really like you to meet.'

Jessica didn't know what to say.

Inside Malestone it was still and quiet. It appeared that everyone else had already gone upstairs to get ready for the fancy dress party.

The entrance hall was empty, though the lamps were lit and a log fire burned in the grate. The flames reflected in the glass baubles on the Christmas tree, added to the soft lighting and the warmth, and made the whole room seem inviting and homely.

Once the driver had unpacked the shopping, Harry stretched and slipped off his coat.

'Such a beautiful house,' he murmured, glancing round the elegantly panelled walls. The whole house discreetly whispered wealth.

Jessica nodded. 'It is, isn't it? What's your house like?'

'In need of some repair,' he said dismissively. 'Damned place burns money.' He stopped and painted on an attentive smile. 'Of course, you can help me put that right once we're married, but it does need some pretty extensive restoration work.' He pulled her closer, his tone becoming more intense. 'It needs the feminine touch to get it round, so we can entertain. You will make the most superb hostess.'

Jessica wondered why it was that almost everything Harry said filled her with a peculiar sense of sexual expectation. He pressed his lips to hers, sliding a hand up under her skirt to stroke the naked contours of her sex.

'And I don't want you to ever wear underwear again,' he whispered. 'I love the idea that you're naked and that all I have to do is reach out and touch you.' As he spoke his fingers divided the lips of her quim, seeking entry into the wetness that lay between. Jessica trembled.

Harry's fingers worked deeper still and he closed his eyes, as if all his concentration was centred on the prize he had found between her legs.

'And it offers such stunning possibilities,' he murmured thickly.

Jessica stiffened and thought about the old man on the train. The memory of his face, and the way he had knelt between her legs while Harry held her, sent another tremor through her stomach. She had no doubt that Harry's mind was working in the same direction. His idea of stunning possibilities, she guessed, included liaisons with total strangers.

She stared up at him, torn between surrendering to the delicate touch that stirred her desire and pulling away from him, clawing herself back from the brink.

His hand slipped out from under her skirt.

'What's the matter?' he said. 'You seem very tense.'

Jessica nodded.

'I'm worried that everything is happening so fast,' she said unsteadily.

Harry smiled. 'You shouldn't. You really should trust me more. I thought perhaps we might go and have a nap before the party begins. Why don't we go up to my room?' His hand slid back up over her thigh. 'You can lie on my bed and sleep while I watch over you. I've got some letters to write.' He paused. 'And then we can get ready for the party together.'

Jessica instantly had a vivid impression of her lying naked on Harry's bed, sound asleep, while he stared down at her. She could see his eyes moving over her nakedness, a soft hand sliding between her thighs, opening her up for his prying gaze. The image was both deeply disturbing and unnervingly erotic.

She shook her head quickly. 'I think I really ought to go to my own room.' She looked down at the shopping. 'I've got presents to wrap, and I'd like to have a bath—'

There was no real excuse for her not to go with him but she pressed on anyway. Harry held up his hands.

'All right, if you insist. I shall come and wake you around seven so that we can get ready.' He grinned. 'We can at least do that together. I want to see you put your costume on.'

Jessica nodded and, snatching up her parcels, hurried upstairs, suddenly desperate to be away from him.

Chapter 17

The Fancy Dress Party

At seven o'clock on Christmas Eve, Malestone House seemed to awaken like a castle being released from a magical enchantment. Downstairs, the footmen and maids quietly set about turning up the lamps and stoking the fires. In the dining room, the butler watched the buffet supper being arranged on the magnificent walnut dining table. Mince pies, roast turkey, pickles, a hog's head - dish after dish, laden with Christmas fare, was lovingly set amongst the candelabra and Christmas decorations. Champagne and wine was brought up from the cellars, ice buckets were filled and glasses polished.

Upstairs, guests and performers began to emerge from their bedrooms, eager to begin their toilette. The noise level steadily rose from a subdued hum to raucous shrieks and whoops, as everyone dressed in their costumes and the party atmosphere filtered through the house like smoke.

Jack Heally, who had repaired upstairs with Alice and Felicia, finally rolled out of bed, where the two women were still sleeping, and went to run himself a bath.

Felicia was the first to wake. She glanced at the bedside clock and pulled a face.

'Damn,' she said. 'I really must get back to George. He said he was going to take a nap. He'll wonder where on earth I've got to if I'm not there when he wakes up.'

She looked at Jack as she slithered off the bed and started to hunt for her clothes.

'Rather a good afternoon, though?'

Jack grinned. 'Absolutely, you were both magnificent. We must do it again sometime?'

Felicia grinned, dragging her skirt up over her hips.

'Did you honestly expect anything less?'

Their conversation woke Alice, who rubbed her eyes and stretched. She looked at them both sleepily and then pulled the bedclothes up around her shoulders.

'I know, I know,' she said, before either had time to speak. 'I really ought to get up and get dressed for the party, but this bed is so warm and so comfortable. Can't I tempt either of you to come back for a little while?'

Felicia, who had now managed to put her blouse on, bent over and kissed Alice gently on the top of the head.

'I really do have to go, darling, see you later.'

Alice groaned. 'I suppose I ought to go too.' She peered out from under the tumble of sheets. 'I don't suppose you'd consider letting me share your bath, would you, Jack? I'm certain, by the time I get back to my room, Bunty will have locked himself in the bathroom and be wallowing around in gallons of steaming hot water, leaving me to get washed in half a basin full of his lukewarm leftovers.'

Jack smiled and pushed open the bathroom door - a column of steam wafted out.

'Be my guest,' he said.

Alice grinned. Still wrapped in the sheets she clambered off the bed to join him.

'Wonderful,' she purred, bedclothes trailing out behind her like a train. 'I'll wash your back if you like.'

'I was rather banking on it,' he said, grabbing hold of the sheets and tugging them away from her. Alice shrieked with delight and pressed her warm body up against him. Her fingers went on a hunt for the knot to the belt of his robe. Jack caught hold of her wrists.

'Come on,' he said playfully, 'the water will be getting cold.'

'Well,' whispered Harry Stolworthy, as he and Jessica stood in front of the full length mirror on his wardrobe. 'What do you think of your costume?'

Jessica stared at her reflection, unable to find any words to describe how she felt. The outfit Harry had chosen for her was a soft, blue gauze harem suit, consisting of a long-sleeved wrap-over blouse, which tied under her bust, and ankle-length trousers, which were gathered at the bottom.

Beneath, she wore a tiny spangled top which was strapless, boned and barely covered her breasts, together with a pair of tight sequinned pants that were cut like a thong, just covering her sex and then lying in the crease between her buttocks. The outfit was completed by a thin veil and sequin-strewn mask, which she had yet to put on, which would render her completely anonymous.

Harry smiled as he stared at her.

'Turn round, let me look at you again,' he said softly. She turned to face him. He was dressed as a sultan, complete with a jewelled turban, a highly embroidered waistcoat over his broad bare chest and trousers like her own, made from heavy, claret-coloured brocade.

In his hand was a small riding crop. Seeing it made Jessica flinch. She wondered if the marks of the whipping he had given her could still be seen through the gauze.

Harry ran a hand over her bare waist.

'Very, very nice. One thing before we go downstairs, I think we have to shave you.'

She stared at him. 'Shave?' she said, uncertain what he meant.

Harry grinned and stroked his fingers across the thin strap that covered her sex.

She froze.

'What?' she managed to stammer.

Harry smiled again. 'When you move I can see a curl or two. It looks untidy. Far better if we shaved it. Slip your trousers off; it won't take more than a few minutes.'

He held his hand out, inviting her to join him in the bathroom next to his bedroom. She hesitated.

'What is it?' he said. 'Don't you trust me?'

Jessica swallowed hard - the simple truth was that she didn't, but she found it impossible to put the thought into words. Slowly she followed him. He unfurled a towel onto the tiled floor and ran a sink of water as she slipped off her trousers and the sequinned thong.

He smiled encouragingly as he lathered his hands. 'Just lie down, it won't take more than a few minutes and it will look beautiful.'

Uncertain, Jessica did as he asked. His fingers worked over her mount, soaping the corona of dark hair. The first kiss of the razor made her flinch.

'Gently,' whispered Harry in an undertone, his mind obviously concentrating on the razor. 'Just stay very still.'

She reddened, as his fingers parted the lips of her sex. She could feel him holding them between his thumb and forefinger while the razor hissed through the dark curls. Each stroke made her more and more nervous, but she lay very still in case he cut her.

'All done,' he said after a few minutes. 'I'll run a little water in the bath so you can rinse the hair off. In fact,' he said with delight, 'I think I'll wash it for you.'

She looked up. He was sitting back on his heels, admiring his handiwork. When she glanced down she was astonished by the result.

She hadn't been prepared for how naked her body would appear without the familiar dark triangle of hair. Her sex was completely exposed, with its plump outer lips visible and the little bud of her clitoris peeking provocatively between them like the tip of a very pink tongue. She felt her colour deepening as Harry stroked the folds with proprietorial ease. Her sex looked so vulnerable.

'What a shame we didn't do this before we went into town. I'm certain our friend on the train would have paid double,' Harry said with a grin.

He offered her his hand and as she got to her feet, he planted a kiss at the junction of the heavy outer lips. Standing in the bath, she let him soap the bare smooth mound, washing away the last of the hair, and tried hard not to let the sense of exposure and vulnerability consume her. Lovingly he towelled her dry.

'You are the most amazing find,' he said with affection. He looked up at her, his grey eyes alight with pleasure. 'Who would have thought I would have found my salvation here, of all places?'

He stroked her thighs, fingers lingering on the cleft mound. 'You know, I almost turned the invitation to Malestone down.' He leaned closer and kissed her sex again. His tongue parted the lips, while his finger spiralled up between her thighs to the depths within.

'You're so tight,' he purred appreciatively, 'and so very, very wet.'

She reddened. It was true, mingled with her fear had been a strange dark pleasure in submitting to him. He stroked her quim, letting his fingers trail the shimmering juices out onto her skin. She could see his cock had hardened under the brocade trousers and shivered as he guided her back down onto the bathroom floor. Eagerly, he stripped off her jacket and the little sequinned top, burying his face in her flushed breasts.

She gasped as he bit her nipples, nibbling and nuzzling with teeth and tongue, while between her legs his fingers worked frantically to free his cock.

Glancing down, she was stunned to see how her sex looked. It lifted towards Harry like an open mouth, seeking out his shaft. He grinned at her and then gently guided his cock home. She saw it re-emerge after the first, deep, breathtaking stroke, wet now with her juices. The image was electrifying. Her outer lips clung onto him, sucking him back deep inside her.

He moved forward a little so that each thrust brushed the tender peak of her clitoris. She almost cried out as he began to move faster, every downward thrust sent a volley of intense sensations through her body. She moaned and lifted her legs, wrapping them around his waist so that his movements were intensified. On and on he went until she thought she would go mad. The waves of pleasure made her thrust herself harder against him, matching him stroke for stroke.

His hands worked over her breasts and neck, his mouth, tongue and teeth now gentle, now fierce, as he lapped and bit at her skin.

Finally, she felt the first shuddering convulsion deep within her sex and called his name as the sensations closed over her, driving away everything but the white hot fire in her belly. A split second later he pulled out of her, making her wail with frustration at being denied the final reward.

His glistening cock spurted over her belly and newly shaved sex. The droplets fell like jewels, making her flesh tingle. Gasping, he leaned forward and kissed her cheek, then slipped his arms around her and held her against his chest.

For a few seconds they lay without speaking, only the sounds of their frantic breath breaking the silence. He was the first to recover and pushed himself up onto his knees. Even now she noticed his eyes moved across her body. He took a towel off the rail and gently removed the traces of his pleasure from her skin. Each brush from the towel was followed by a light kiss. When he was done he helped her to her feet.

'We really ought to be getting ready now,' he said. Jessica felt a rush of tenderness that surprised her. Kneeling beside her, Harry looked like a beautiful, vulnerable boy. Perhaps she had misjudged him, after all. He offered her so much and had shown her things she never knew existed. But, even as the thoughts formed, she knew what they had shared wasn't enough to sustain a relationship that would last a lifetime.

She looked into his eyes, aware that he was studying her face for some kind of reaction. She looked away, afraid that he might sense what she was thinking.

Harry ought to be a light dalliance, a scintillating, magical flirtation with danger. Realistically, what they had between them wasn't the stuff of which marriages were made. She bit her lip, wondering how she could tell him and make him understand that she meant it. Perhaps, when she was back at school, tucked up tight in her little bed at St Winifred's and they were miles apart, the relationship would die a natural death.

Harry got to his feet and handed her the little sequinned pants. She pulled them on, together with the harem trousers and turned again for his comments.

He smiled, running a hand over her breasts. 'I think I prefer it without the top.'

Jessica laughed and turned to look at her reflection. As she did, he scooped the gauze blouse up off the bathroom floor and slipped it over her shoulders.

'Try it with this,' he purred.

Jessica shook her head but Harry was insistent and so she slipped the little wrap-over blouse on.

Harry grinned at her reflection. 'That looks much better.'

Jessica started to protest, but Harry had already turned and was heading into the bedroom, taking her little sequinned top with him.

'Harry, I can't wear this on its own,' she called after him.

He reappeared, seconds later, carrying a tray of theatrical make-up and the sequinned mask and veil. In his other hand, he held a paste jewel and a little tube of glue.

'Turn and face me and stand still,' he said, still grinning.

Bemused, Jessica did as he asked.

He undid her blouse and outlined each pert nipple with lipstick, rubbing the scarlet colouring over her areola. Gluing the jewel, he gently pressed it into her navel and then loosely retied her blouse. Reaching into the make-up box he took a stick of kohl and outlined each of her eyes and then added a smear of the bright scarlet lipstick to her mouth. Finally, he slipped the mask over her eyes and adjusted the veil so that her face was totally covered.

'Now you can look,' he whispered triumphantly, turning her round to face the steamy mirror.

Jessica gasped at the transformation. Her breasts were barely covered by the folds of sheer fabric, which accentuated rather than covered her nakedness. Her skin was still flushed with excitement and her nipples, stained scarlet, peeped through the material like ripe cherries. The kohl Harry had rubbed around her eyes made her look Egyptian and her lips, as scarlet as her nipples, just showed through the thin veil - the overall effect was quite astonishing. She barely recognised herself.

'Harry,' she said again. 'I don't think I can go downstairs like this.'

He grinned. 'Of course you can. No one will take a blind bit of notice. Do you think that the costumes are going to be demure? Can you imagine what someone like Bunty has got planned?' He leaned closer to her. In the mirror she watched as he planted a kiss to her neck.

'Trust me, it will be all right. Besides, you're wearing a mask. Masked, no one will know who you really are - and tonight you're my willing, obedient slave girl.

Which reminds me—' he went into the bedroom and came back with a pair of ornate gold coloured wrist bracelets, joined by a short length of chain between them.

'Here we are,' he said with a smile. 'The finishing touch. Give me your hands.'

He took one of Jessica's wrists and snapped the bracelet shut. As he was about to close the second one, she saw they fastened into a little lock. When the fastening closed, she realised that she couldn't get out of them unless Harry had the key. Another thought dawned on her too - unless he let her out of the ornate bracelets, there was no way she could take off her blouse and put the sequinned top back on.

As if he could read her mind, he lifted an eyebrow. 'I think we're just about ready to go down, aren't we?' He went back into the bedroom and she followed him.

'Harry, please take these off and let me put the top back on.'

He looked up at her, his expression impish.

'I don't think so, Jessica. And have you never heard that slaves should be seen and not heard?' He picked up the riding crop and flexed it speculatively. 'Or would you prefer it if I taught you the lesson another way?'

Jessica stared at him, as he took his turban off the chair.

'Oh, sandals,' he said lightly, 'I had quite forgotten,' and took two pairs of soft slippers with curled up toes out of the box beside his turban. 'Sit down on the bed, my dear. And then, when I've put yours on, perhaps you'd like to get on your knees and help me with mine?'

Jack Heally was amongst the first to arrive downstairs and cast his eye over the preparations that had been made for his guests. As all of the musicians from Alice's troupe had been invited, one of the footmen had been stationed by the gramophone.

The house, with the tree and decorations, looked quite splendid.

A few early birds had already found their way to the breakfast room, where the servants were serving drinks. Jack glanced in the hall mirror and smiled at his reflection. The frock coat, the ruffled shirt and tricorn hat, together with black breeches, stockings and buttoned boots, suited his swarthy, dark complexion.

Alice had lent him a brace of stage flintlocks to finish the outfit off. He was pleased by the effect and, drawing the pistols from his pockets, struck a pose just as Alice, dressed as Cinderella, appeared at the foot of the stairs behind him.

She had made some subtle adjustments to the costume, so that the low, lacy bodice only just retained her breasts. She grinned at him as he turned to welcome her, pistols still in his hands.

'You're supposed to say, "Stand and deliver", or do I have to work as prompter on my night off, as well?' she said.

He reddened. 'Just thought I'd just try them out. You look beautiful.'

She spun round for his inspection and then dipped a mocking curtsey. Unlike Miranda in the pantomime, Alice had chosen to wear a white powdered wig, which, with the high-heeled glass slippers, made her at least a foot taller than Jack.

She grinned again. 'Now, are you going to hold me up, rob me and steal my virtue or have I got time for a drink first?'

Jack offered her his arm. 'A drink, I think; after all it's early yet.'

Behind them, several other guests had appeared and as Jack and Alice found a drink and began the round of social niceties, Bunty Redknap made his entrance. He was dressed as a circus strong man and descended the stairs to a flurry of applause. His huge torso and belly were oiled and glistened in the lamplight. He had glued on an enormous handlebar moustache and his groin was covered by a leopard skin apron which left very little to the imagination. As he reached the bottom step he bowed and flexed his muscles, which made everyone clap again.

Slowly, the rooms downstairs began to fill.

George and Felicia arrived dressed as Roman emperor and empress. Felicia's costume was cut to mid-thigh, and it was obvious as she moved that she had nothing underneath.

Miranda had unearthed a mermaid costume from somewhere, and was carried downstairs, bare-chested except for scallop shells over her tiny breasts, by the Haywood twins, who were covered in green body paint and had bundles of fishing net tied around their waists.

As they settled her on the *chaise longue* they joyfully announced they were drowned sailors, lured onto the rocks by Miranda's siren call. Behind them, arm in arm with a young woman clad as a nymph, came Prince Charming, dressed as a soldier, complete with fine moustaches and a chest full of medals.

In the ballroom, the music began to play, and Jack excused himself from Alice and started to make the rounds, glass in hand, eyes working around the bizarre assortment of characters. Although he tried not to admit it, he wanted to find Jessica. Many of the less flamboyant guests had decided to wear masks which made his job all the more difficult. Almost every step was dogged by someone wishing him merry Christmas or making small talk.

He finally managed to make his way into the ballroom. In a quiet corner, a rather risqué Little Bo Peep was being seduced by a winged, masked Mercury, while on the dance floor a nubile young witch was rubbing herself suggestively against Friar Tuck, who didn't seem to object in the least. Beside them a bear was pawing a fairy godmother and two masked women dressed as cats purred along in time to the beat.

Jack drained his glass. Jessica and Stolworthy had to be there somewhere. Finally, when the party was well underway, he spotted them. In the shadows, by the door which led to the anteroom of the ballroom, Jessica sat on a cushion beside her sultan, cradling a champagne glass.

Jack felt a plume of anger in his belly as he noticed the chains that linked her wrists to a belt around Stolworthy's waist. Without thinking he made his way towards them, his anger and jealousy drawing him like a magnet.

Stolworthy looked up at his approach and lifted his glass in salute.

'Good evening,' he said pleasantly. 'Wonderful party.'

But Jack's eyes were on Jessica. Her costume was an erotic masterpiece, and even as angry as he was, he felt his cock stir as her naked breasts moved beneath the sheer gauze.

Stolworthy coughed, interrupting Jack's train of thought.

'Interested in my little slave girl, are you?' he said with a salacious wink. 'This way,' he added, shaking the chain that linked them, 'you can't whisk her away without me knowing about it. How much will you offer me for her?'

Jack glared at him, feeling his anger solidify into a tight, explosive knot.

Stolworthy rattled the chain again. 'Of course, I usually charge by the hour, but I'm sure we could come to some arrangement if you wanted to have her for the night.'

Jack glanced down at Jessica, who was watching the exchange with astonishment.

'Harry?' she said, getting to her feet. 'Stop it, this is only a game.'

Harry's expression hardened, his eyes still firmly fixed on Jack's. 'It might be a game to you, my dear, but I am deadly serious.' He lifted the chain again. 'How much then, Jack? How much is she worth to you? I'm open to any reasonable offer.'

Jack took a step towards him but realised, even before he raised his fist, that this was neither the time nor the place to conclude his business with Harry. Instead he held out his hand.

'Give me the key to Jessica's chains,' he said in a low voice, edged with steel.

Stolworthy pulled a face. 'Oh no, you misunderstand me, Jack; there are no free trials in my harem,' he said.

Jack realised, as Harry got up and lurched forward, that he had already had a lot to drink. Jessica held out an arm to steady him and Harry grinned.

'See, Jack, such devotion. What more could any man want from any woman? Isn't she perfect? We're going to be married, you know.'

Jessica attempted to quieten him but Harry would not be silenced. He dipped his hand into the drawstring bag he was wearing on his cummerbund and produced not a key, but an engagement ring. He fumbled for Jessica's hands, torn between using her to support him and trying to slip the ring onto her finger. Jessica's face was ashen.

'Stop it, Harry, please,' she snapped, trying to jerk away from him, while staring down at the ring.

Harry grinned. 'But I want us to announce our betrothal, my dear. What better time than Christmas Eve? I want everyone to know that we're engaged.' His voice rose sharply, so that the crowd of partygoers around them turned to see what the fuss was.

Jessica's eyes hadn't left the ring that Harry was holding between his fingers.

'Where did you get that?' she said unsteadily.

Harry grinned. 'Why, I bought it today, my dear, you saw me, didn't you? From that little jeweller chappie in Church Street.'

Jessica shook her head. 'No, Harry, I didn't see you buy it.' Her voice was low and tinged with disbelief. 'You stole it, didn't you? While you had that man hunting high and low for something bigger and better, you slipped this one in your pocket.' She stared at him, almost as if she couldn't quite believe what she'd said. 'That's why you gave him the other man's calling card, wasn't it?'

Watching them, Jack Heally could see the drunkenness clear from Harry's eyes.

'Wasn't it?' Jessica repeated, her voice getting louder.

Before Jack could stop him, Harry drew back his hand and slapped Jessica hard across the face. The surprise as much as the pain felled her.

'How dare you call me a thief, you little vixen,' Harry roared and lifted his hand again. This time, Jack was too quick for him and grabbed his wrist, jerking it high up behind Harry's back. Harry let out a mewl of pain but didn't resist. Jessica, still chained to him, crouched on the floor, rubbing her face, eyes bright with shock and tears.

Jack nodded towards her. 'Reach into that pouch and get the key out while I hold him.'

Wordlessly, Jessica did as he asked and then froze as she opened her hand - inside, besides the small gold key, were two other rings.

Jack jerked Harry's arm higher.

'You thieving little bastard, what else have you taken?'

Stolworthy spat onto the polished wooden floor. 'The woman you love, I think, wouldn't you say, Jack? Here, Jessica, help get this bloody oaf off me. I think we ought to leave. Perhaps Bunty or one of the other chaps would run us down to the village.'

Jessica shook her head. 'No, I don't think so, Harry,' she said in a tiny voice.

Harry stared at her in amazement. 'What the hell do you mean no? We're going to be married. You said—'

Jessica shook her head again. 'No, we're not, Harry.'

Jack, with a sense of relief, was about to release Stolworthy when a footman appeared with Alice by his side. She looked at Jack, then Stolworthy and Jessica, and rolled her eyes heavenwards.

'I think,' she said calmly, 'we ought to go to your office, Jack. Charlie's borrowed a car and motored down from London.'

As she spoke, Stolworthy slipped out of Jack's grip and turned to glare at her.

'Who the hell is Charlie and what's it got to do with Jessica and me?' he said, attempting to salvage his dignity as he hurriedly straightened his clothes.

Alice smiled coldly.

'Quite a lot, actually.' She stepped to one side and indicated the others should follow her. Jack took the key out of Jessica's fingers and unlocked her wrists. She was blushing and seemed unable to meet his eye. Gently, he took her hand, and in silence they followed Stolworthy and Alice across the ballroom.

Chapter 18

The Last Act

Jessica felt strange as she walked between the groups of guests. She had so many thoughts in her head it was difficult to think clearly. Around her the people talked and chatted, resplendent in their costumes, totally unaware of what was happening. Jessica could hardly believe it herself. The idea that Harry could have stolen the engagement rings shocked her so much that she couldn't bear to let the thought surface.

Conscious of her nakedness, she pulled her hand away from Jack and wrapped her arms across her chest.

He smiled down at her and slipped off the highwayman's jacket.

'Here, why don't you put this on?' he said gently. 'You're shivering.'

She didn't know what to say and was afraid that she might cry. With his arm around her shoulders, Jack guided her upstairs.

Jessica looked ahead at Harry and Alice. With every passing moment it seemed that Harry's confidence was returning. There was a definite swagger in his step as they reached Jack's office door.

Inside, sitting on the desk, illuminated by a single lamp, Charlie Foster sat with his back to the door. Jessica, though she had only met him briefly in Alice's flat, would have recognised him anywhere. The lamp had been arranged to emphasise his stunning profile.

He turned as he heard them come in, and smiled.

'Jack, how very nice to see you again,' he said, getting to his feet and extending his hand.

Jack nodded his welcome and shook his hand firmly, then Charlie turned to Jessica.

'And Jessica, you look a little different. I thought perhaps you weren't as—'

Stolworthy cut the niceties short.

'Can we stop all this small talk? Would you care to tell me why the hell I have been dragged up here?'

Charlie sucked his teeth and then sighed, looking Harry up and down.

'You must be Harry Stolworthy. Alice rang and asked me to find out what I could about you.' He paused for dramatic emphasis and Jessica realised, in spite of her discomfort, that Charlie was really rather enjoying holding centre stage.

'It's taken me ages, what with Christmas and all,' he began.

Stolworthy said, 'This is completely and utterly ridiculous. I've a good mind to leave now; I've never been so insulted in my life. What is this, some kind of kangaroo court?'

Charlie smiled, cutting him short, and carried on as if Stolworthy hadn't spoken.

'I'd asked around, put a few feelers out, then last night I went to Ushers after the show and discovered that Mr Stolworthy isn't quite what he seems.'

Harry was about to speak and then seemed to think better of it.

Charlie spun round to face him. 'There's quite a lot of gossip about you, if you know the right people to ask.'

Jessica leaned forward, unable to bear the suspense.

'Please,' she murmured, sick of Charlie's carefully staged build-up to his revelations. 'What is it?'

Charlie shifted position. 'Your friend, Mr Stolworthy here, is up to his eyes in debt. He's frittered away most of what his parents left him and is now trying to get his hands on a rather large trust fund set up by his great uncle. The old man is on his last legs and Harry is desperate to try and fulfil his uncle's conditions of inheritance.'

Jessica turned and stared at Harry, who was struggling to maintain his composure. Even though he appeared to be unmoved by Charlie's comments, his face had drained of colour.

'What conditions?' Jessica managed to ask.

Charlie's eyes never left Harry's face.

'Great Uncle Stolworthy, apparently, is a great believer in family values. Rumour has it that he suspects Harry of being a homosexual. To get his hands on the family fortune, Harry just has to get himself married.'

Jessica gasped and for an instant the room seemed to go out of focus.

Charlie Foster was still talking. 'The old boy may be ill but he's fairly sharp, and before he ties up the details of his will, he would need to convince himself that the young lady in question was respectable, which stopped Mr Stolworthy here from setting himself up with some showgirl or tart.' He turned and looked at Jessica. 'A decent, upright school teacher would be an absolutely perfect choice.'

Jessica felt an icy chill trickle down her spine. She stared at Harry, whose face was now ashen.

'And meanwhile,' Jessica said unsteadily, 'until his uncle dies, Harry could drum up some funds by stealing and selling his fiancée to complete strangers.'

Harry squared his shoulders and stared at Charlie. 'Rather a melodramatic story, sir,' he said confidently. 'But it's complete and utter nonsense. You're right, my uncle did suggest I ought to get married. He wanted to see me settled and happy before he died, which is only natural. But nothing was further from my mind when I came to Malestone. I met Jessica and fell in love, it's as simple as that.'

Charlie pulled a face. 'How very convenient. So, your wooing Jessica hadn't got anything to do with having a row with your lover over the terms of your uncle's will, and betting him ten pounds you could find someone to marry you before the new year?'

Harry's face contorted into a furious mask.

'How dare you, you arrogant little bastard,' he snarled, leaping forwards and making a grab for Charlie. Charlie was too quick for him and took a side-step, leaving Harry to crash into the desk. Harry took a wild swing and then froze as a slim, blond man stepped in from the side door.

'Pip?' Harry gasped, caught mid-stride, with his fist raised. 'What the hell are you doing here?'

The man stepped into the light. He had a kind of androgynous beauty, his thin angular face emphasised by a pair of enormous blue eyes. Jessica could see he was close to tears.

'I drove down and brought Charlie,' he said, in a voice that trembled with emotion. 'How could you behave like this, Harry?' A tear spilt over his dark lashes and trickled down his cheek. 'When Charlie told me about you getting engaged to some woman I could hardly believe it.' Biting his lip, he stepped towards Jessica and caught hold of her hands.

'I'm really so sorry,' he said, struggling to fight back the tears. 'In some ways I feel responsible. Harry and I have been lovers for years. I just wanted him to sort out his finances, get a job - something to get him out of debt. I had no idea he would try something like this.' He folded her into his arms and murmured. 'I'm so sorry. I really am.'

Harry, his face like a mask, rounded on Pip.

'You stupid little bugger. If you could have kept that mouth of yours shut for another week or so we'd be home and dry. She was putty in my hands.' As he spoke he launched himself towards Pip and Jessica. Jack stepped between them before Harry could set a hand on the younger man.

'I think we've seen and heard quite enough,' Jack said calmly. 'It would be better for everyone if you left, Harry. I'll have a footman help you pack.'

Pip nodded to Jack. 'I've brought my car; we can be back in London by late tonight. I'm so sorry about this.'

Harry, all the bluster finally ebbing away, turned and left the room, followed by Pip.

Jessica watched them go, feeling raw and terribly empty. She had been completely betrayed by Harry. Jack reached out to touch her but she turned away, tears coursing down her face. Without a backward glance, she ran out of the office, passing Pip and Harry on the way, and fled to her room.

Once inside, she tore off the slave costume and threw her clothes into a suitcase. She had seen the look of pity in Jack's face and couldn't bear it. Dragging on a thick woollen suit, coat and shoes, she hurried back out on to the landing. As she turned the corner, she almost fell over Alice, who had obviously been sent to find her.

Alice grabbed her arms. 'What the hell are you doing?' she said.

Jessica shook her head. 'I can't stay here, I have to go. Please, just get out of my way.'

Alice stared at her. 'Don't be so ridiculous. Where on earth are you going to go at this time of night?'

Jessica shook herself free. 'Into the village. There's bound to be a train, if not tonight, then first thing tomorrow morning. I can't stay here - everyone will think

I've been a complete fool.'

Before Alice could protest, Jessica broke into a run and hared away down the stairs. Everywhere was crowded with guests from the party. Forcing her way between them, she made her way across the hall and wrenched open the heavy front door.

The cold night wind hit her like a body blow, sucking the breath out of her chest. She shivered and then without a backward glance stepped out into the darkness.

Outside, after the noise of the party, the night seemed almost magically calm and quiet. What she needed was time to think and plan what she would do next. It wasn't too late to go back to the school in Somerset for Christmas. No one but her need ever know about her disastrous encounter with Harry Stolworthy.

Parked in front of her on the gravel in a neat row, were the guests' cars. As she approached them, struggling with her suitcase, a man in uniform stepped out from the shadows.

'Leaving already, miss?' he said pleasantly. 'Good night, was it?'

She nodded, too nervous to speak.

'Which one is yours?' he said, nodding towards the cars. 'I'll get it started up and bring it round for you.'

Jessica stared up at him and then realised borrowing one of the cars would make her escape far easier. The nearest village was miles away. She coughed, struggling to clear the tight knot in her throat.

'The red one,' she said as confidently as she could, pointing out Bunty Redknap's soft-topped roadster.

'Right you are, miss,' said the man. 'Won't be a minute.'

As he headed off into the darkness, Jessica struggled to catch her breath. A plan formed in her mind. She would go to the village and if there wasn't a train, she would take a room in the local pub; surely someone would take her in on Christmas Eve.

Across the drive an engine roared into life. She took another deep breath, trying to steady the mixture of pain, fear and humiliation in her stomach. The headlights on Bunty's car flickered and then slowly the car crept alongside her.

The man got out and touched his cap. 'There we are, miss. Safe journey home, and a very merry Christmas.'

'And to you too,' she muttered, and then nervously slipped into the driving seat and tried to remember what she'd seen Alice do when she'd picked her up from the station.

It wasn't the first time she had been in a car but it was the first time she had driven one. As she let out the clutch, the car lurched forward and she was off. The driveway looked quite narrow; carefully she negotiated the first bend, her unhappiness temporarily forgotten as she struggled to control the steering wheel.

She crept along at first, trying not to panic as the trees hurried past her in the headlights.

Beginning to feel more confident on a long straight section of the roadway,

Jessica changed up a gear, wincing as the engine complained. She bit her lip and pressed the accelerator a little more. Ahead of her, in the distance, she could see the road swung round sharply to the left. The car was on the bend almost before she had time to think. Desperately she pressed what she thought was the brake. At that instant, the car hit a rut and seemed to snatch itself away from her. As she struggled to regain control, the wheel was wrenched out of her hands.

She shrieked as bushes and trees headed towards her - and then there was a sickening crunch as the car slewed into a dry dyke. The engine roared impotently for a few seconds and then faded and died.

Shaking, Jessica slumped forward and rested her head on the steering wheel - this was complete madness. There was nothing left now but to walk. Out beyond the bright cones of the headlights, the night looked very dark and uninviting. As she sat, trying to regain some sense of control, heavy raindrops fell on the cracked windscreen.

Jack Heally grabbed hold of Alice on the landing outside his office.

'What the hell do you mean, Jessica's left?' he snapped. 'She can't leave.'

Alice jerked herself out of Jack's grasp. 'She has. When I went upstairs she was coming down with her case. I couldn't stop her.' She paused and then smiled. 'But don't worry, she can't have got far on foot.'

Jack sighed, thinking about Jessica out alone in the park, in her present state of mind. He ran through the hallway, pushing his way between his guests, who were now almost too drunk to notice. It would be a hell of a job to catch Jessica on foot. He knew Harry and Pip would be leaving soon. He'd already sent a footman up to ensure Harry only packed what belonged to him.

It occurred to him that Jessica might try and hide if he went after her in a car. She would assume it was Harry and Pip. And if they met her on the road, God alone knew what might happen. He looked up and down the driveway and then hared off towards the stables.

Inside the stable, a single lamp was lit above the door. Grabbing a bridle out of the tack room, Jack opened the first stall he came to which housed his favourite hunter. He slipped the bit into the horse's mouth, praying that it would be enough to control the huge beast once they got outside.

Leading the gelding out into the darkness, he held it steady and then clambered up onto his back. The horse complained at being dragged out into the cold, dancing back and forth until Jack settled himself down. Kicking it into a brisk trot, he set off down the drive, wishing he'd had the sense to bring the lantern.

Away from the house, the night closed in around him like a shroud. Overhead, dark clouds promising rain slunk ominously across the moon. The wind suddenly shifted, and Jack felt the first drops of rain on his face. It was no night to be out in the open. Jack shivered. The horse was as apprehensive as he was and whinnied nervously.

Jack kicked his mount on again, praying he would find Jessica quickly. Rounding a particularly sharp corner he was confronted by Bunty's car, stuck nose-up in a shallow ditch, headlights ablaze. His stomach lurched as he drew closer, his fear vanishing almost instantly when he saw the driver's seat was empty.

'Jessica? Jessica are you there?' Jack called anxiously, his voice whipped away by the wind, which was edged with icy rain.

She couldn't be far, he convinced himself. It hadn't occurred to him that she might take one of the cars. The rain began to fall more steadily, soaking through the thin jacket he had snatched off the rack in his office. He called again, praying Jessica would answer him.

As he was about to leave the abandoned car, the horse skittered nervously from side to side. Jack knew it could sense something in the darkness that he couldn't see. Ahead of him there was a scuffling sound in the bushes, then, into the arc of the headlights stepped Jessica Harper. Her hair was already soaked, clinging to her ivory white face like a sleek pelt.

'Jack?' she said, in a tiny miserable voice. 'I think I've broken Bunty's car.' The words released a great dam of tears.

Jack slithered down off the horse's back and hurried over to her. She was frozen, and curled up against him like a frightened child, sobbing softly.

'How could I have been so stupid?' she sniffed. 'You must think I'm a complete and utter fool.'

Harry kissed the top of her damp hair. 'No, no,' he whispered gently. 'I don't think you're a fool at all. I'm just so glad that you're all right, and so glad you didn't go off with Harry. I don't think I could have coped knowing that you were with him.' He guided her back towards the car and pulled a travelling rug off the passenger seat.

'Here, wrap this around you. You need to get warm,' he said, 'you'll catch your death out here.'

Jessica, eyes bright with tears, looked up at him.

'I can't go back to Malestone,' she snuffled. 'I really can't.'

Jack looked around to get his bearings and then nodded. 'The Old Lodge cottage is just around the next corner. It's empty. We'll go there.' He glanced back into the interior of the car, wondering if Bunty had thought to carry a spare coat.

Jack leant inside - apparently Bunty had been prepared for every eventuality. Besides carrying a heavy driving coat, between the seats was a large box, which on closer inspection appeared to contain a bottle of champagne, candles and matches and the makings of an ad hoc picnic.

Beside him, Jack could see that Jessica was beginning to shiver violently. Her eyes were glazed and she looked almost feverish. He wrapped the heavy motoring coat around her shoulders, caught hold of Bunty's box and the reins of his horse and guided her towards the Old Lodge.

In the darkness, with rain and wind beating on their faces, the two or three hundred yards to the little cottage seemed to take forever. Jessica leant heavily against him, trying hard not to stumble in the ruts. Even over the sound of the wind he could still hear and feel her muffled sobs and felt a wave of tenderness as she curled closer to him.

He saw the moon reflected in the cottage windows as they rounded the next bend.

'It's all right, we're here now,' he said, leading her up the cinder path and then tying the horse up under the little lean-to that adjoined the cottage. It took a few seconds to force the door and then gratefully, both of them stepped into the shelter and calm of the little kitchen.

Jack set Bunty's treasure box down on the floor and opened it, while beside him he could hear Jessica's teeth chattering.

'Give me a minute, I'll try and get us some light and see if we can get a fire going.'

He struck a match, and lit one of Bunty's candles.

The candle bathed the room with a soft, warm glow. The interior was bare except for the bales of meadow hay that, a day or two earlier, he had shared with Felicia Gudgeon and his friends. In the grate someone had laid a fire, and on the mantelshelf stood a paraffin lamp.

Jack grinned triumphantly and within seconds managed to kindle the sticks into life. The bright blaze filled the hearth. Jessica, still in a state of shock, watched him work with huge unhappy eyes.

He smiled up at her from the fireplace.

'Come over here and get warm. I'll just go and see if there's anything else we can use in the cottage. I'm certain there are more logs in the shed.' He stretched up and got the lamp.

She bit her lip as she huddled beside the hearth.

'Please, don't go,' she whispered. 'I really don't want to be on my own. I feel so awful.' As she spoke her voice broke again and she curled up under his jacket, her tears warm against his skin.

'Don't cry,' he said in an undertone. 'I'll get Bunty's box for you to sit on. I won't be more than two minutes, I promise you.'

She sniffed. 'All right, you'll have to excuse me.' She forced a throaty laugh. 'I'm not usually like this. Everything is such a muddle at the moment. You know, the stupid thing is I never intended to marry Harry. It would have been a complete disaster. I planned to tell him, but I just couldn't find the words. But all the rest of it—' She rubbed her eyes, trying hard to compose herself. 'All the rest, all that stuff about Pip and Harry's uncle, and the engagement rings. It is such a shock. I feel so used.'

As she looked back up into his face, Jack saw the flash of need in her eyes and closed his arms tight around her.

'It's all right,' he said tenderly. 'It's over now. There's only you and me here.' He pushed himself to his feet. 'Let me get the logs. I won't be long.'

Outside, the rain fell in a continuous icy sheet and the wind roared furiously amongst the trees, tearing back and forth between the cottage chimneys. Jack worked quickly, stacking up an armful of seasoned logs before going back inside.

As he did, Jessica turned. Framed in the fire's glow she looked like an angel. She was sitting on the hearth with the coat wrapped around her. He felt his heart flutter and hurried over to her, dropping the logs in a heap.

He could see in her eyes that the fear and the shock were receding fast. Neither spoke as he reached out a hand to cradle her face. It felt, in that first fleeting second, as if they stepped outside of time, leaving behind all the pain, the deceit and the uncertainty. In the firelight, there was only a man and a woman he desired, with no past, no future, only a breathtaking, all-engulfing present.

She leaned forward, her lips seeking the reassurance of his, and he moaned as her mouth opened to the lightest caress of his tongue.

She was still shivering, or was it trembling, as he pushed the damp coat away. He realised with complete certainty that everything he wanted was in his arms. He kissed her damp hair, excited by the way her fingers lifted to unbutton his shirt and pull it down over his broad shoulders.

'Oh Jack,' she whispered, nuzzling against him. Her tongue was like a butterfly, lapping back and forth across his throat and the tiny dark buds of his nipples. He groaned and struggled to keep pace with her. His fingers, still cold and damp, fumbled with her blouse, finally ripping away the tiny pearl buttons to reveal her pert breasts.

In the soft glow from the lamp and the fire, he could still see the dark outline of the lipstick around the tight, cold peaks. He bent forward, drawing a nipple in his mouth, his hands working at the folds of her skirt.

She moaned and threw back her head, relishing his attentions. There was a feeling of rightness and completion about the eager way they undressed each other. It seemed as if Jack was reclaiming her for himself, and he knew from the rapt expression on her face that she felt the same way.

Her hands made short work of his breeches, dragging them down over his muscular thighs, exposing his engorged cock. She grinned at him, and licked her lips, all fear finally gone. In the firelight she looked magnificent, her dark hair in a tumble of damp curls, her naked shoulders rising above the remains of the blouse he had torn undone. Leaning forward, she pressed a kiss to the angry crown of his cock and then drew it into her mouth. He shuddered as her lips closed around him and then lay back on the hay, letting her take him deeper and deeper into her mouth.

Gathering up her skirt she clambered across his hips and with cool hands guided his throbbing shaft between her legs so that it nuzzled against the heat and wetness of her quim.

For an instant she hesitated and looked down at him, her eyes twinkling in the flames. 'Jack—' she began unevenly.

He shook his head.

'There's no need to say anything,' he said, as his hands reaching to caress her breasts. She groaned and lifted her body so that his cock slid effortlessly into the heat that brewed deep inside her.

His mind was full of her smell, the way she felt as she began to move with him, the intricate shadows of the fire as they moved across her breasts.

He knew that Harry Stolworthy had been right. She was the woman he loved. Her sex nipped at him as she tightened the muscles to draw him deeper. She ground her hips down against him, pleasuring herself as they rode on and on towards the point of no return.

The shy, gauche schoolteacher he had first met had vanished, the beautiful woman that knelt astride him now was self-assured and completely in control, sharing her body with the man who moved beneath her. He wanted to say something but knew there were no words big enough or powerful enough to describe the sensations and the emotions that filled his mind.

Jessica hunched over him, slipping her hands under his buttocks, and it seemed to Jack as if they were completely at one, joined flesh to flesh, mind to mind.

As the first waves of pleasure hit them both, she threw back her head and let out a wild banshee scream. The sound echoed around the tiny room, joining with the wind that roared through the chimneys.

As Jessica's cry faded, Jack felt her sex closing rhythmically around his shaft. Her orgasm engulfed them both like a storm and he knew then he was lost. Wave after wave roared through him, driving away everything except for the image of her moving above him.

Finally they were still, and the sound of the wind and the rain filled the room. She curled up against him, making soft noises of pleasure as he stroked her damp hair. Rolling over he pulled the heavy coat over them both and closed his eyes.

Jessica was woken by the sound of church bells and struggled to remember where she was. She opened her eyes, blinking against the sunlight, fighting to keep control of the thoughts that threatened to drown the waking calm.

Jack Heally was sitting beside her. Crouched down on the hearth, dressed in just his breeches, he was feeding the glowing fire. He smiled as she began to stir. The cottage kitchen was deliciously warm. She stared at him, trying to focus her eyes and her thoughts.

'Good morning and merry Christmas,' he purred, leaning over to kiss her forehead. His eyes were alight with love.

She shivered, wondering what she ought to say. She felt an intense glow of warmth in her chest, ignited by his tender touch.

Jack uncurled himself slowly and slipped back amongst the crush of hay under Bunty's huge coat.

'I've been thinking,' he said, taking her in his arms. 'Perhaps we ought to move in here after we're married.'

She stared at him. 'After we're married,' she whispered.

He nodded, grinning, as his hand worked down over her belly. 'Well, before if you like. You can take as long as you like to say yes, as long as you stay with me while you make up your mind. I've been thinking about what we ought to call our children. What do you think of Rory as a name? Or maybe George, that way we could ask George and Felicia to be godparents.'

She pulled herself up on to one elbow. 'You're serious, aren't you?' she said.

He nodded. 'Never been more so. Now come back here and make love to me again before everyone up at Malestone decides to come looking for us.'

Jessica smiled and curled up against his broad chest.

'What about Bunty's car?' she said, as she found the buttons on his breeches.

Jack smiled. 'Maybe I'll buy it for you as a wedding present. Now stop talking and snuggle down, we've got the rest of our lives to talk.'

Also by Carol Anderson and available as paperbacks at AMAZON...
A Private Affair
A Private Education
Flood Tide
Invitations
Passion Beach